CLOCKED
OUT

CLOCKED OUT

A Josie Posey Mystery

ANNA *St.* JOHN

LEVEL
BEST BOOKS

First published by Level Best Books 2024

Copyright © 2024 by Anna St. John

This novel is entirely a work of fiction. The names, characters and incidents portrayed in it are the work of the author's imagination. Any resemblance to actual persons, living or dead, events or localities is entirely coincidental.

Anna St. John asserts the moral right to be identified as the author of this work.

Author Photo Credit: Steve Rasmussen

First edition

ISBN: 978-1-68512-564-6

Cover art by Level Best Designs, Shawn Reilly Simmons
Illustration by Lyndsey Mbwauike

This book was professionally typeset on Reedsy.
Find out more at reedsy.com

To my Bruce,
always.

In Loving Memory of
My mother, who taught me to read,
My father, who encouraged me to write,
And my sister, Kim, who believed I could do anything.

Praise for Clocked Out

"An absolute 'I-can't-put-this-down' delight of a mystery!"—J.C. Eaton, author of The Sophie Kimball Mysteries, The Wine Trail Mysteries, The Charcuterie Shop Mysteries, The Marcie Rayner Mysteries

"Anna St. John strikes gold again…with plenty of twists and turns, the reader will wind up guessing until the very end. Don't waste time—buy your copy today!"—Gayle Brown, author of *A Deadly Game*

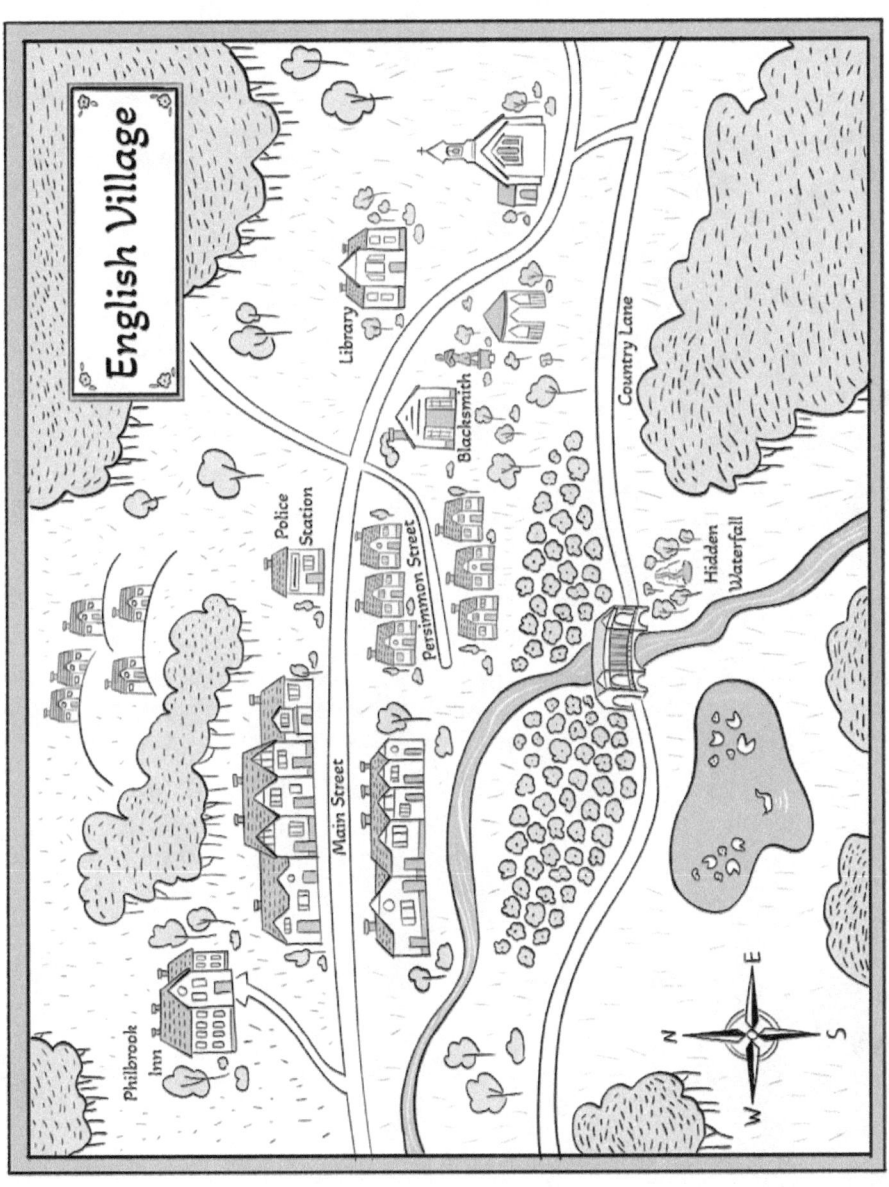

Chapter One

Wednesday Morning

At the flashing yellow lights, I pulled Piper to the side of the narrow intersection where Persimmon joined Main. A huge dump truck was parked crosswise on the road just ahead. Two orange-vested workers stood beside it. A third further blocked my view with a handheld stop sign. From the vantage point of my little red VW convertible, I couldn't see what the problem was.

"Arrgh. We don't have time for this." I tightened my grip on Piper's steering wheel. Yes, I'm aware that most people, even those who name their cars, don't speak to them aloud. But I figured it couldn't hurt to share my frustration with the little vehicle, especially when we were at a total standstill in a village far too small to have traffic jams.

I craned to peek over the top of the convertible's windshield and catch a glimpse of the intersection. Even now, in what might be considered rush hour, cars flowed easily down Main Street just beyond the work crew. Only Persimmon Lane was at a standstill. A second car came to a stop behind me.

I checked my watch for the umpteenth time since my editor had called just after breakfast.

"Josie, you need to be at The Curiosity Shop in an hour," she'd commanded. Leslie Anderson's voice carried a familiar edge of urgency. The woman was a bundle of high energy who thrived on tight deadlines and a steady stream of caffeine. "One of our biggest celebrities is in town and agreed to an interview if we can accommodate her schedule."

"It's Wednesday," I reminded her as I hand-washed my favorite coffee mug. "Mahjong Day."

"She is five minutes from your house," Les said, skipping over the sanctity of my plans.

"In one hour?" I tried appealing to her often-repeated desire for professionalism. *The Village Gazette* looks bad when you send a reporter who isn't properly prepared. Can't this wait until tomorrow?"

"Not gonna happen." Leslie's flat response left no room for arguments. "Ella McGregor Benjamin is only available *this* morning. After today, she has blocked time to spend with her former college roommate, who will be in town for the art show. Then she's off to New York for a few weeks. I heard she rented a place here in English Village. We need to find out whether she's moving home or just taking a sabbatical from her high-pressured career."

I sighed heavily into my cell phone. When Leslie Anderson wants a news story, she won't take no for an answer.

"The details are in your email."

"But, Leslie—"

"She requested you, Josie."

"All right. All right. All right. But it's on you if this article looks like a cub reporter did it."

Leslie's laugh carried into my ear, and I pictured her in the newsroom, spinning a pencil between her fingers as she leaned back in her chair. "You've got this, Josie. You're a pro."

"Well, first, I need to get dressed," I said, "then I'll read whatever you sent me about Mr. McGregor's daughter. I've heard him talk about her, but I definitely need to see her bio."

"One more thing," Leslie added.

"I'm listening."

"Don't be one second late. This lady is deadly serious about being on time. She makes watches for a living."

"Got it."

I raced through my shower, powered up my laptop, and printed out the

2

background information from Leslie with twenty minutes to spare. My sweet Old English sheepdog, Moe, watched my frenzied activities with mild interest. From a cursory glance, I learned that Ella McGregor Benjamin was indeed a very big deal—a rising, rare talent in the watchmaking industry. At a quarter till ten, I grabbed my purse and car keys from the kitchen island and turned to see Moe waiting at the door. He sat with his fluffy head cocked at an angle, his leash in his mouth. My heart melted at his eager pose.

I knelt to wrap my arms around him. "Sorry, boy. You have to stay here and take care of the house. We'll go out and run errands later. I promise." I returned his leash to the basket beside the coat rack, locked the door behind me, and hurried to back Piper out of the garage.

With a breezy fifteen minutes to make the five-minute journey, I pulled out of my driveway, confident I would arrive early. Instead, I traveled only a few blocks to the intersection of Persimmon and Main, where I now thrummed my fingers on the steering wheel and counted from twenty to zero, backward.

If this had happened to me in Kansas City when I worked for *The Star*, I might have beeped my horn and flashed my silver press badge to bypass the delay. But here in English Village, I was officially retired and carried only a FREELANCE REPORTER business card that came with no special privileges and impressed only my mahjong friends. I decided to try a polite request instead.

After unbuckling my seat belt, I raised my head to peer over the windshield. "Excuse me!" I waved at the traffic director.

Mr. Stop Sign kept his arm raised but took a few steps in my direction. "Hang on, lady. This will only take a minute."

"Could I maybe scooch around the truck while you're working?" I flashed my sweetest smile. "As you can see, my car is quite small."

"Scooch?"

"Yes, please. I'm running late for an appointment."

He shrugged. Walked closer. "Wait. Aren't you that reporter who writes for the *Gazette*?"

I was astonished that the guy in the orange vest recognized me. I shoved

3

my outstretched hand over Piper's side mirror toward him. "Yes. I'm Josie Posey. Pleased to meet you."

He extended a gloved hand for a clumsy grasp and then motioned toward the congested intersection. "There's a shallow pothole ahead. We like to repair them before they get bigger. Safety first. We'll be finished here in five minutes."

I glanced at my watch, confirming my fear. I'd be late to the interview.

"Pretty please?"

He studied my hopeful expression, then turned his back and walked over to his team. I returned to my seat and debated whether to rev my engine and race over the curb. I was pretty sure Piper could zip along the sidewalk and bypass the truck entirely. Then I heard shouts ahead. The big truck inched forward in an awkward turn.

Mr. Stop Sign reappeared beside my car. The corners of his eyes crinkled as he waved me forward. "Scooch ahead, ma'am. My mother reads every article you write. She would never forgive me if I made you late for your appointment."

I grinned at him and put Piper into first gear. She purred into action. "Let's go, girl," I said to the little car. "With any luck, we can still make it."

We circled the work truck and turned left onto Main Street, traveling past the popular Cozy Cups Cafe run by my friend Lorene, beyond the quaint old-fashioned bank and toward the end of the next block. Three minutes later, I parked in front of The Curiosity Shop and dashed inside. My watch read 9:59 a.m.

As soon as I entered the shop, I felt I had stepped back in time. A familiar Frank Sinatra song drifted from a Victrola record player. Sunlight filtered through the front windows, bathing rows of antiques and collectibles in a dim golden light flecked with tiny dust particles. The place was jam-packed with treasures displayed in artful clusters that encouraged browsing. Beneath the crooning, I heard the rhythmic tick-tock of a multitude of clocks. Altogether, it was a pleasing combination.

I spied a young woman across the large showroom, partially hidden by shelves of clocks in all shapes and sizes, and headed in her direction. She held a clipboard in her hands as she bent slightly toward a mantle clock that rested on the glass counter.

As I moved toward the woman, all the clocks struck the top of the hour, pointedly announcing my on-time arrival. Now close enough to recognize from my brief research, Ella turned from her work and smiled a greeting. Neither of us attempted to speak over the cacophony of chimes, bells, and chords. She was slight in stature, about five foot four, with a heart-shaped face. Her shiny dark curls were tied back with a bright red bandana. In faded jeans and a simple white T-shirt, she looked about twenty-one or twenty-two. I never would have guessed her true age of thirty-one had I not glanced through her bio in preparation for our meeting.

When the clocks quieted, the young woman set the clipboard on the glass countertop, walked toward me, and extended her hand. "You must be the reporter," she said. "I'm Ella."

I grasped her hand and smiled. "Please, call me Josie."

"I've prepared tea on the patio. We can talk there."

Ella poked her head in an office door on our way toward the exit. "I'll be outside, Dad. Don't forget to listen for the bell."

She unlocked the shop's back door and motioned for me to precede her. "I'm pretty sure my dad's the one who contacted the *Gazette* to let them know I was home," she said modestly. "He wants to tell the world how proud he is of his little girl."

"He was a clockmaker for many years, wasn't he? Like father, like daughter."

"Yes. He spent hours assembling them. That was a long time ago. When he still had a steady hand and 20/20 eyesight."

We sat across from each other at a small wrought iron table in the shady garden. Bright blue ceramic pots lined the brick pathway that extended another thirty feet to a small wooden shed. It had been painted to resemble a child's fairy-tale playhouse.

I set my phone on the table to record the interview. "Okay?"

Ella nodded her approval, then poured us tea and insisted I take a biscuit. Afterward, she motioned toward a nearby sundial. "As a child, I played out here and learned to tell time by the shadows on that sundial."

"You began your career early," I said.

A smile lit her face, revealing one charming dimple in her right cheek. "You could say that. I've always been fascinated by the movement of time."

A small gold pendant on a simple chain caught my eye. I peered at it more closely. A lustrous yellow sun studded with diamonds and sapphires in a familiar pattern.

"Is that a sundial necklace?"

Ella reached up to touch the beautiful piece where it rested elegantly at the heart of her collarbone. She caressed the medallion lightly between her thumb and forefinger. "Yes. It was a gift from a friend."

I eyed the diamond slider clasp. "Must be a close friend. It's lovely."

Ella turned a light shade of pink, lowered her eyes, and reached for her teacup. "He is."

Clearly uncomfortable with the subject, Ella didn't volunteer any further details. I took the hint and returned to the topic of her career. "I've been told you are one of the top watch and clock designers in the world."

Ella's laugh was infectious. She began with a giggle and proceeded to lean her head back to laugh long and hard. She laughed until tears streamed down her face, and I happily joined in her merriment. When she had caught her breath, I raised my eyebrows at her and asked again.

"What? Was I misinformed?"

She smiled and shook her head slowly. "Not entirely. I'm at Level III of my training, which is a big deal. Similar to completing a medical degree. Now, I have to decide whether to continue the equivalent of a residency to attain the next level.

"Sounds impressive to me."

"I can tell you aren't from English Village. Few locals would ever think of me as a superstar. How long have you lived here, Josie?"

"We're not here to talk about me," I reminded her. "First, tell me more about the clock industry and your meteoric rise in a company known for quality timepieces. Later, when we've finished, I'll answer your questions about *my* background."

It seemed like a good plan at the time. But if I had known Ella was embroiled in a high-stakes controversy, I would have conducted the interview differently. Instead, I asked all the wrong questions. Later, I wondered whether I could have prevented her death.

Chapter Two

Wednesday Mid-Morning

During our two-hour conversation Ella described her career path as the result of persistence and luck. "In school, I was one of those kids who pushed the limits. Easily bored, I saw no reason to turn in repetitive daily assignments and thought I knew more than the teachers. My parents tried everything to motivate me, but secretly they wondered if I would ever find my way."

"Yet, here you are. *World Famous*, according to my editor."

She shook her head. "More like infamous here in English Village. People know me too well. I'll always be that little girl who asked too many questions and made my own rules."

I lifted the china teacup to sip my tea and studied her over the rim. "They may see you differently after this story is published. What would you like the locals to know?"

Ella fidgeted with her napkin before her eyes met mine. "That all their efforts weren't wasted. My teachers. My dad. The school counselor. I heard what they said. It just took me a while to understand."

"To understand?"

"To realize the journey is as important as the destination. Every step takes you closer to where you want to be, and the people you meet along the way will guide you."

"What opened your eyes?"

"I fell in love with the most intricate, complicated, fascinating subject of all: keeping time. Today's luxury watches are truly works of precision and art. They are far more complex than the clocks my father built. I was lucky to find others as passionate about this crazy business as I am."

"You traveled a long way to discover what you already knew from your childhood sundial."

"Uh-huh. From the moment I stepped into the design lab at Adler Minetti Timepieces, I felt at home."

A splinter of sunshine glinted off the young woman's wrist. I glanced down. It was a small moment. A fraction of a second. But it changed the course of our conversation. "Your own watch is lovely. Did you design it yourself?"

Ella's eyes lit up. "Yes. You are the first person to ask about it. Even my father hasn't realized how unique it is. His eyesight isn't what it used to be."

She proceeded to describe, in detail, the steps involved in creating the watch. Then she spoke of her dreams for the future, her challenges as a female in a male-dominated career, and the competitive nature of the business. I noted a hesitation in her voice. At the time, I assumed she paused to consider how to explain her world in a way that I would understand its complexities.

Ella stood as though to change the subject, offering to show me several clocks that influenced her own designs. We left the sunny patio to reenter the shop, and it took a moment for my eyes to adjust to the darkness. Which is probably why I didn't initially notice Alex McGregor standing near a ladder at the front windows.

"Oh!" I cried out when I saw him in the shadows. "You startled me!"

Ella was quick to introduce her brother. "Josie, this is my big brother and my personal hero our entire childhood."

Alex rolled his eyes. "Everybody knows Ms. Posey, little sister. You're the one who's new in town."

I swiveled my head to observe their playful exchange. "I'm happy to know both of you," I said. "From what I've heard, Ella will soon be the famous one."

"Wouldn't surprise me," Alex said. "Now that she's graduated from that fancy school in the Big Apple." He turned to adjust the ladder and then snapped the safety lever into place. I noted a limp in his step, and my eyes slid down to his work shoes. One sole was thicker than the other. I recalled my friend Nellie mentioning Alex had injured his leg in a fall from a tree when he was a child. The bone fracture healed in an abnormal position and caused a deformity.

"Thanks for bringing my tools inside." Ella motioned toward a leather case and several tins of cleaning solutions atop the glass counter beside her brother.

"No problem. Don't forget to wear gloves. Wouldn't want you to get those expensive hands dirty." He tipped his ball cap to her as he walked from the room.

Ella grinned at me. "See what I mean? Nobody is famous in their hometown. Especially not to their brother."

She walked me through the shop, talking knowledgeably about the history of clocks and pointing out her favorites. I marveled over a brass cage model clock with annular enamel dials, silver hands, and a mercury pendulum.

"This one was completed in 1901 by the clockmaker Antoine Thomas-Dubret," Ella said.

"It was inspired by a new way to divide time during the French Revolution. There were one hundred minutes in an hour and ten hours in a day."

When we passed a clock with the brass figure of the mother holding her child, I paused to touch the baby's cheek. Ella stopped beside me. "This one is a treasure," she said fondly. "After my mom died, I used to sneak into the shop at night to visit this clock. It made me feel closer to her. When my dad found me here one morning asleep on the floor, he told me the story that inspired the clockmaker to create it. The next day, he tagged it 'NOT FOR SALE.'"

"He saved it for you all these years."

Ella ran her finger along the rim of the clock face and nodded.

At that moment, while she seemed deep in reflection, I asked the question my editor most wanted to know. "What's next for you, Ella? Will you stay with Adler Minetti Timepieces? Complete the next level of training? Return home to the family business? Begin something new?"

She flashed her dimpled smile again. "Ah. That's the big question, isn't it?"

I waited, my pen poised over my notepad.

Ella sighed. "The truth is, I haven't decided. While I'm here for the art show, I plan to help clean and catalog Dad's clocks. My brother shouldn't climb ladders. Besides, he was never good with details, and this is long overdue. Every clock is numbered, but the collection hasn't been appraised in years."

"And after the clocks are inventoried?"

She shrugged. "I've rented a place here for the summer while I figure out my future. It's complicated, I'm afraid."

I looked into the young woman's eyes and tried to decipher the emotion there. Worry? Fear? Instead of pressing her further, I backed away. "I'm sure you will succeed whatever path you choose."

When we paused next to admire a row of tall, stately clocks, I asked, "Do you ever work on grandfather clocks like these?"

"We call those *long clocks*," Ella said. "Real clockmakers would never refer to it as a grandfather clock. The nickname became common after the songwriter wrote his famous lyrics in the late 1800s." She waved her arm to indicate the full row of clocks. "As you can see, my father loves them. I prefer to focus on much smaller timepieces, the kind people wear every day."

As we moved beyond the "long clocks," Alex stepped back into the showroom. "I'm off to drive Dad to his pinochle game. Will be back after lunch. You okay here?"

Ella shooed him away with both hands. "Go. Dad enjoys the time with his cronies. I've got this."

He nodded. Walked out. Then, returned to the threshold again. "Forgot to tell you some guy called for you. Said he might stop by later."

I smiled at Ella. "See? Everyone wants your attention."

She shrugged. "Probably someone in town for the art show. Or a friend of Jack's."

"Jack?"

"My ex-husband. He's here too."

Ella laughed at the surprised expression on my face. "Purely a coincidence. But that's another story."

I tapped my index finger on my wristwatch. "I have time if you do."

At the end of our morning together, Ella handed me a small backpack heavy with books. "Here's some reading material to get you started on the article."

I peeked inside to see a half-dozen books and two or three spiral notepads. Mentally, I groaned at the thought of reading them, but I accepted the bag without comment. No need to hurt Ella's feelings.

Ella also offered to share some of her drawings, which she intended to ship home from her New York City apartment. She hinted she might have a special announcement soon. I assumed the young designer was on the brink of a new creation, but she didn't disclose any details. I wrote my address on the back of my business card and handed it to her. "Send me all your trade secrets," I joked. "They will be safe with me."

She smiled as she accepted the card, but her voice took a serious tone. "Be careful what you promise. You might get more than you bargained for."

At first, her comment gave me an uneasy feeling, but when I tried to study her face, she had already turned away, and my unspoken fears vanished into thin air.

Ella walked me to the door and agreed to talk again later in the week. Then she gave me a small wave as I drove away. She looked so young and innocent. I wouldn't discover until later after I had researched Ella's full bio, that her watches sold for upwards of a half-million dollars… and her trade secrets might be worth killing for!

Chapter Three

Wednesday Afternoon

Though intrigued by Ella's story, my only goal for the rest of the day was to run a few errands and play my weekly game of mahjong. This week, we had agreed to share little-known facts about the game we all enjoyed. I was eager to see what the ladies had discovered. But first, Moe and I would take care of the errands.

I retraced my route down Main Street all the way to Persimmon Lane. The only sign of the earlier work crew was a freshly patched pothole at the intersection. Cruising along with the top down, I turned my radio to sixties music and sang along. It was ideal convertible weather with a glorious blue October sky, temperatures hovering around 72 degrees, and a light breeze that barely gusted to five miles per hour.

As I drove, I thought of my grandmother and how much she loved this small town. When she bequeathed her lovely little cottage to me two years ago, she outdid herself on the perfect-timing scale. Our adult sons had both moved to faraway places. My husband and I were considering retirement. We were ready to downsize and escape big city life. Then, a few days after Grandma Molly's attorney contacted me with keys to her cottage, a tragedy occurred.

"Mrs. Posey?" I could still hear the officer's voice on the mid-afternoon phone call. "It's about your husband, Kenneth. He's been rushed to the hospital." The rest of that call was a blur. A heart attack as he left his office building. CPR from a passerby. An ambulance.

I arrived at the hospital too late. In the blink of an eye, the love of my life was gone. Suddenly, Grandma Molly's cottage became more than a gift. It was a godsend. I adopted sweet Moe, a fluffy ball of fur at that time, and moved to English Village.

Bright red maple trees stretched their leafy arms toward the sunshine as I rounded the corner and pulled to a stop in my driveway. Inside the cottage, I dropped the heavy backpack onto the floor beneath the coat rack.

Moe greeted me with an enthusiastic wag that shook his entire body. It was time to make good on my promise. I grabbed his leash and ushered him down the sidewalk. Mrs. Abernathy, our newest neighbor, waved from across the street.

"Are you off to the park?"

"Just running a few errands. Need anything?"

The elderly woman shook her head. "No, but I saved a ham bone for Moe. Send him over when you return. I'll have it ready."

Moe heard the word "bone" and cocked his head to look up at me. "We will stop by later," I assured both my neighbor and my dog.

Together, Moe and I climbed into the car. He sat in the back seat like a prince in Her Majesty's Royal Parade, his floppy ears soon flying in the breeze. My own graying curls were tied back in a ponytail. No muss. No fuss. We often ran household errands like this together. He enjoyed the ride, and I welcomed his company.

As we made the short drive toward the library, I thought again of my grandmother and her uncanny sense of timing. She always showed up at precisely the right moment in my life. Even when I was a little girl, she magically knew when I needed to hear from her. It was as though she had a direct line to my mind and my heart. When I grew older, the invisible thread became even stronger. I'd barely ripped open the envelope of my college acceptance letter when Grandma Molly called me to chat. "I've been thinking of you, dear. Do you have any good news, by chance?"

Outside the library, I pulled Piper up to the book return bin, still smiling at the memories that danced in my head. Moe waited patiently while I dropped a couple of Louise Penny mysteries into the slot. Then, we rounded the corner of our favorite park and drove toward Main Street. Just ahead was The Curiosity Shop, where I'd spent the morning with Ella.

The charming old building reminded me of the historic restaurant where Kenneth had proposed many years ago in another city. That evening, Grandma Molly called to leave an answering machine message before I made it home from our date to announce my engagement to my parents. "You're on my mind again, Josie. What's new?" The memory still made me smile. Grandma's timing was legendary.

I slowed to peer into the plate glass window of The Curiosity Shop. Inside, Ella stood midway up the old wooden ladder with her clipboard and a feather duster, hard at work on the inventory of her father's treasured clocks. I looked forward to our follow-up call later in the week after I'd had more time to research her accomplishments.

Moe's ears perked up when we pulled into the drive-through lane at the bank. He was on his best behavior for my favorite teller, Maryanne, who, per routine, passed him a biscuit before she handed me my receipt. We circled onto Main Street again and drove another two blocks to the post office.

"That's it, Moe." I shoved a stack of envelopes into the big blue box. "Time to go home for lunch."

Back at the cottage, I put Moe in the backyard while I crossed the street to retrieve Mrs. Abernathy's ham bone. She readily answered the door with a brown lunch bag in her hand. "Here you go. I couldn't bear to toss it out when I knew Moe would enjoy it. The butcher assured me it was safe. No splinters to worry about."

By this time, the only thing that worried me was that I might be late for Wednesday mahjong. I ate a quick sandwich and pulled my game card from the desk drawer. I'd better hustle, or the mavens would scold me. Never mind that I qualified for the senior discounts at the movie theater; those ladies treated me like a little sister who needed their guidance. Funny how bossy they could be, just because they were a decade older.

Leaving Moe to his afternoon nap, I climbed back into my car and drove to Kate's. Every week, the same four women played together. And every time, someone shared information the rest of us didn't know. Others might call it *gossip*. Our mavens called it *news*. They took pride in staying connected to community events.

The most adventurous of our Mahjong Mavens, Kate traveled extensively and often had new stories to tell or a road trip to suggest. If there was a concert in town, Kate encouraged us to attend. She was the most likely of the mavens to push us out of our comfort zone—though some would say *I* held that distinction.

Kate greeted me at the door. "Come in, Josie. We're setting up the game."

She motioned to Sharon and Nellie, who had already taken the colorful racks and tiles out of their cases.

"You've arrived in time to help build the walls," Nellie called out to me.

Sharon poured drinks from a crystal pitcher. "Water or tea?"

In no time, we mixed the Chinese tiles and stacked them into two-story walls around the four trays that formed the traditional square: East, South, West, and North. With four experienced players, the game moved quickly. Whoever sat at the East position rolled the dice for the first hand. Each time a player won a game, she marked her score in the book, and we rotated the dice. This group didn't play for money—it was a friendly competition for bragging rights.

"Ladies, I have come to win today." Nellie tucked her perfect gray bob behind her right ear as she declared her intentions. "Please note that I'm wearing green—which, as you know, is a lucky color for Wednesdays."

I couldn't help laughing. "That theory didn't work for Sharon last week. But it's worth a try."

Kate rolled the dice to start the game. "Did everyone bring a mahjong fact to share?"

"I did," Nellie answered. "Some people believe mahjong was invented by Confucius. The three dragon tiles correlate with Confucius' three noble virtues."

"Pretty sure that's a myth," Kate said. "But it makes a great story."

"I've got one you won't believe." Sharon's blue eyes sparkled with excitement.

"Tell us," Nellie and I said in unison.

Sharon waved her arms as she spoke, nearly knocking her full glass of water off the table. "Mahjong began in China during the Qing dynasty. It didn't arrive in the US until the Roaring Twenties. It has been one of the most popular games in China forever, and..." She paused dramatically.

"And what?" Kate swatted Sharon with her game card.

"And now they have banned it!" Sharon claimed with a flourish.

"You're kidding," Nellie said.

"It's true," Sharon insisted. "The government declared mahjong to be illegal gambling around 1949. But, they actually banned public mahjong parlors fairly recently, in the fall of 2019."

I smiled. "You should hear our friend Lorene's opinion of that."

"The chief's wife?" Nellie asked. "She grew up in China, so she would know."

"Lorene says her mom still plays mahjong with friends in Chengdu. The city is famous for their love of the game."

"The ban must not extend to private homes," Sharon said. "I'm glad we can still play it here. Let's get started."

Although our conversation was limited while we concentrated on the game, we found time to share small bits of news between hands.

Nellie reminded everyone the English Village International Art Show would be held the upcoming weekend. "Yes, Nell," Kate said. "You've been talking about it for months. We'll be there."

Nellie was known for her ability to execute major events in the village. For decades, she had helped raise money to support community nonprofits. Somehow, the Mahjong Mavens always ended up on her committees. We had all pitched in to help with the Summer's End Festival a few months earlier. The art show was Nellie's most ambitious project yet, because it involved international guests and several days of activities.

"I want it to be a successful fundraiser for the Art Foundation," she said.

"It will be," I assured her. "Would it make you feel any better if we met to go over the details again?"

"Yes, please," Nellie agreed. "I have a checklist ready."

"My cottage at seven tonight?" I proposed.

"Perfect."

Kate looked up from her tile rack. "Josie, you haven't told us about your latest profile interview for the *Gazette*. Who is it?"

"Mr. McGregor's daughter, Ella. I spent most of the morning with her."

"What did you think of her?" Sharon asked. "She was a bit of a brat in grade school. I taught her in my second-grade classroom."

"I heard she had a run-in with her brother on her first day back in town," Nellie said.

"Whoa." I looked up from my game card. "I didn't sense any of that. She was friendly. Intelligent. Down-to-earth. And from what I saw, her brother appeared to be quite proud of his little sister."

Nellie took a sip of her water. "It's always good to have our young people return to English Village. What made her decide to come back? Will she stay?"

"You invited her, Nellie," I said. "She's here for the art show."

Nellie's smile lit her face. "She planned her trip home to coincide with our event? How nice!"

"As for the future," I continued, "Ella isn't sure yet. At least, not sure enough to tell me." I planted my elbows on the table and rested my chin on my clasped hands as I reflected on Ella's words. "For now, she wants to help her dad with an inventory of their rare vintage clocks at The Curiosity Shop."

"You think she will take over the business?" As always, Kate was first to get to the heart of the matter.

"Maybe."

"That could set her brother off," Sharon said. "He has worked in the shop since he was a kid. He might not be thrilled to have his little sister return home and edge him out of the business."

I threw my hands apart in the universal "I don't know" gesture. "Ella did have something she wouldn't, or couldn't, share with me. Something big."

"You'll figure it out," Kate said. "You always do."

My mind was preoccupied as we played our final game. The more I thought about the interview with Ella, the more certain I was that I should have probed deeper. The young woman had skillfully avoided several of my questions.

She was hiding something.

I wanted to know why.

As we cleared the tables, we heard a heavy knock on Kate's front door.

"Expecting someone?" Nellie raised an eyebrow to Kate.

"Never on a Wednesday." During the two hours we played each week, no one scheduled appointments. We didn't even answer our phones on Wednesday afternoons.

Kate pulled open the door. The rest of us were atypically speechless as Police Chief Earl Marshall stepped inside.

"Sorry to interrupt your game. I need to talk to Josie."

"Me?"

"Yes." The chief's serious dark eyes found mine. "The woman you interviewed this morning took a tumble."

"Ella?" I was startled by the chief's comment. "We were just talking about her," I said.

"I tried to reach you by phone, but I'm told you ladies are inaccessible on Wednesday afternoons." He nodded to the mavens who had gathered into a tight circle around him. Chief Marshall's dry sense of humor was not lost on me. He could try to lighten the mood all he wanted, but the fact that he stood at Kate's door told me the situation was serious.

"What happened?" I asked.

"Mr. McGregor's daughter fell at The Curiosity Shop. She hit her head pretty hard."

"How terrible. She planned to inventory the clocks today," I said. "In fact, I saw her through the window when I ran errands around noon. She was standing on a ladder."

"And now she is in a coma at the hospital."

"*What?*"

"I'll need you to make a statement."

"Why?" I asked. "Surely this was an accident, right?"

"That's what we need to determine. You spent several hours with Ella McGregor this morning. Might have been the last person to speak to her before she fell."

"It's Benjamin now. Ella Benjamin." A small shadow of fear crossed my mind as I considered that someone might have intentionally harmed Ella. Confused, I stared back at the chief. "All my notes are at home."

Chief Marshall's head pivoted to the three mavens who stood listening to our conversation. He returned his gaze to me. "Could we step outside, please?"

I huddled with the chief beside the ivy-covered trellis that framed the far end of Kate's veranda. He kept his voice calm and low.

"Sometime after you saw Ella at noon, she fell from the ladder and landed on her back. When her brother found her unconscious, she was still wearing the thin jeweler's gloves she used when handling their antique clocks. Tools from her kit were scattered across the floor."

The chief's vivid description made my heart hurt. Tears filled the corners of my eyes. "Poor Alex, to discover his sister that way. But it *had* to be an accident."

"Most likely, she lost her footing and fell," the chief agreed. "However, it's unusual for someone as young and fit as Ella to lose her balance on a ladder she's probably climbed a hundred times."

"Anyone can have an accident," I said.

"True. It's just...well, the ER doctor called to alert me that she noticed something unusual in Ella's injuries."

"What—"

The chief raised his hands in the air. "And before you start peppering me with questions, let me say that she did not provide details. She wants more time to study the X-rays. All I know is that there may be irregularities about the way Ella struck her head. I need to rule out foul play."

"What does that mean?"

"It means I have to consider other scenarios. Maybe Ella was distracted and fell. Maybe it was more complicated than that. I'm on my way to the shop to take a look around."

"You think something *caused* her to fall?"

"I don't know yet, Josie. That's why we call it an *investigation*."

I gave him what I hoped was a withering look. "How can I help?"

"Tell me what you recall about Ella's tool kit, her plans for the day, any people she expected to see. *Think, Josie.*"

Taking a deep breath, I closed my eyes and pictured myself with Ella at the shop. "Her tool kit was leather. Heavy. Her brother laid it on the counter...." My eyes popped wide open. "Oh! I remember that Alex said 'some guy' called for Ella. He didn't leave his name, just said he would drop by later to see her!"

"See?" Chief Marshall gave me a nod of approval. "This mystery man could be a person of interest."

I shook my head. "You're on the wrong track. Nobody would harm Ella. From what I could see, everyone loved her."

"Come to the station tomorrow to make a statement. Meanwhile, I'll check out the ladder and the showroom where she fell," the chief replied.

He took a few steps toward his car before he turned back to me, his eyes dark as coal. "And Josie," he said, "*No one* is loved by *everyone.*"

With the chief's words thundering in my head, I returned to Kate's living room, where she, Sharon, and Nellie waited at the mahjong table.

"Come here." Nellie motioned for me to join them. "Tell us what's happened."

I looked helplessly into the eyes of my concerned friends. "I don't know many details. Thomas McGregor's daughter, Ella, fell off a ladder. Her brother found her unconscious. But there's more. Ella's doctor contacted the chief about irregularities in the injury. Now he's on the case."

"Irregularities? What the heck does that mean?" Sharon asked. "The girl fell off a ladder."

"Her injuries are serious. The chief wants to 'rule out foul play' so he can file an official report if necessary.

Nellie reached out to touch my arm gently. "Surely he doesn't think *you* were involved?"

"That's absurd." Kate shoved her chair back from the table.

I shook my head. "Nothing like that. He's determined to figure out whether anything prompted her fall. He wants to learn as much as he can about Ella. Her lifestyle. Her health. Her career. The chief thinks I might uncover a clue from the conversation I had with her this morning."

Nellie handed me a glass of water. "Sit down. You look pale."

"Did he say what the irregularities were?" Kate asked.

"No. Just that Ella was young and strong. Not the most likely candidate for an accidental fall. The doctor noticed something unusual about her injury, but didn't clarify her suspicions."

"That man is like a dog with a bone. He won't let go until he's satisfied there's nothing left of it." Sharon's blue eyes sparkled across the table. She adored a good mystery and appreciated Chief Marshall's desire to solve unanswered questions.

"The chief is headed back to The Curiosity Shop now. He wants to take a closer look at the ladder."

"Anything we can do to help?" Nellie's sincerity touched my heart.

"Let's talk about it tonight," I said. "You ladies may be able to fill in a few details I missed in the interview." The mavens knew far more about the residents of English Village than Google or our local police department.

My heart raced as I considered what might have caused Ella to fall. Whatever—whoever—it was, the chief needed help with his investigation. The mavens and I were on the case.

Chapter Four

B y mid-afternoon, I had returned home and changed into comfortable clothes to search the Internet for additional information about Ella McGregor Benjamin's career. Moe rested his head on my feet while I worked. It didn't take long to confirm that Thomas McGregor's daughter was an extraordinary young woman.

Although Ella mentioned her scholarship to the Adler Minetti horology school during our interview, she had glossed over the details. Google delivered more than twenty articles about the prestigious program, including several that mentioned Ella by name. The facts were impressive.

Adler Minetti Timepieces maintained one of the industry's highest quality ratings worldwide. As part of their commitment to the retention of talented artisans, the company offered a free education to a small class of students each year. When Ella submitted her application, she was one of five hundred would-be watchmakers considered. Two hundred were interviewed. Ella made the cut.

After a rigorous testing program, ten students were accepted to the class. Ella was the only woman to receive a coveted spot in the history of the program.

"Wow!"

I didn't realize I had made the comment aloud until Moe raised his head to nudge my knee. I scratched his favorite spot behind his ears. "Sorry to startle you, boy. Ella is a bigger superstar than I realized."

I reviewed the notes I'd made earlier in the day. Ella stated she was lucky to get into the program, but she didn't disclose that she was the first woman apprentice in 170 years.

One article quoted a student who had graduated from the program a few years before Ella began. "It's grueling," the young man said. "We spent the first seven months of our training hand-making our own tools. It was nearly a year before we were allowed to touch a watch."

Ella had already achieved Tier III of the training. If she decided to continue, she would spend another three years as an apprentice before she reached the top level of craftsmanship. I wondered what she would choose. I rubbed my eyes and closed the laptop. It was time for a break before the mavens arrived for our final preparations for the big art show.

Moe and I took a short walk around the block, pausing to admire the red and gold chrysanthemums our neighbor had planted along her sidewalk. I vowed to purchase a few for my back deck soon. The bright blooms would add fall color to replace my fading geraniums. On our way back to the cottage, a patrol car approached from the opposite direction, its blue light rotating atop the vehicle. I froze in my tracks, squinting to see where it was headed. Could there be a burglar in our quiet neighborhood?

Seconds later, the car turned into my own driveway, and Chief Marshall walked up the sidewalk toward the front door. Moe and I hurried to catch up to him.

"Why are you here, Chief?" I was slightly out of breath from scurrying the half-block to my porch. "Has something happened? Your patrol light is on."

The chief's dark eyes took in my scruffy jeans and tennis shoes, noted Moe's blue leash, and swept back up to my flushed face before he answered. "I've tried to reach you for the past hour. I get perturbed when someone goes missing. Especially when she spent the morning with another woman who may have been assaulted. Finally decided to stop by for a visit."

"I wasn't *missing*. I'm right here. Wait! Did you say Ella was *assaulted*?"

"Possibly." He swiveled his head to scan the quiet neighborhood while I attempted to make sense of his answer.

"Possibly you said it? Or possibly she was assaulted?"

Chief Marshall scowled at me. "If you'd answered your phone when I called, we wouldn't be having this conversation on your front porch."

"Sorry. My phone was off for mahjong. Must have forgotten to turn it back on."

He nodded. "Could we talk inside?"

"Of course. Yes. Let's do that." While I unlocked the door, the chief turned off his flashing light and rejoined me on the porch. Mrs. Abernathy peered from her window across the street, and I gave her a friendly wave to prove she had nothing to worry about, hoping she couldn't discern that my own worry meter was sky high.

Moe bounded over the threshold ahead of us, snatched a toy from his basket, and stretched out on the cool tiles in front of the refrigerator. I placed my house keys on the counter and turned to the chief. "I can make coffee…"

"How about a glass of water instead?" Chief Marshall set his hat on my kitchen island and pulled up a barstool.

I studied his face as I filled two water glasses and took a seat across from him. It had only been a couple of hours since we'd talked at Kate's house, but the chief's countenance had changed. Earlier, his bearing reflected the weight of sadness as he shared the news of Ella's tragic fall and the doctor's speculations. Now, he faced me with grim resolution.

"After studying the area where Ella fell, I'm fairly certain it wasn't an accident."

I gripped my water glass between both hands and waited for him to continue.

"For one thing, the top rungs of the ladder were broken," he said.

"It was an old ladder," I countered.

"There were no signs of overall rot or decay. Why would the least-used rungs at the top be weaker than the others?"

The chief's question was a good one. I shrugged my shoulders. "I don't know."

"Me, either. I've asked the crime lab to take a closer look."

I shivered as the word 'crime' settled uncomfortably into my brain. "Anything else?" I asked.

Chief Marshall pulled a small notepad from his front pocket, squinting to decipher his own handwriting. "In addition to the fracture on the back of her head, the doctor identified one small cut near Ella's left temple and an indention of an unusual shape."

"Huh? I thought she landed on her back."

The chief took another sip of his water. "That's how her brother says he found her. It's possible she hit her head, then bounced onto her side—slamming her temple against one of the tools that scattered from her case."

"I can see how Ella might have struck her head on an unknown implement when she fell, making the accident more serious," I said. "What is the shape of the indentation?"

He tore a sheet of paper from his pad and sketched a rough design, sliding it across the table toward me. "The markings don't match any of the tools at the scene. Did you see Ella use a gadget this shape?"

I peered at the drawing, baffled by the symmetry of the chief's design. "Looks like streaks going outward from a circle, but there's no mark in the center."

Chief Marshall tapped his pencil on one of the streaks. "Yeah, probably not some kind of gear you'd find in a clock because those are generally thin. We would see the entire imprint. Instead, the marks are evenly spaced, but the streaks aren't well-defined. No edges. Must be something smooth with tubes like miniature wind chimes."

"Have you asked her dad or brother for an opinion?"

"Not yet. Suddenly, everyone is a potential suspect. I'd like to identify it ourselves if we can."

"Leslie Anderson will need a story," I said. "Care to comment?"

"Keep it short. Ella Benjamin fell from a ladder today in what is believed to be a tragic accident. We're looking into it to determine what might have caused the fall."

"With all due respect, she's going to want more, Chief."

"That's all I've got," he said.

As soon as he walked out the door, I made a quick phone call to Leslie with Chief Marshall's statement and promised a more complete story soon.

Though he ended our conversation with an admonition to "keep the details confidential," I was in such a dither I knew the mavens would spot my anxiety from a mile away.

As it turned out, Nellie saw the chief pull out of my driveway. She carried a huge duffle bag into my cottage and peppered me with questions before even saying hello.

"The chief was here about Ella again, wasn't he?"

"Come inside, Nell. Would you like coffee?"

"Don't try to distract me."

"I wouldn't dream of it. Cream?"

"Anyway, the word is all over town. When Ella tumbled from the ladder, she cracked her head on a 'foreign object'—whatever that means. My neighbor's son is an intern in the emergency room at St. Anthony's. He told his mom that Ella is still in a coma there."

I set the mug of coffee on my kitchen island and slid it closer to Nell. "If you already knew all about it, why ask me?"

"You know why." Nellie's eyes flashed daggers at me. "The chief didn't drop by your house for a neighborly chat. He must think her accident is suspicious."

"Sorry. I can't confirm that."

She put her hands on her hips and frowned. "You may as well tell us. We will find out anyway."

I pinched my thumb and forefinger together and slid them across my sealed lips.

"Funny, Josie. Very funny."

"Seriously, Nell. I don't know any more than you do. The chief asked again about my interview with Ella at the shop this morning. He wondered if I'd noticed what *you called* the 'foreign object' while I was there."

"And had you?"

"No."

Nellie huffed a little when I refused to describe the 'foreign object,' but she rebounded quickly. "Anyway, she will most likely wake up within forty-eight hours. Then she can explain it herself."

I opened the fridge to remove a platter of fruit and cheese. "Can we talk about the art show now? Kate and Sharon will be here soon. Art first; Ella discussion later."

Nellie rolled her eyes and took a handful of grapes from the tray before glancing out the kitchen window. "They're pulling into your driveway now."

I watched Nellie empty the contents of her duffle bag onto the kitchen floor. The International Hank English Juried Art Show was Nellie's brainchild—a happy accident of sorts. Our local English Village Art Foundation had been successfully hosting a fall workshop to honor the village namesake for several years. The event was well managed and attracted more applicants each year. Under the leadership of experienced volunteers, the weekend activities had become rote. At the conclusion of the event, committees simply set new dates, confirmed new presenters, and moved forward for the next year. Easy peasy. Until this year, when Nellie had the brilliant idea to invite someone from the Hank English Estate in London to attend the show.

Her goal was admirable: to better connect the workshop to the talented young painter who died long before there was a community named after him. Nellie imagined Hank's granddaughter traveling to the heart of America to make a brief speech at the opening session. Instead, the descendants of Henry Nolan "Hank" English eagerly offered to sponsor a juried art show tied to the event. Nellie found herself organizing an entirely new component that required far more work.

Kate and Sharon knocked on my door as they bustled inside with bags of their own.

"Knock knock. We're here," Kate announced.

"You're right on time." I waved them into the kitchen. "Almost ready."

Sharon carried a bulging shopping bag over one arm and a glorious apple pie in the other. The aroma of cinnamon and sugar made my mouth water before she crossed the kitchen to set it on the countertop.

While Nellie organized the contents from her duffle, I shoved my interview notes and laptop into a briefcase and carried them to my bedroom, away from any prying eyes.

"Take the table," I told Nellie. "We'll turn my dining room into a boardroom for tonight."

Nellie had come prepared like the former teacher and PTA leader she had been for more than thirty years. She snapped a portable easel into place and set a flip chart onto the rack. She laid a handful of colored markers beside the chart, placed a set of stapled papers neatly on the table in front of each chair, and provided a ballpoint pen for every guest.

Finally, she added a bell at the head of the table. "Just in case someone needs to get our attention."

Kate laughed when she saw it. "There are only four of us, Nellie. We should be okay without the bell."

Sharon pulled paper plates and napkins from her bag and set them beside the pie. "Let's get this party started."

I studied the plates as Sharon sliced into the fragrant dessert. Their design featured an artist's palette with dabs of paint around the outer rim and a handful of brushes scattered in an array of colors across the center. The paper napkins looked like squares of drop-cloth fabric from an art studio decorated with messy splashes of "paint."

"How do you do it?" I asked Sharon, in awe of her selection. My friend always brought perfectly-themed party supplies to our gatherings. I was convinced she had a secret warehouse filled with party décor and accessories for every occasion.

"I have my sources." She wiggled her eyebrows, a la Groucho Marx, and struck a mysterious pose.

"Must be good ones." Kate admired the colorful plate, then served herself a large slice of pie.

I savored my first bite of the flaky crust and sweet apple filling. "Delicious. What is this?"

"It's a Dulce de Leche pie." Sharon handed me an index card. "I brought you the recipe."

Nellie called the group to order, and we made quick work of the art show assignments. "Who wants to welcome the family?" she asked. "We will have

Hank English's granddaughter and her husband for three nights."

Sharon took a forkful of pie before she answered. "They're staying at the Philbrook Inn. They will be comfortable there. The food and service are wonderful. Let's have a guest basket in their room when they arrive."

"I can chauffeur them around town," Kate volunteered. She loved to introduce visitors to the highlights of the English Village. "I will show them the statue in the park. Give them the grand tour. Get them to the event on time."

Nellie used a broad black marker to draw a line through the first two items on her flip chart.

"I'll assemble the gift baskets," I added, running with Sharon's idea. "Lorene at Cozy Cups would probably supply coffees and teas. We can add a mug. Plus, a candle and some small items with English Village engraved on them. I'll also ask Jill at The Garden Cart to send flowers to their room at the inn."

"Thank you, Josie." Nellie jotted the details onto her flip chart.

"What about the guest judges?" Sharon skipped to the next item on the list.

"Good question." Nellie read from her printed handout sheet. "We've scheduled a private reception for the judges, to include the Art Foundation Board of Directors and a few other community leaders. Invitations were mailed to the mayor, the banker, the college art department—everyone on our foundation VIP list."

"Need us for anything?" Kate sat with her pen poised over her own list.

Nellie waved her papers in the air as she spoke. "This afternoon, I realized we haven't ordered refreshments for the reception. Can't believe I've sent an invitation and made no plan to feed the guests."

I wasn't surprised to hear Sharon, our party queen, ask, "What's the theme?"

"Totally casual," Nellie said. "Sunday afternoon. Light finger foods would be enough."

Sharon pointed to the flip chart. "Cross it off the list. Just give me a headcount, and I'll take care of the food. We can order beverages from Cozy Cups."

"Probably should have invited Lorene to this meeting," I said and added coffee and tea to my task list. "I'll handle that when I call about the gift baskets. Anything else?"

"A couple of volunteer opportunities." Nellie sketched a diagram of the gallery entrance on the flip pad.

She indicated two sets of double doors where guests might enter. "We'd like to have a couple of people at each of these to direct visitors to the registration tables."

"I'm happy to do that." I waved my pen in the air. "I'm sure Harvey would join me for the afternoon."

Nellie rolled her eyes at me. "I *told* you the two of you would be good partners. You should have listened to me earlier."

"Yes, Nellie." I grinned while she scolded me like a teenage schoolgirl. "You were right. But Harvey and I are friends, not partners." Harvey Jacobs owned the local hardware store and filled his spare time creating iron artwork at the blacksmith shop in our historic district. He and I had become good friends this summer and had recently begun dating – although I hesitated to call it that. It seemed like an odd word for people in their mid-fifties, and I had no intention of taking our relationship beyond friendship.

By now, our pie plates were empty, so we snacked on the fruit and cheese platters.

Kate rang the bell. "Time out. Let's get back to the assignments. Any other volunteer greeters?"

"I can do it," Sharon said. "I'll get Terry to help. He knows everyone, and he's great at directing people." She popped a grape into her mouth.

Nellie made a final check mark on her list. "That should be all we need, except for one thing…" She looked at Kate. "Anything you wanted to share?"

Kate stood motionless and turned a pale shade of red. "Er, ah, yes. I did. I mean, I do. Have something, that is."

"For goodness' sake, what is it?" Sharon prompted.

"I entered a painting in the amateur category, and the judges named me a finalist!" Kate blurted out.

"What?" I said, taken aback. This was big news. "Kate, I didn't know you were an artist!"

"I'm not. At least, I wasn't. But I took a beginner's painting class at the art museum this summer, and they encouraged me to enter the competition. There were only a few in my age category, so I might win an honorable mention by default."

"Tell them what you painted." Nellie practically glowed with excitement.

Kate broke into a huge grin that looked ever-so-much like the Cheshire cat from *Alice in Wonderland*. "I think you'll like it, Josie. You inspired my choice."

She pulled a draped canvas from behind the easel and set it in front of the flip chart. Then, dramatically, she removed the cloth that covered the painting. The mavens' collective gasp silenced the room.

Chapter Five

Wednesday Evening

W e stared speechless at Kate's watercolor.

"It's an Amaryllis belladonna!" I jumped from my seat to take a closer look. This was Kate's first painting. I couldn't tear my eyes from the canvas. The delicate pink blossom stood perched on a singular wisp of green stem, looking every bit like the "naked lady" it was called by those of us who used the more informal name.

"We have to show it to Miss Betty," Nellie said.

Our local dance instructor loved this particular flower, even though her husband had died from ingesting its poisonous blooms. Kate was all too familiar with the story, having helped with last summer's murder investigation. "I hope she will hang it in her studio," Kate said.

"I'm sure she will appreciate the gift," Nellie assured her.

"It's beautiful, Kate." I looked from the painting to my friend's glowing face.

Nellie covered the canvas with the drape again. "You'll need to return this to the exhibition tomorrow so they can hang it with the other entries. We've borrowed extra ladders from the hardware store. With additional crews, we will complete the job in half the time."

"That reminds me," Sharon said. "Did you hear about the chief finding a 'foreign object' at the base of the ladder where Ella fell?"

I replied without a reference to the foreign object. "Yes. Chief Marshall stopped by earlier. Hopefully, Ella will recover quickly. That young woman has quite a career ahead of her. She told me she had been interested in clocks and watches since she was a little girl, playing hide-and-seek in The Curiosity Shop."

Nellie packed her markers into the duffle bag she had slid under the dining room table. "Have to admit, I'd never heard of watchmaking as a career before Ella won that scholarship."

"You're not alone," I said, recalling my article research. "The profession is fading fast. Twenty years ago, there would have been plenty of options for science and watch-obsessed high school students like Ella. But the number of watch schools in the U.S. has dwindled from forty-four to fewer than ten."

"What happened?" Sharon asked.

"Apparently, when the digital watch was invented in Japan in the seventies, everyone assumed the mechanical watch industry would fade away. Cheap quartz watches flooded the market. Students chose other careers. Enrollment tanked. Schools closed down."

"Makes sense." Kate removed her painting from the easel and zipped it into a case.

I carried the cheese tray back into the kitchen. "Especially in the Midwest, where recruitment was more challenging. One program at Oklahoma State University–which ran for seventy-two years–closed its doors. Another at Saint Paul College, in Minnesota, followed soon after."

"Colleges can't continue to invest in programs if there's no job market for their graduates," Nellie said.

"Except they underestimated the demand for luxury brands." I rattled off the names of several well-known watchmakers. "Cartier, Rolex, Patek Philippe, and Adler Minetti sales skyrocketed. Their wealthy customers still appreciate fine craftsmanship and are willing to pay for it."

"Now the cycle is turning back the other way?" Kate asked.

"When Ella told me she was lucky to get into the Adler Minetti watchmaking program, she wasn't exaggerating," I explained. "The brand built its own training course and offers full scholarships to a select number of students each year. They hardly had a choice: the customer base for extremely fancy watches expanded, while the number of craftsmen who made them had cratered."

Sharon wrapped foil over the remains of her pie. "I guess you could say they are training a new generation to create watches that will stand the test of time."

"Anyone for more coffee?" I refilled our cups and set the pot back onto the burner. "If you still have time, I'd love to hear what you remember about Ella as a young girl."

Kate swept her gaze around the table. "Not sure I will be of much help since I left town after college. What do we know about her? Anyone?"

I was happy to have Kate take the lead. She had been an attorney in the United States Marine Corps and knew how to keep everyone on track. When I led a conversation, it tended to be circuitous. Kate's style was far more direct.

"Let's begin with her childhood," she suggested, pointing first to Sharon. "You were her second-grade teacher. What was she like?"

Sharon was precise with her answer. "She was smart. She learned quickly. She loved math."

"Anything else?" Kate asked.

"She adored her older brother," Sharon added.

"The same one she had an argument with?" Nellie asked.

"She only has one brother," Sharon confirmed. "She followed him everywhere when she was little. He always had a slight limp from an injury as a boy. He had climbed far too high in a tree. When he fell, he broke his femur in several places. They screwed in a titanium plate, but he never healed properly."

"How about you, Nellie?" Kate turned to the one person in the room who knew our town's history inside out.

"Ella won a science award when she was in the sixth grade," Nellie said. "It was a big deal. Part of the National Science Bowl. Her middle school team won the regionals—mostly because of her work."

Sharon nodded. "I remember that. Didn't their team go to the nationals in Washington, D.C.?"

"They won an all-expenses-paid trip," Nellie said. "The national events included several days of science activities, sightseeing, and competitions. They brought home a bunch of medals. Tom McGregor told me all Ella could talk about were the science seminars."

"How did they do at nationals?" I asked.

"That was the best part," Nellie said. "They took first place for sixth-graders! The whole team—five students and one coach—won a science trip to some exotic place. I don't remember where now. Maybe the Galapagos Islands? They studied microbiology in marine life. Mr. McGregor was so proud of her."

Kate took charge again. "Okay. We know she was smart. Anything else from her school years?"

Nellie began to speak and then paused.

"What is it?" I asked.

"I'm not sure when it happened, but Ella's mom was diagnosed with some kind of rare disease. Her name was on the prayer chain at our church for a long time."

Sharon agreed. "That's right! I was in a yoga class with her back then. She got progressively worse until she had to drop out."

Kate pulled us back on topic again. "Ella was a smart little girl. She loved her big brother. Their mother was ill. That's not much information. Does anyone recall her high school or college years?"

Sharon raised her hand.

Kate laughed at the gesture. "You don't have to ask permission to speak, Sharon. What do you remember?"

"It's about her brother and her dad. When my mother-in-law gave us her grandfather's clock, we took it into The Curiosity Shop for cleaning and repairs."

"Did they do a good job?" I asked. "I still have Grandma Molly's antique wall clock on a shelf in my spare bedroom. Maybe Mr. McGregor could get it ticking again."

Kate held up both hands to interrupt my interruption. "Stop. We need to stay focused on Ella McGregor."

"Sorry." I folded my hands on the table, but couldn't resist correcting her. "Kate, Ella's name is Benjamin now. Ella Benjamin. Please continue, Sharon."

Sharon gave me a wink. "We'll talk later."

Turning to Kate, she blurted out her speculations. "We were in the shop several times over the course of a few months. Each time, Mr. McGregor and his son, Alex, greeted us together. Alex didn't repair clocks, but he handled nearly everything else in the shop. I noticed a huge family scrapbook on the counter and flipped through the pages. It was filled almost entirely with photos and articles about Ella. She was clearly the celebrity of their family. Alex sort of faded into the background when his dad spoke of Ella. There were barely any pictures of Alex on those pages."

"Makes sense." I remembered the backpack I hadn't yet opened. "I'll bet I have copies of most of those articles from files Ella gave me."

Nellie sighed. "I'm afraid we aren't adding much to your research, Josie."

"You've probably helped more than you realize. Ella seemed fine with her brother when I interviewed her." My mind flashed briefly to the comment Alex made about Ella's expensive hands. "Though it's possible something happened to their relationship after she went away to college. Or that he resented her position as her father's protégé."

"Did she talk to you about her career?" Nellie asked.

"Yes. We spent nearly two hours discussing her education, her work, and her marriage to Jack Benjamin. Now I need to sort through those notes for Chief Marshall."

Nellie tucked her stylish bob behind her ear. "You better get moving. The chief can be pretty intense when he's working a case."

"I know."

"And you'll give us the latest?" Sharon prompted. "Like the description of the 'foreign object' everyone assumes was used as a weapon?"

"I'll tell you everything I can." My answer was the best I could do since there were details the chief insisted I keep quiet—even from the mavens.

We cleared the table, and I walked my friends to the front door.

"What do you think will happen to Ella now?" Sharon asked.

I flipped on the front porch light. "I'd say Adler Minetti is fortunate to have Ella as a student. She is passionate about designing state-of-the-art watches for the next generation. That young woman has a bright future ahead of her."

I truly believed Ella McGregor Benjamin could become the next big name in the watch world. Right up until my phone rang late that night with very bad news.

Chapter Six

Late Wednesday Night

"This is Josie," I answered Chief Marshall's call on the first ring. It was nearly midnight. The call must be important.

"How's your research coming along?" The chief's voice was as strong as always, but I heard beeping noises and blurred conversations in the background.

I looked at the papers spread across my grandmother's huge antique dining room table. "I'm halfway through my notes. How about you?"

"There's been a new development on my end."

"Anything you can share?"

I heard his heavy sigh and pictured him at his office, pouring another cup of stale brew into his stained *Cops Rule* coffee mug. "Ella regained consciousness for almost thirty minutes this evening."

"That's great. Is she feeling better?"

His deep voice filled the space between us with sorrow. "No, Josie. She was awake for long enough to say goodbye to her dad and her brother. Then, she slipped away again. Her heart stopped at 9:45 p.m."

A lump formed in my throat, and I had to swallow hard to reply. "I'm so sorry."

"Her doctor called with the news shortly after it happened. I've been at the McGregors' since then, taking more pictures and securing the scene," the chief said. "This wasn't an accident, Josie."

My mind flashed an image of Ella's bright face as she sat across from me on her patio. Twelve hours ago, she was filled with life and hope.

"Could it have been an attempted robbery gone wrong? I saw several valuable clocks throughout the showroom."

The chief lowered his voice. "Mr. McGregor said all the inventory is intact. It wasn't a robbery. Someone wanted Ella dead. This was murder."

"*Murder?*" My mind reeled as I processed the chief's words. "How do you know?"

"I suspected it after I went to The Curiosity Shop for a closer look at the ladder. Several of the upper rungs were definitely unstable. Plus, Dr. Grant shared the X-rays. Ella's temple had unusual markings in the shape I described to you."

"Er, about those marks," I stammered. "Word is already around town that Ella hit her head on an unknown object."

"Thought I told you to keep it quiet," the chief's voice simmered with anger.

"It wasn't me, Chief!" I leveled my tone to match his. "Sharon told me her neighbor's son works in the ER at the hospital, and he said the marks on Ella's head had to be caused by a *'foreign object.'*"

After what seemed like a really long pause, I looked at my phone to be sure it was connected. Then I spoke again. "Chief. You still there?"

"I'm here," he growled. "And if *the son of a neighbor of one of your mavens* says there was a *'foreign object'* involved, I guess I have to accept that the rumors are flying. But I don't have to like it."

"No, sir," I answered. "Just wanted you to be informed."

"Yeah. Well, I still don't want to fuel the gossip by describing the marks or commenting on a *'foreign object'* before we know what really happened."

"It was an old ladder. She could have lost her balance as she reached for a clock on the top shelf. Maybe she landed on one of her tools when she fell." I wasn't willing to believe Ella had been murdered.

The chief countered with another theory. "Or, the killer tampered with the ladder so she would fall, then finished the job with a blow to her temple."

Sharon was right, I thought to myself. Once Chief Marshall had an idea in his head, it was impossible to persuade him otherwise. "Who would do such a horrible thing?"

"Whoever it was, they went to a lot of trouble to give the appearance of an accident. We found no sign of a forced entry. No fingerprints. No evidence of a struggle."

"My vote is still for an accident." I could be as stubborn as the chief, I decided.

"There's something else." The chief pulled another surprise out of his bag of tricks. I should have known he wouldn't insist Ella's death was a murder without solid evidence. Now, he shot the harsh words into my ear without warning.

"Dr. Grant told me when Ella woke from the coma, she was agitated. The girl said three phrases to the doctor before her family came into the room. With a tremendous effort, she raised her head and grasped Dr. Grant's hand. Then, she looked into the doctor's eyes and spoke each word clearly."

"What did she say?"

"The doctor preferred to give the list to me in person to avoid any confusion or misinterpretation. She wrote everything onto a prescription pad and tucked it into the pocket of her lab coat. I'm on my way there to get it now. A face-to-face hand off is a safer way to handle confidential information and protect our chain of evidence for a court of law if the words lead us to Ella's killer."

My mind raced as I tried to guess what clues Ella might have given us from her deathbed. "Will you call me when you have it?"

"It's midnight, Josie."

"I know, but..."

Chief Marshall's voice was weary on the other end of the line. "By the time I retrieve the information and take Dr. Grant's statement, it will be the wee hours of the morning."

"But you'll share her words?"

"Most likely, I'll need you to help me decipher them. Dr. Grant said they made no sense to her, but they might to you."

My voice caught in my throat. "Chief, I'm really sorry."

"There's nothing to be sorry about." His normally gruff voice took a gentler tone. "Unless you rigged that ladder. You didn't do that, did you, Josie?"

"Of course not." I gulped to quash the sob that threatened to escape from my throat.

"Then I'm going to need your help finding out who did."

"Where should I start? I just met her for the first time this morning."

"Think about it, Josie. You were one of the last people to speak with Ella before her fall. You spent two hours with her. No doubt you will find something from your interview that leads us to the next clue."

"I hope so."

"You'll know it when you see it. Hold on...." I heard voices in the background again, and the chief covered the mouthpiece with his hand to muffle the conversation. Then he returned to our call. "Let me give you my cell number so you can call me at any time."

"That's not necessary."

"What?"

"I don't need it, Chief Marshall. I already have your cell number."

The chief and I had developed a mutual respect for each other from the first day I moved to English Village. In fact, we had already worked together to solve a murder case. Sort of.

When the husband of our local ballerina died from poisoning, I had been linked to the murder—not directly, thank goodness—but in a way that helped to solve the case. Mostly, the chief told me to turn over the notes from my interview with the ballerina. Like he was doing now with my notes from Ella's interview.

Which I did. But I had my own job to do, writing the story for *The Village Gazette*. Naturally, I ran across more details in the process. Then the chief insulted my mahjong friends, and we had to prove we weren't worthless old biddies.

In the end, even though he hated the thought of relying on help from outsiders, Chief Marshall accepted our input.

"You kept my phone number?" I could hear the surprise in his voice.

"I have you on speed dial."

The next thing I heard was a deep chuckle. "You remind me of Lorene." I considered this a compliment because the chief's wife is my friend. Until he added a final comment: "You are both exasperating women."

He ended the call, and I went back to my notes. The chief had a way of insulting me that only made me more determined to figure out Ella's murderer before he did. I renewed my efforts to dig into her background so I could make a list of everyone who qualified as a suspect.

Moe stretched onto his side and groaned to tell me it was way past his bedtime, but I couldn't stop until I'd sorted through the full set of notes. Ella's murder changed everything. What was once a light feature article about a smart hometown girl had become a crime story. By morning, my editor, Leslie Anderson, would demand an update, and Chief Marshall would expect new details.

I listened to the recording of our interview and jotted down the names of people who knew Ella best. The list was an interesting mix of educators, family, and friends.

At the top, I wrote the names of family members the chief already knew: her father, Thomas McGregor, and her brother, Alex McGregor. On the surface, both seemed to love her dearly, but the mavens insisted there were rumors of friction between Ella and her brother.

Next, I added her ex-husband, Jack Benjamin. Ella married Jack while they were both horology students. The hours were long, and the pressure to perform was intense. Ella told me the marriage was a mistake. "We were too young and too competitive to devote ourselves to our relationship," she had said. "Our marriage was in trouble six months after our wedding day. We hung on for another year and a half, but divorced after only two years."

The fourth name on my list was Logan Lavender, Ella's mentor and friend. She was a watch collector who appreciated fine craftsmanship. Ella mentioned her several times in the interview; the woman had accompanied Ella home from a recent trip to Geneva, Switzerland. If anyone could tell us more about Ella, it would be Logan.

The final name was Ella's professor, Daniel Davis. A scholarly man in his early sixties, Dr. Davis had spent the past seven years training Ella. He knew her better than most.

Pouring through the interview tapes and my notes, I found only a few other places where Ella provided specific names. She briefly mentioned a classmate named Carlos, but did not include his last name. She recalled a doctor's appointment with a specialist named Rosenberg—but only to say she was late to class one day because of an appointment with Dr. Rosenberg. And she told me a funny story about her ditzy landlady, Lucy Buttons. None of these people had a significant connection to Ella, but I included them anyway.

When I'd completed the list, I typed out a quick news story for Leslie, incorporating the facts as we knew them. Ella Benjamin was pronounced dead at 9:45 p.m. as the result of complications from a fall earlier in the day. Police are investigating the accident. Foul play is suspected. I fired the brief news release into Leslie's email and closed my laptop.

Moe nudged my knee, and I rubbed my bleary eyes.

"I see you." I placed my palm under his chin and lifted his face. "Are you ready to go to bed?"

My wall clock ticked toward 2 a.m. Only seventeen hours had passed since I walked through the door of The Curiosity Shop to interview Ella McGregor Benjamin. I wondered how long it would take to find her murderer.

Chapter Seven

Thursday Early Morning

I awoke to the insistent ringing of my cell phone and fumbled to reach it on the nightstand next to me.

"Hello?" I answered with my croaky early-morning voice.

"'ello thar! How are ye? Is it Josephine Posey I'm speakin' to?" A lilting voice with a slight Irish accent greeted me.

"Yes. Who's calling?"

"Me name is Lucy Buttons, and I need to confirm yer mailin' address."

"Wait a moment, please." I sat up, rubbing my eyes. Moe snored softly on his own bed across the room. A quick glance at my alarm clock confirmed my suspicions: it was barely 7 a.m., earlier than usual for my cell phone to ring.

"Miss Buttons?" I resumed the call. "What time is it there?"

"Time?" The woman's voice registered surprise at the question. "Why, it's 8 a.m., of course. Top 'o the mornin' to ye, Ms. Posey."

"Ah, yes. Good morning to you, as well," I said. "We're earlier in this time zone, so I apologize for not being fully awake."

"Oh, my!" I heard the consternation in her tone. "I've called you too early, then?"

"No, no," I assured her. "I'm awake now. But, could you tell me again who you are and why you are calling?'

"Of course." The perky voice did not sound familiar. "I'm Lucy Buttons,

45

yer know."

"Do I?"

"We haven't met, but Miss Ella told me to send yer a couple of her things."

"Ella McGregor? I mean, Benjamin?" Good grief. I had scolded others for using Ella's maiden name, and now I was doing it.

"Ella Benjamin is how I know 'er," the woman continued in an upbeat tone. "I'm 'er landlady, yer see."

"Excuse me. But, Ella told you to send me something?" I repeated what the women said earlier. I had assumed Ella fell before she was able to contact her Irish landlady.

"Yes, ma'am," Lucy confirmed. "I've finished packin' 'er things, and she requested I mail the package directly to ye. Did she not mention it to you, then?"

"Only that she intended to contact you."

The landlady carried on in the same endearing accent. "She provided yer phone number but not yer address. Now she's not answerin' 'er phone."

"Ella fell off a ladder in her father's shop yesterday." I spoke quietly, as though it might help soften the news for this helpful woman who clearly had a good relationship with her renter. "She died last night."

"Oh!" Lucy Buttons exclaimed. "Oh, no! I'm so sorry."

"Me too," I said.

"How tragic. She was a wonderful young woman and a perfect tenant, she was." The landlady lowered her voice to the respectful tone used by many elderly folks when they spoke of the deceased. "I didn't know 'er family, so it's not likely they would think to contact me."

"May I ask when you last spoke to Ella?"

"Sure 'an she sent me a text with 'er wishes," Lucy said. "It was just after you interviewed 'er. She said to send the reporter—that's you—a few things to help with yer article." She paused, thinking. "Do you still want me to send 'em?"

"I'd like that very much." I gave her my address and promised to notify her of plans for a memorial service."

"She was a lovely girl," Lucy said again. "Please tell 'er father I'm sendin' an Irish blessin' fer the family."

"I will," I promised. "May I also phone you with any questions about Ella after I receive the box?"

"Of course. And Ms. Posey...." She paused as though not certain whether to continue.

"Yes?"

"I think Ella may have been ill. I found a prescription bottle in 'er medicine cabinet." If the landlady struggled with her conscience over sharing too much information with a stranger, she apparently decided Ella's death freed her from any confidentiality clause. "I don't mean to pry, but it looks like she never opened the bottle. Shall I send it along?"

"Yes, please. Her family may want to contact the physician who prescribed it." Plus, any details about Ella's life could prove helpful in the chief's search for her murderer.

"Very well." Lucy's voice was drained of energy as she absorbed the reality of her young renter's death.

I heard her brief sob and waited a couple of beats before I pushed for more information.

"Ms. Buttons, was there anyone who might have argued with Ella? Or perhaps disliked her?"

"Never. The girl was a saint. Ever-one loved her."

Now I had even more questions, and the day had barely begun. Moe was awake with his head resting on my knee as I ended the call. I let him out the back door, turned on the coffee pot, and retrieved my newspaper from the front porch. I barely needed to open the door to reach it. Little Johnny Fletcher, my paperboy who lived a few houses down the block, had a great pitching arm. He consistently landed the newspaper directly outside my door.

While Moe ate breakfast, I stepped into the shower. The steaming water failed to clear my head. Too much had happened in the last twenty-four hours to absorb it all. I felt a huge responsibility to sift through the details of Ella's life and find solid clues for my murder investigation. Technically, it was the chief's investigation, but I was involved, just the same. I wondered what items Lucy Buttons would send me. She had offered to ship UPS Next Day Air so I would know soon enough.

Meanwhile I'd promised the chief I would scour my interview notes for any reasons someone would want to harm Ella. I spread the pages in front of me and buried my head in my hands. The task was impossible. Nothing pointed to an enemy or a conflict. Even Ella's divorce was amicable. I shoved away from the table and stood to pace the floor.

Moe followed behind me. Back and forth. I was still pacing when the chief called at nine a.m.

"I met with Dr. Grant last night. Could you come to the station?"

"Be there in ten minutes."

Chief Marshall sat across from me in the cramped police station conference room. Frown wrinkles etched his ebony forehead. He gripped the stub of his pencil in his right hand and slid a yellow slip of paper toward me with his left.

I squinted at the three items, written in blue ink. Dr. Grant's graceful handwriting surprised me. Didn't all physicians scribble indecipherable hieroglyphics when they wrote? This penmanship flowed across the page in precise curves. Unfortunately, the perfectly-formed letters did not enhance the meaning of the words.

The message was an odd combination.

32

Complicated

Long Clock

"I hope you can figure this out." The chief laid his pencil beside the spiral notebook in front of him and picked up his coffee mug. Took a sip. "It means nothing to the doctor, or to me."

"Did you show this to her dad or brother?"

"Not yet. Dr. Grant believed Ella's final words might lead us to her murderer. Until we decipher her message, I'd prefer not to share them with anyone."

"Did she say anything to her family before she died?"

"Only that she was sorry."

"Sorry for what?"

The chief ran his hands through his closely cropped hair. "Josie, the woman said two words to her father and brother. That's all. If she had provided details, I would have shared them with you."

"Sorry, Chief. I don't understand it."

He leaned back in his chair and clasped his hands behind his head. "Unfortunately, neither do I."

No matter how long I stared at the yellow slip of paper, Ella's dying statement meant nothing to me. I turned the words upside down, flipped them over, and held the paper to the bright overhead light. Nothing. After I puzzled over the yellow note for several additional minutes, I asked the chief one more question. "Could Ella have been talking in her sleep?"

"Not likely. Dr. Grant said Ella woke up from her coma, raised her head, and looked directly into the doctor's eyes as she spoke. She struggled to say each line. She said them only once, but the doctor felt they were important. Then, Ella sighed and closed her eyes. She didn't open them again until her father and brother arrived. At that time, she squeezed her father's hand. He bent closer to her. She whispered, 'I'm sorry,' before she passed away."

Something nagged at the back of my mind since the chief handed me the note. I had already spent several hours sifting through every word of my interview notes. My entire conversation with Ella was fresh in my memory, but the clue still made no sense. I studied the message again:

32

Complicated

Long Clock

This time, a small buzz of familiarity stirred in my temple. Yes! Ella had referred to one of these items when we talked. I wasn't sure which one or how it related to her murder, but I felt confident I could connect the dots somehow.

"I might have something." My voice was barely a whisper, but the chief pounced on it with hope.

"I knew you could do it!"

"Not yet. I need time to dig into it. But I'm certain Ella commented on at least one of these subjects when we talked. I'll find it. Give me a few hours."

"Take this with you." The chief handed me a bright yellow file folder with three dozen sheets of phone records inside. "My guys are working on the recent calls to our area code. Let me know if you run across anything else we should review."

My optimism faded after I'd returned to my cottage and stared at the messy stack of notes that cluttered my dining room table. I dropped the yellow file folder into the mix, collapsed into my favorite reading chair, and leaned back to stare at the ceiling. Sweet Moe cocked his head and raised one paw to rest it on my knee.

"What was I thinking, Moe? This is an impossible task. I don't know where to begin."

Moe looked at me with sad brown eyes, strolled to his toy basket, and returned to drop Lamb Chop at my feet. The stuffed toy smiled up at me with red felt lips and long eyelashes.

I accepted his gift and knelt to wrap my arms around his fluffy body. "You are the best friend ever."

He squirmed out of my embrace to stretch onto his back on the floor, paws waving in the air. Which forced me to scramble to my hands and knees where I could give him a proper belly scratch. And while I was there, in an awkward position halfway under the dining room table, I saw a scrap of paper had fallen from my briefcase. I snatched it up to read: Logan Lavender. Ella had given me her mentor's name and phone number to contact regarding the feature story about her career.

"That's it, Moe!" I held the paper in front of his furry face. "I need to call Ella's friend for help."

Chief Marshall's IT specialist was already on the case, reviewing calls to The Curiosity Shop, as well as Ella's phone calls, texts, and emails. The process would take a while. Their primary focus was on potential suspects who lived nearby or had been in town the past few days. It might be a week or longer before they contacted Ella's co-workers and friends from New

York or Switzerland. Meanwhile, if I could reach her mentor and friend, Logan Lavender, I might be able to track down an interpretation of Ella's final words.

But first, I called the chief to check-in.

He answered with a question: "Have you solved the case?"

"No. I'm more confused than ever. I'd like your permission to interview a few of her friends."

"Are they people you would contact in the normal course of writing your story? Or potential suspects?"

"Honestly, I don't know. They include people I would call for the article I was supposed to write. But, each of them could be considered suspects. You taught me everyone is a suspect until we have a confession or a solid case."

"Er, yes, I did." The chief cleared his throat, and I figured he wasn't thrilled to get me any deeper into his investigation. "Who's on your list?"

"Her father and her brother."

"I'll take those. We're already talking to them." The chief's answer didn't concern me. I knew Nellie and Sharon would deliver a casserole to Thomas and Alex McGregor before the end of the day. Those two would learn more than the chief's detectives anyway.

"How about her ex-husband? He lives out of town, but is visiting friends in English Village right now."

"He's ours, too. An ex-spouse is always a prime suspect."

"Could I call her friend Logan Lavender? She was with Ella in Switzerland a few weeks ago, and she's an expert on watches and clocks."

The chief spoke slowly as though he were talking to a child. "Interview her as you had planned for the article. Don't tell her Ella's final words. And don't treat her like a suspect. Anyone living in another country is unlikely to have killed Ella in the heart of America."

"Yes, sir. Can I mention the words Ella used, as long as I don't say why I'm curious about what they might mean?"

"Don't push it too far, Josie." I heard the chief's words as a "yes" but decided not to ask for further clarification.

"How about her professor, Daniel Davis?"

"Another logical person for you to call. Besides, I will have my hands full with the local folks and the unidentified caller who said he planned to stop by the shop."

"You found him?"

"Not yet, but we have a list of all the incoming calls from that day."

While the chief was feeling generous, I shared the remaining names from my notes with him. "There's also a landlady named Lucy Buttons, a physician named Dr. Rosenberg, and a student she admired named Carlos."

Chief Marshall sounded doubtful. "Those all seem a little far-fetched. Speak to them if you would like, but I doubt they would be connected to her murder."

"And the Mahjong Mavens?"

I couldn't see him, but somehow I knew was giving me the exaggerated eye roll he always did when I mentioned the mavens. "Tell them I said to stick to the art show and stay out of this investigation."

"But I can brainstorm with them about hypothetical stuff, right?"

"Hypothetically?"

"Hypothetically. You know, for the purpose of figuring out theoretical possibilities."

"I know what 'hypothetical' means, Josie."

"I knew that."

The chief sighed heavily into the phone. "You'll consult the mavens even if I don't approve, won't you?"

"Chief, I would never do anything to compromise your investigation."

"Use some common sense, will you? I don't want the mavens sniffing around where they don't belong. They already have their noses into everything, as it is."

"But in a good way."

"Uh-huh." Something in the chief's voice told me he had doubts about involving the mavens, but I plowed ahead.

"Okay, Chief. I'll get right on this. No delays on my end."

I set my cell phone on the table and turned to Moe. "Guess what, boy? The chief can't wait to see how we can help him." Moe raised his eyebrows as though to question me, but I ignored his quizzical expression. He was a dog. He couldn't possibly have understood the one-sided phone conversation.

Chapter Eight

Now that I had the chief's approval, I placed the call to Logan Lavender in New York. She answered in a poised and professional tone. "Logan Lavender speaking." The woman's voice was so rich and full I wondered whether she had ever considered a singing career.

If Ella hadn't described her mentor to me as a mature woman in her sixties, I would have guessed Ms. Lavender to be in her early forties. I introduced myself. "My name is Josephine Posey. I'd like to talk to you about Ella McGregor Benjamin, if you have a moment." Though I intentionally neglected to say I was a reporter, Ms. Lavender immediately reacted in a negative way.

"Why are you calling me?" There was a note of anger in her voice and I wondered why she sounded so defensive. "I heard about Ella's death this morning from a mutual friend. I know nothing about it."

I tried to soothe the woman. "I'm not an investigator; I'm a feature writer for our small-town newspaper. I talked with Ella shortly before she died, and I'm reaching out now to the people she admired most."

"Oh." The anger left her like a deflated balloon. "Did Ella say that about me?"

"She considered you one of her closest friends and mentors. I hoped you could give me insights only a good friend would know."

Ms. Lavender's voice softened. "It's interesting she described me as her mentor. Although I'm considerably older than Ella, it often seemed *she* was the one teaching *me.*"

"That's exactly the sort of detail I need for the story I'm writing."

"Give me a moment while I move closer to my desk, where I can recharge my cell phone," Logan said. "Forgive me for being a little cranky. I've just returned from a rather stressful trip and need to recuperate." I pictured Logan Lavender walking across the room to a beautiful mahogany desk and sliding into a comfortable leather chair. She returned to the call. "Do you mind if I put you on the speaker?"

"Not at all," I agreed. "I'll do the same. It's always easier to have a conversation if your hands are free."

Ms. Lavender laughed gently. "That sounds exactly like something Ella would say. She always claimed I talked more with my hand gestures than I did with my voice."

I admitted Ella had mentioned Logan's animated speaking style during our interview. "Your enthusiasm was one of the things she loved most about you."

Logan sighed. "We were close. Sometimes, I felt Ella knew what I was thinking before I knew it myself. She was the kind of friend who doesn't come along very often."

I flipped on my recorder and set the phone on the table. "How did the two of you meet?"

"It was remarkable," Logan explained. "I have been a patron of the Marco DeLuca Watchmaking Competition for many years. The year Ella won the award, I hosted all the honorees for an evening at my home in Geneva. Ella sat next to me during dinner, and we talked as though we had known each other for many years."

I knew Ella received the Excellence award, but I wasn't familiar with the details of the contest. "I read the DeLuca competition takes six months to complete."

"Yes," Logan said. "It's an opportunity offered exclusively to students at watchmaking schools worldwide. It is sponsored by DeLuca & Piazza of

Florence. Each school can recommend up to three participants, but only the best are invited to participate. They spend the first week of June in workshops. Afterward the students have six months to develop a solution for the assigned task."

"They are judged on their ability to solve a specific problem?" I asked.

"Yes. In early January, the expert jury scores them on originality, innovative character of the idea, functionality, technical and artisanal execution, and aesthetic appeal of the design."

"Sounds complicated." My brain pinged me a reminder to be on the alert for the use of the word "complicated," but I shook off the mental interruption.

"It's quite challenging," Ms. Lavender agreed. "Over the years, the assignments have ranged from the construction of a moon-phase display to date, time zone displays or power-reserve indicators. Ella's competition was focused on the construction of a calendar-week display in combination with a dual time zone."

I heard the excitement in Logan Lavender's voice and realized the accomplishment must involve a great deal of skill and effort. "No wonder her father and brother are so proud of her," I said.

"Her entire country should be proud of her," Logan said. "Ella is the only woman ever to receive the award and one of only two Americans. This is a male-dominated industry, and the $10,000 prize often goes to someone from Germany, France, or Finland."

"Wow," I said, immediately regretting I had no better word to express my astonishment. "It's too bad the watchmaking industry doesn't receive greater recognition from the public."

Logan Lavender sighed. "It's one of those scientific fields that is rarely mentioned," she said. "People tend to think watches today are all mass-produced digital styles. They have no idea there is a huge market for the craftsmanship and detail of an expensive handmade watch or clock."

While I had Ms. Lavender on the phone, I decided to explore other areas of Ella's life. "I've been told Ella was remarkably intelligent, with a passion for both watches and clocks. What can you tell me about her personal life? Did you know her ex-husband?"

"Oh, yes," Logan said. "I knew from the beginning it wouldn't last. Jack was a nice young man, but he would never have been happy living in Ella's shadow. She was clearly far above him, intellectually."

"Did she enjoy traveling, or have any other interests or hobbies?"

Logan paused before answering. "Ella was secretive about her other interests," she said. "We talked once about her failed marriage and briefly about her family in English Village, but nothing else."

"That seems odd since the two of you were close friends," I said.

"Yes," Logan agreed. "I believe Ella was involved in something she was unwilling—or unable—to share with me. In the last six months, she appeared to be carrying a heavy burden."

"What do you mean?" I scribbled notes onto the pad in front of me.

"She became quiet and moody when I asked about her work," Logan said. "She stopped eating. I cautioned her about losing too much weight, and she snapped at me. Something was on her mind, but I don't know what it was."

I thanked Logan Lavender for her time and ended the call, perplexed. Then I stood to pace the length of my Grandma Molly's dining room table. Moe lay on the floor beside the couch. He turned his head from side to side as I crossed in front of him.

The new information from Ms. Lavender had only added to my confusion. Ella had a secret she had not shared with anyone. Could it have led to her death?

Determined to find a clue to Ella's secret, I refilled my coffee cup and gathered my interview notes into a pile. I stacked the 4x6 index cards and shuffled them like a deck of playing cards. Then I tossed them, one by one, onto the surface in front of me. I was halfway through the deck when an underlined phrase caught my attention.

Aha, I thought. *This is the connection I was searching for.*

Quickly, I read through the scribbled notes. During one part of my interview, I had asked Ella if she ever worked on grandfather clocks like the ones in her father's shop.

"We call those *long clocks*," she had said. "Real clockmakers would never refer to it as a grandfather clock. The nickname became common after the songwriter wrote his famous lyrics in the late 1800s."

I turned the card over in my hands, inspired to do additional research. My friend Google provided answers immediately: *Grandfather clocks—with their long cases, pendulums, echoing chimes, and Roman numerals—seem to belong to the world of courting parlors, Model-T Fords, silent movies, and going out on a date for an ice cream soda. In short, the world of grandparents. But, the real reason these timekeeping devices—technically called* longcase clocks—are known as grandfather clocks is because of a songwriter with a vivid imagination.

I skimmed the lengthy article and jotted notes for future reference. The songwriter was an American traveling in England. Henry Clay Work checked into the George Hotel in North Yorkshire in 1875. There, he noticed a large pendulum clock in the lobby, motionless. When he asked about the clock, the innkeeper explained the clock had belonged to the two previous owners—the Jenkins brothers. When the first brother died, it was said that the clock began to lag in its timekeeping. When the second brother died, the clock stopped completely at the precise moment of his death. No repairman had been able to bring the clock back to life.

Fascinated by the story, the songwriter wrote "My Grandfather's Clock" and released it in 1876. When I read the lyrics, they stirred an early memory of my grade school music teacher, Mrs. Crenshaw. I smiled to myself as I recalled her rapping on the wooden tick-tock block to make clock sounds as we sang the rhythmic song.

> *My grandfather's clock was too large for the shelf*
> *So it stood ninety years on the floor*
> *It was taller by half than the old man himself*
> *Though it weighed not a pennyweight more*
> *It was bought on the morn of the day that he was born*
> *And was always his treasure and pride*
> *But it stopped, short, never to go again*
> *When the old man died*

Probably, this was another of my often-traveled rabbit holes, but I found the story fascinating. The original longcase clock that attracted the songwriter's attention wasn't even owned by a grandfather. I wondered whether Henry Clay Work realized he had renamed an entire category of clocks simply by writing his memorable lyrics. And I speculated on how the information related to Ella's secret.

It seemed too soon to bother the chief with a random thought, but I called him anyway. A clue was a clue. My call went to voicemail.

"Chief, it's me. Josie. I thought you should know when Ella said 'long clock' she probably referred to a grandfather's clock. Don't know where this leads us, but it's a start."

I ended my message and leaned back in my chair, laptop open. The clock above my mantle ticked steadily forward. My mind whirred with unrelated thoughts.

As I stared at the blank computer screen, Moe leaned against me to rest his head on my knee.

"I see you, boy. Is it time for a break?"

He nudged my hands away from the keyboard, and I laughed at his persistence. "Let's go for a walk."

I grabbed my phone and door key before I fastened his leash and dialed Kate's number. Moe and I often walked with Kate and her goldendoodle, Bacon. I still smiled at the origin of the dog's name. "It's the only name he responds to," Kate had explained.

I was relieved when she answered. Kate had a matter-of-fact way of helping me sort through complicated problems. Even a short walk with her could help clear my mind.

"We're headed to the park," I said. "Come join us. Moe wants to spend some time with Bacon, and I could use a distraction from Ella's murder case."

Kate didn't let me down. "Meet you at the statue."

Chapter Nine

Thursday Afternoon

Hank English stood, bronze arms crossed, gazing down toward the bench where Kate and I sat. "Do you think he knows the answers?" I motioned toward the prominent statue in the center of our park.

Kate looked doubtfully up at the community's namesake. "I don't think so. Frankly, I'm a little baffled, myself."

"Me too. We need more information."

"What could the number 32 mean?" Kate stood and paced back and forth in front of the statue. Then she stopped and turned to face me. "How old was Ella?"

"She was thirty-one."

"Could it have something to do with her birthday?"

"Hypothetically." I smiled as I thought of how the chief might react to this conversation.

"Or, it could be the number of a storage locker, or maybe a code only a clockmaker understands." Kate was on a roll.

"Like when a police officer says *ten-four*, to signal he understood the message?"

"Or, when the military says *eighty-six* it, meaning, throw it out." My Marine friend was quick to offer some jargon of her own. She once scolded me for referring to her as an "ex-Marine" when I introduced her to Chief Marshall.

60

"There's no such thing as an ex-Marine," she corrected. "Once a Marine, always a Marine."

"But what if you are no longer on active duty?"

"Then you are a retired Marine or a Marine veteran."

The distinction sounded like hairsplitting to me, but I accepted her explanation. After all, she was also a Harvard grad and one of the smartest women I'd ever met.

While I wasted time reflecting on Kate's status as a retired U.S. Marine Corps officer, she remained focused on Ella's deathbed statement.

"The words must have been important if they were the first thing she told her doctor," Kate said.

"I don't have a clue." I returned to the bench at the base of the statue, Moe at my feet. "Thirty-two means nothing to me."

"It will," Kate assured me. "Maybe you should work on the other words first."

"Unfortunately, all I have figured out so far is a possible reference to a grandfather clock." I bent to stroke Moe's head. "Ella told me a long clock is the official name for a grandfather clock. Considering how many of those are in The Curiosity Shop, it's not much help."

"Hey, that's one out of three," Kate said. "You're making progress."

"Ella said it would be complicated." I groaned, and Moe was quick to nuzzle my cheek with his wet nose.

"You didn't really expect it to be simple, did you?" Kate laughed and handed me a fresh tissue to wipe my wet face.

"No," I admitted. "I don't mind working it out. I'd just like to know if I'm pointed in the right direction."

"Give it some time," Kate said. "You just started yesterday."

"I'll talk to some of her friends," I said. "Maybe Ella's last words will mean more to them."

We switched our conversation to the preparations for the art show scheduled for the coming weekend. Kate pulled a small notepad and pen from her shoulder bag. She used the pen to point to the Hank English statue beside us. "This guy will be the main attraction for the judges when I take them on the tour of English Village. What else should I show them?"

I thought of the areas I enjoyed most in our small town and offered Kate a suggestion. "I know we don't have major tourist attractions, but all of the judges are artists. English Village is filled with beautiful spots an artist might want to see."

"You're right!" Hurriedly, Kate scribbled onto her pad. "I can take them to see our covered bridge and the hidden waterfall. They would never find those scenic spots anywhere else."

This time of year, the area Kate mentioned would be ablaze with fall foliage. Harvey and I had driven over the bridge on our way to the nursery when we shopped for shrubs over the weekend.

I blushed as I recalled that afternoon. Shumard Oaks, Autumn Blaze Maples, and spectacular Golden Rain trees stood tall along the winding roadway to the bridge. Vivid reds and oranges intermingled with bright splashes of yellow; the color was so exquisitely beautiful we pulled the car to the edge of the road so I could grab snapshots with my phone.

When I'd finished, Harvey stood behind me, his strong arms wrapped around my waist as we took in the view.

"It's glorious!" I said. "Harvey and I took pictures this weekend." I ignored Kate's raised eyebrow reaction and handed her my phone to share the photos. "There are also a few of those flowering cherry trees they might enjoy. No blooms this time of year, but their bark is dark red, and the pointy leaves are bright orange. From the bridge, you could take the country lane and circle back past the wildflower fields and Crystal Pond."

"I wonder if I could convince the Philbrook Inn owners to drive us in their open carriage?" Kate studied the series of photos and returned my cell phone. "The judges will be guests there."

The Philbrook carriage was frequently used for garden tours and wedding parties. It held bench seating for three rows of people and enough space for a tour guide to sit beside the driver in the front. "It might take longer than a car, but the ride would be lovely. There's a canopy over the carriage, so it should be comfortable even in the afternoon sun."

"I thought we might stop at the chapel for tea," Kate said. "Pastor Pinkerton would be happy to show them the view from the bell tower. The judges could see all the way across the village. The horses could take a break before we drive back toward the Historic Park and the Hank English statue."

While all of English Village had quaint architecture, with neighborhoods that mirrored the Cotswold Hills area of England, our chapel was truly spectacular. It was constructed of the same distinctive yellow limestone of my little cottage, native to our area. I was certain the judges would enjoy seeing the church, surrounded by its acreage of green parks. The soaring steeple and bell tower attracted architectural scholars from around the world. Pastor Pinkerton loved to share its beauty with visitors.

"You might include a stop at the blacksmith shop," I suggested. "There are only a few still open in the country today. Plus, what Harvey creates there *is* magnificent artwork."

"Magnificent, huh?" Kate shaded her eyes and gazed toward the quaint little blacksmith shop where Harvey had just stepped outside to toss some metal scraps into a bin. "Have you looked at that man of yours lately? *He's* the work of art."

I raised a finger to my lips. "Hush, Kate. He'll hear you. Besides, it's a huge exaggeration to label him 'my man' when we haven't even kissed."

"Whose fault is that?" Kate tossed her head.

"Pa-lease!" I gave Kate "the look" that had always silenced my sons when they were young.

"Yeah, yeah. It's none of my business," she said, backing away from the discussion. She made a show of studying her notepad and ticked off the itinerary.

"The tour would only include three stops. Once to see the waterfall, once to rest at the chapel, and once to visit the Hank English statue and the blacksmithery."

I hoped the Philbrook would agree to provide the carriage ride; it would assure a memorable experience for the visiting judges. "Ask Nellie to call the Philbrook owners. She and Tim know them best."

"The entire route would take about an hour. I could easily have them at the art show in time." Kate's enthusiasm was infectious. With the art show only a few days away, she had a solid plan in place. I wished my efforts to identify Ella's murderer would come together as easily. Instead, my head was filled with bits of unrelated information that led nowhere.

We walked together to the water fountains so the dogs could drink deeply before we separated to return home. Kate and Bacon had barely disappeared down the sidewalk when Moe decided to veer off the path to poke his nose into a damp pile of leaves beneath an oak tree. He shoved the leaves aside with his huge paw and reached deeper to retrieve a bright yellow tennis ball. He was so proud of his new toy I couldn't bear to take it from him. Instead, he pranced happily beside me, the ball tucked firmly into the corner of his jaw.

Then Moe heard a door slam at the blacksmith shop on the edge of the park. He dropped the tennis ball and made a beeline for the door, dragging me behind him.

"Whoa!" The dog was slightly smaller than a pony, but I often used the equine command to get his attention. This time, it did no good. We rounded the corner, and I understood why. Harvey Jacobs stood beside the blacksmith door, a dog biscuit in one hand and a single daisy in the other.

"Good afternoon, Josie. I saw the two of you deep in conversation by the statue and figured you'd come this way."

"And you have gifts." I motioned to the items he carried.

"One for each of you." He handed the biscuit to Moe and the daisy to me.

"Thank you, sir." I did a quick curtsy in my blue jeans. "We're off to have a quiet evening at home."

"What about the murder?" Harvey raised one eyebrow as he spoke. "Aren't you going to help Chief Marshall solve it?"

Startled, I looked up into his kind eyes. "How did you know?"

"It's a small town. Everyone knows everything before it hits the newspaper."

"Right." I was sure we'd had this same conversation before. "Yes. I'll talk to the chief again later this afternoon. So far, we have no suspects."

"Be careful." I saw the genuine concern in his expression. "Call me if you need anything."

"I will."

I waved at him as Moe, and I crossed the street toward Primrose Lane, eager to reach our cottage. It was a typical Thursday afternoon. A few mothers pushed strollers toward the library. Children rode their bikes home from school. In a couple of hours, families would head into their homes for dinner. For now, the village was quiet and peaceful under the bright blue October sky. Harvey was right. We all needed to be careful. Someone in our village might have murdered the clockmaker's daughter.

I filled my lungs with the clean fall air and marveled at the beauty around me. Inevitably, my mind turned again to Ella McGregor Benjamin. It seemed impossible anyone from our community would have murdered the lovely young woman. The whys of an investigation always puzzled me. If I could understand *why* Ella had been killed, I should be able to determine *who* took her life. Moe and I were barely inside our door when the chief called my cell phone.

As I rushed to dig my phone from my purse, I got tangled in Moe's leash and stubbed my toe on the backpack I'd brought home from The Curiosity Shop. I shoved it aside and sat on the floor beside it.

"Hi, Chief," I answered, thankful it wasn't a video call so he couldn't see I was sprawled on the floor with a dog leash wrapped around my legs.

"Got your message, Josie. And I had a thought." Chief Marshall never wasted time talking about the weather.

"Tell me," I said, still sitting on the floor where Moe now rolled onto his back expecting a belly rub.

"The grandfather clocks in The Curiosity Shop are all numbered. How many do you think there are?"

"Thirty-two?" My heart raced a little as I threw out the number.

The chief's booming laugh caught me off-guard. "That would be way too easy. No. There are forty-one *grandfather* clocks, twelve grand*mother* clocks, and a multitude of wall clocks."

"I guess I'm not following you." I nestled the phone between my chin and my shoulder while I unhooked Moe's leash from his collar and untwisted it from around my ankles.

"Mr. McGregor used a numbering system to keep track of the clocks," the chief explained. "If a customer sees a clock he likes, he can jot down the number for future reference. Apparently, shoppers often return two or three times before they make a purchase. The number helped Mr. McGregor to identify the clocks a customer liked best."

I dragged the backpack closer so I could lean against it and stretch my legs in front of me. "I see how this helps Mr. McGregor. How does it help us?"

"The thing is, only one clock has a sticker with the number 32 in the corner of the glass door over the pendulum," Chief Marshall said. "Clock number 32 is a grandfather clock."

Now I understood his excitement. "Ella could have been telling us to find a clue inside clock 32!"

"We have moved the clock to our evidence room at the police station," the chief said. "An expert will take a look inside. If he finds anything, I'll let you know."

I promised the chief I would do the same if my calls to Ella's friends resulted in useful information. Now, all I had to do was find out how to contact those friends. Ella had provided only Logan Lavender's number during our interview. I stood up and gathered the leash, purse, phone, and backpack to place them on the kitchen island.

Suddenly, I recalled that Ella's bag contained a few spiral notepads and folders in addition to the textbooks. I unzipped the backpack and reached inside. A quick peek at the notebooks revealed nothing of immediate interest—just handwritten class notes, from what I could decipher. I shoved the jumble of textbooks aside and discovered a smaller blue book hidden beneath them. When I fished it from the backpack, I let out a loud "Woohoo!" that startled sweet Moe, who came running to see what I'd found.

Ella's personal address book.

Chapter Ten

Thursday Evening

"This is it, Moe. This is the treasure I've been searching for."

Moe and I settled into our favorite spot. I pushed the recliner into position, and he scooted under the raised footrest. With my notepad and pen ready, I flipped through Ella's little blue book to find additional contacts. Before I could choose one, my cell phone rang again in my hand.

I smiled when I saw the caller ID.

"Hello, Harvey."

"I have a great idea, Josie."

It's funny how the sound of a voice brings an instant picture into our minds. I could see Harvey's familiar lopsided grin as he talked.

"I'm listening." Harvey was pretty much the opposite of me. Tall and lanky, while I was short and, well, not thin. A man of few words, to my woman of never-ceasing words. He created works of art, and I struggled to design posters for the library story hour. All of which were reasons the Mahjong Mavens declared Harvey the perfect man for me to date. Those meddling ladies never stopped trying to get the two of us together. While I agreed Harvey was a great guy, I wasn't ready to move our friendship to the next level, whatever that meant. Still, I liked the warm sound of his voice in my ear, and his smile gave me butterflies in the pit of my stomach.

"How about I make dinner tonight? I'm trying a recipe Nellie gave me, and it's too much to eat by myself."

This man never failed to surprise me. When I first met Harvey at the local hardware store, I noticed his easy smile and kind eyes. I assumed he was a nice guy interested in hardware stuff. Later, I discovered he and his dad owned the store. But Harvey was an artist at heart. He created beautiful metal works at our little village blacksmith shop in his spare time—including the gorgeous chandelier which now hung over my walnut dining room table. After we became friends, I learned he often explored nearby antique shops, he enjoyed flying kites, and he loved to cook.

"I'm in," I told him.

"Don't you want to know what I'm making?"

"Nope."

"Not even a hint?"

I laughed. "Not unless you want me to bring something as a side dish."

"Actually, I'd like to bring it to your house. Then Moe can help us with any leftovers. Okay with you?"

A man who cooked *and* liked my dog. Maybe the mavens had the right idea. "I have wine. Seven o'clock?"

"See you then."

I rolled my eyes and glanced over at Moe. "Your buddy is bringing dinner," I told him. Moe cocked his head to the side and smiled back at me, his tongue hanging out like it did when he was happy.

It wasn't long before Moe and I both heard Harvey's car pull into the drive. We raced to the door to greet him. Harvey handed me a covered casserole dish. "Careful, it's hot. I need to put it in the oven for a few minutes to melt some cheese on top. Nellie insisted I shouldn't skip the final step."

"It smells delicious. Garlic and tomatoes. Is it Italian?"

Harvey's laugh filled the room. "I thought you didn't want to know the menu."

"I've changed my mind."

"Josie Posey, you are incorrigible." He uncovered the foil to sprinkle shredded pepper jack cheese over the top of the casserole. "This is called

Santa Fe Pie. It's a Tex-Mex dish, not Italian."

"It sounds wonderful."

"I made it with shredded chicken, but Nellie says it's also delicious with ground sirloin. She and Sharon delivered the sirloin version to the McGregors this afternoon."

"Those ladies always know what to do when there's really nothing anyone can do."

For the next several minutes, Harvey and I were silent. Lost in our own thoughts, we worked comfortably side by side in my kitchen. I appreciated his ability to sense the times when no words were necessary. This guy was easy to like.

While Harvey mixed olives and tomatoes into his Mexican salad, I opened a chilled bottle of Kendall Jackson chardonnay. Finally, I broke the silence. "Moe and I had planned leftover ham sandwiches for dinner tonight."

Harvey nodded with understanding. "It's hard to justify cooking a bigger meal for just one person."

He set the warm casserole onto the kitchen island beside the freshly tossed salad. "Hope you like avocado dressing."

We filled our plates and dug into the meal. I'd been so distracted by the murder case I'd barely touched my food the last couple of days. Suddenly, I was ravenous. I finished my salad in record time.

Harvey added a dash of pepper to the steaming food on his plate. We should do this at least once a week to make sure we're receiving the proper nutrition."

"Absolutely." I scooped another large bite of the chicken and cornbread concoction into my mouth. "This is the most delicious meal I've had since Sunday. And the healthiest."

Harvey gave me a knowing look. "Hey, our pot roast was nutritious. You were the one who pulled Sharon's Peach Blueberry Crisp out of the freezer."

"I did." I dabbed at my mouth with a napkin. "And we ate every last crumb."

"Speaking of crumbs," Harvey said, "what's the latest on your murder investigation? I saw Lorene at the coffee shop, and she said you were following a trail of breadcrumbs through the forest."

I sighed. "There's no forest involved, but Lorene is right: I'm tracking down tiny details, trying to find a solid clue."

"Anything interesting yet?"

Harvey leaned forward and gave me his full attention as I explained my three critical clues to Ella's murder. He was as puzzled by them as the chief and I were. "I wonder why Ella told these things to the doctor and not to her father or brother?"

"I've thought about that too." I took another sip of my wine. "Maybe they were part of a dream, and she simply told the first person she saw when she woke up?"

Harvey held his fork in the air like a pointer and suggested a theory I hadn't considered. "Or she knew she only had a few minutes of consciousness. She wanted to make sure someone had this information."

I tried again to make sense of the list. The number 32. The word "complicated." And, the third message, "long clock." Finally, I admitted my fears to Harvey. "It's possible these words don't mean anything at all. Ella might have been hallucinating."

"Strange words to hallucinate," Harvey said.

I moved the last of my casserole around the plate, too full to take another bite. As I stared at the nearly empty dish, it occurred to me Logan Lavender was not surprised to learn of Ella's death. I wondered who might have contacted her with the news. And then I realized I had forgotten to ask Ms. Lavender the most important questions of all.

"Fiddle-de-dee! I have to call Ella's friend again."

"Forget something?" Harvey was accustomed to my outbursts.

"I never mentioned Ella's last words to her friend, Logan Lavender, in Manhattan." I carried my empty plate to the kitchen sink. "As someone in the same profession, she might know why Ella said them."

"Didn't the chief tell you not to share this list with anyone?"

"No. He said not to talk about her dying words. I can ask hypothetical questions about what these words might signify to a watchmaker."

"Pretty sure you're pushing the limits, but you know Chief Marshall better than I do." Harvey looked at his watch. "It's still fairly early in New York. I'll head home so you can get back to work."

I walked with Harvey to my front door, where he took my hands in his and looked directly into my eyes. "Be careful, Josie."

I rolled my eyes. "I won't do anything dangerous. I'm mostly calling people and searching for clues on the Internet."

Harvey gave me a doubtful look. "I've seen you get into trouble by waving to someone on the street. Remember the time you stood face-to-face with the guy who turned out to be a killer?"

I brushed off his concerns. "That was months ago. Anyway, I'll be busy with the Art Show the next couple of days. There won't be time for amateur investigations."

He gave me that lopsided smile and tucked a stray curl behind my ear. Then he bent forward as though to kiss my cheek. I ducked my head and backed away, but not before I breathed in his woodsy scent and felt my knees buckle a little.

A shadow crossed Harvey's eyes. "Just the same, lock your doors and stay safe," he said, turning to walk away.

Which I did, not realizing someone dangerous might have already entered my house.

Chapter Eleven

Thursday Night

As soon as Harvey drove away in his truck, I turned back to my notes and redialed Logan's number. The phone rang seven times, finally going to voicemail.

I waited for the beep. "Logan, this is Josephine Posey. I forgot to ask you something important. Please call me back as soon as you can."

Since Logan wasn't available, I decided to call Nellie. The chief had instructed me not to interview Mr. McGregor or Alex, but he hadn't told me not to talk to others who had seen them.

Nellie and I were close. We even shared a childhood nickname—something I learned when we first worked together to solve the case of the ballerina's husband. Nellie helped me track down important clues to his murder simply by asking hundreds of questions to nearby neighbors. She laughed when I thanked her. "They didn't call me Nosy Nellie for nothing."

"As a child, I was Nosy Josie. What are the odds two nosy children would become friends as adults?" I joked.

"Apparently, about 2 to 1." Nellie's declaration resulted in even more laughter.

I dialed her number, and she answered promptly. "Hi, Josie. What's up?'

"Harvey and I just finished your *Santa Fe Pie*."

"And?"

"It was delicious."

"I'm glad you enjoyed it. Particularly since you shared it with Harvey. You know how I feel about the two of you."

"Yes, I know." Nellie had been the first of the mavens to insist I spend more time with Harvey. She loved matchmaking. "Harvey said you took one of your casseroles to the McGregors."

"I wondered when you would ask," Nellie said. "I expected your call. I even made notes so I wouldn't forget anything."

I laughed. "Are they on 4x6 note cards?"

"No, ma'am," Nellie said. "But they are important, just the same."

"Tell me what you noticed. The chief won't let me visit them yet."

I heard the rustle of paper over the phone and pictured Nellie lowering her reading glasses onto her nose as she studied her notes. "First, it was obvious both of these men really cared about Ella. Her father was grief-stricken. He couldn't stop talking about what the world has lost with her death. Her brother was stunned. His hands shook. He adored his little sister. Neither of them believed Ella had any enemies."

"Normal reactions. I would have been surprised if they weren't still reeling from her sudden death. What else?"

"Ella arrived home last weekend. She brought a few personal items in a suitcase and moved into her former bedroom. It was a temporary arrangement. She had already found her own apartment. Mr. McGregor said most of Ella's belongings were being shipped to her from New York, where she had just completed her studies. They should arrive this week."

"Did he mention whether Ella planned to work in The Curiosity Shop?"

"Her dad was happy to have her home. He said he never knew how long she would stay."

"And Alex?"

"Her brother said he hoped Ella would move home permanently. He choked up when he told me they needed her help. He thought Ella might create some of her own watches for the shop. Not the luxury models, but handcrafted styles to attract customers from across the country."

"No mention of any conflicts?"

"Nothing."

I tried to imagine why Ella's presence at the local shop would be a threat to anyone. There had to be a reason someone tampered with the ladder. "Did he say anything about her fall?"

"Only that he regrets not testing the ladder before she used it. He's the one who brought it inside for her. He feels responsible."

"Did he use those words? Did he say he *feels responsible*?"

"Yes."

"And the 'foreign object' at the base of the ladder?"

Nellie's reply was edged with irritation. "Not a word. I still don't know what the object was, if you'd care to enlighten me."

"Sorry. Guess I hoped Alex would mention it. I can't talk about it until someone else does."

"Talk to Sharon if you want more insight into Alex," Nellie said. "She had a longer conversation with him while I carried the casserole into Mr. McGregor's office. We both noticed Alex seemed nervous. He was polite, but he shifted from one foot to another like he couldn't hold still. Then he moved us toward the door like he was eager to get us out of the shop."

"Why would Ella's brother be nervous about having you and Sharon in the shop?"

"Maybe he has something to hide."

"Exactly! I want to find out what it is. And I know just how I'm going to do it."

"Josie," Nellie scolded, "you need to let Chief Marshall handle this part."

"Don't worry. I only want to send him a sympathy note. There's no harm in that."

"*Uh-huh.*" Nellie knew how to dish out sarcasm in two short syllables.

"Gotta go," I said.

My next call was to Sharon. When she answered, I heard joy in her voice and the rattle of tin pans in the background.

"You're up to your elbows in flour, aren't you?" I said.

"You know me too well. I promised to help with refreshments for the Art Show reception, so tonight, I'm making appetizers to put in the freezer. Nellie is in charge of Bacon and Asiago Cheese Straws and Crispy Polenta

Bites. I'm doing miniature tarts. What do you think? Shall I fill one batch with lemon and the other with pecan? If I bake the shells tonight, the rest will be quick and easy."

"People love choices," I said. "Make them both. Though neither sounds easy to me."

"I'll have them in the oven before you can get over here to watch."

"No. It's late. I don't want to interrupt your baking. Call me tomorrow morning when you have time. I need your impressions of the McGregor family."

"Let's meet at Cozy Cups Café at nine-thirty," Sharon suggested. "We can talk there, and I have a surprise for you."

"See you then."

After the conversation with Sharon, I couldn't wait for morning. Her surprises were always good ones. Maybe she would let me be the taste-tester for her latest dessert. Whatever she had in mind would have to wait till morning.

I slipped into my pjs and settled in for a few hours of research.

It was past ten. Moe already snored at my feet, and I still needed to check in with Chief Marshall and write my sympathy note to the McGregors.

I drafted several versions before I settled on one that might have the desired effect.

> *Dear Thomas and Alex,*
>
> *Please know I am thinking of you as you mourn the loss of your beautiful Ella.*
>
> *After the hours I spent with her, I have no doubt Ella leaves behind an extraordinary legacy. I will do everything possible to ensure the true story of her brilliance is told.*
>
> *Only time will tell how famous she may become.*
>
> *Sincerely,*
>
> *Josie Posey*

If Alex was innocent of any wrongdoing, he would read this note as the heartfelt message I intended. But if his intense grief was rooted in a guilty conscience, Alex might interpret the sympathy note as my promise to expose her murderer.

I set the note aside and walked through the house, turning out the lights. I still hoped Chief Marshall would call with news about "Long Clock #32." Maybe that's why I didn't check the caller ID when my cell rang. Instead, I slapped it to my ear, expecting to hear the chief's familiar voice.

"This is Josie."

The harsh noise on the other end of the call sent chills down my spine. The words were distorted by one of those phone apps I'd seen in crime shows, but I understood them.

"Accidents happen every day."

"Who is this?" I shouted into the phone, but the call had ended.

I rushed to check the locks on my doors. Then I dialed the chief.

"This may not be anything," I said when he picked up the phone.

"What happened?"

"Someone prank-called me tonight." I described the details of the call, and Chief Marshall insisted I repeat them.

"It was a short call, Chief. There's nothing more to tell."

"Humor me."

I took a deep breath and repeated my story. "I was sitting in my chair with my laptop open. I just finished reading an article about Ella's school. Moe was asleep at my feet. My phone rang. I answered. His voice was muffled, but he said: 'Accidents happen every day.' Then he hung up."

"He didn't actually threaten you?"

"No."

"Did you hear anything in the background?"

I thought about it for a moment, then shook my head as though the chief could see me over the cell phone. "No. Nothing."

"Okay, Josie. Get some rest. This guy is most likely just a prank caller, as you said."

"I know."

"If you receive another unidentified call, remember to record the conversation on your cell phone. That fancy app you added is worthless if you don't use it."

"I will."

The chief took another minute to tell me he had nothing to report on Long Clock 32. "My experts haven't found anything unusual inside. They will remove the back panel and make sure nothing is hidden there. At this point, it's another dead end."

We agreed to start fresh tomorrow. Then Chief Marshall reminded me again of the procedure we'd relied on when someone else had once threatened my safety.

"You know the drill. Turn on your porch light, and leave it on tonight. We'll have a patrol car drive through your neighborhood to be sure you're safe. If you need help, call. If you can't call, switch off the porch light, and the officer will come in to check on you. Got it?"

"Yes, sir."

"And make sure your phone is charged so we don't have an issue like the last time."

"Got it."

The chief's reassurance was just what I needed to hear. Logic told me the caller was most likely someone who simply wanted to rattle me. But, try as I might, I could not sleep. I fought the urge to pick up Ella's blue notebook and flip through the pages in the hope that her precise handwritten names and numbers might reveal something new. Instead, I set it on my nightstand. The task could wait until morning.

Just before I drifted off to sleep, while I was "not thinking" about the notebook, the seed of another idea planted itself in my mind. I knew where I might look for clock tuning instruments that might match the "foreign object" the chief had described. I sat straight up and jotted it on the pad beside my bed. Then I pulled up the covers and closed my eyes.

Moe sensed my uneasiness and stayed close by my side. He slept on the rug beside my bed, raising his head throughout the night to make certain I had not moved.

Chapter Twelve

Friday Early Morning

By dawn, Moe and I were awake and ready for breakfast. When my phone rang at seven thirty it startled me so much I jumped up from the table, knocked over my mug and sent a pool of coffee across the kitchen counter. Good thing the cup was almost empty.

I grabbed the phone with one hand and sopped up the coffee with a napkin in the other. The caller ID displayed an unfamiliar number, so I took a deep breath and turned on the recorder app as I answered, just as the chief had instructed.

"Hello, this is Josie." I hoped the caller couldn't hear the sound of my heart pounding in his ears the way I heard it in mine.

"Ms. Posey?" It was a male voice. No crazy disguises or weird sound effects.

"Yes."

"This is Professor Davis. I believe you wanted to speak with me about Ella Benjamin?"

At his words, I breathed a sigh of relief and slipped comfortably into my reporter mode. "Yes, Professor. Thank you for returning my call. I wanted to get a sense of the kind of student Ella was, and I thought you might be able to help."

"Have you already spoken to her directly?" His tone was abrupt. Impersonal. Almost cold. I wondered if this was how he addressed all news reporters or just the ones who asked about Ella. Then I realized he had probably not been informed of Ella's death.

"Ms. Posey?"

"Yes. I'm here." I stumbled over the words. "Professor, the truth is I interviewed Ella earlier this week. But she was in an unfortunate accident later that afternoon."

"How terrible!" The professor's shock appeared genuine. "What happened? Is she okay?"

I answered as gently as I could: "Sadly, she fell off a ladder and hit her head. She was hospitalized...but passed away the next day."

The professor's crisp, professional manner disappeared as he reacted to the news. "Oh, no! I can't believe it. We just spoke last weekend."

"Can you tell me why you talked? I thought she completed her coursework with you more than a year ago?"

"She did. She is...er, *was* exceptional." He stammered, and I heard the disbelief in his voice. "I admired her creativity and her work ethic. Ella was truly a wonderful young woman."

I remained silent, allowing him to absorb the news. "A student with her level of dedication comes along once in a lifetime," he said. "The world has lost a rare talent."

"Professor, please tell me why you talked last weekend?" I repeated my original question.

"Did I say we talked?" He seemed confused.

"Yes," I assured him. "Just a moment ago. You said you spoke to Ella last weekend."

"Perhaps you misunderstood." His tone returned to the clipped, professional voice.

"I don't think so," I said as warmly as I could muster. "In fact, I'm positive you said you talked to Ella over the weekend."

He backtracked slightly at my persistence. "Well," he huffed, "it wasn't actually a call. We conversed via email. We do that often. Just to stay in touch, you know."

"I see."

"Do you?" he said. "I'm sorry, Ms. Posey, I have to take another call. Could we finish this conversation another time?"

"I had hoped you would tell me more about any projects Ella was working on and answer a few additional questions."

"Another time," he repeated.

"Would Monday be better?" I pressed for a firm commitment.

"Monday morning at ten." Now, he spoke with a confident air more consistent with his position. "I've written it on my calendar."

"Thank you."

"Ms. Posey," the professor continued, "if you learn anything about who murdered Ella, could you let me know?"

"I will," I answered.

After we hung up, I listened to the recorded conversation. I wanted to hear the nuances in the professor's voice, but more importantly, I wanted to verify his statement about having spoken to Ella last weekend.

I also had a nagging thought.

After replaying the recording three times, I was certain of two things: The professor lied when he denied talking to Ella. And I never mentioned Ella was murdered. He did.

It was obvious Professor Davis knew more than he revealed to me. I wondered how much. Had someone already told him about Ella's death? If so, who? And if not, why would he assume her fall was not an accident?

I set aside my notes and finished my breakfast deep in thought. It seemed I had more loose ends than ever. The call with Professor Davis was incomplete. Logan Lavender had not returned my follow-up call. I hadn't even attempted a call to Ella's student friend, Carlos. And the chief had provided no additional information about his conversations with Ella's father and brother.

On the bright side, today promised to be a good one. I had a meeting with Sharon at nine-thirty for her impressions of the McGregors. Afterward, I planned to shop at Harvey's hardware store to see if he carried any common clock repair instruments. His shelves were jam-packed with all sorts of unusual items.

I wanted to make a couple of additional phone calls and work the murder case before Harvey, and I attended Nellie's tasting party in the evening, And with any luck, UPS would deliver my package from Lucy Buttons.

Now that the sun was shining, I felt a little foolish about my reaction to last night's prank phone call. It wasn't the first time someone had tried to discourage me from assisting Chief Marshall with a case. Most likely, it wouldn't be the last. I vowed not to ruin Nellie's event by mentioning the call to any of the mavens. The ladies were already nervous about my involvement. The prank call would set them all on edge.

With time to spare before my coffee date with Sharon, I dialed Logan Lavender's number. She surprised me and answered on the second ring.

"Logan Lavender." Her rich voice floated across the line as though she were standing in the room next to me.

"Hello, Logan, it's Josie." I attempted a friendly, non-threatening tone.

"Yes, Josie. Sorry I missed your call yesterday. I've been racing from one engagement to another. You know how it is. If you want a task to be done correctly, you have to do it yourself."

"I understand. You're a busy woman."

"Still, I meant to return your call this morning. How can I help?"

"As I've researched the watch industry, I've come across a few words I don't understand. I hoped you might enlighten me."

"Like any specialized profession, we have our own jargon that can be confusing to outsiders. Which ones have you baffled?"

I cleared my throat. "It's not that I don't comprehend the three words individually. I just want to know if they mean something unique to your industry."

"Not sure I understand."

"For example, in journalism, the number '30' means the story is over. It's an abbreviated way of saying 'the end' when the article concludes."

"Ahh. I see. What words did you discover related to watchmaking?"

"The number *32. Complicated.* And *Long Clock.*"

Logan barely hesitated before she answered. "I'm afraid the only one that makes sense to me is *Long Clock.* It's a term we use for a traditional

81

grandfather's clock. The others have no special meaning."

"Very well. I'm sorry to have bothered you," I said.

"No problem. But now I'm curious. Where on earth did you see those three terms together?"

"It doesn't matter," I said. "They were just words I came across in some notes I reviewed for the article about Ella's career."

"I'm impressed that you attempt to track down every detail," Ms. Lavender said. "Few people take the time to delve so deeply into a subject. You must be a perfectionist."

I laughed. "Some say I'm obstinate."

"I've always admired a woman who knows what she wants and goes after it."

As we ended the call, I had a good feeling about Logan Lavender. Ella's mentor was a strong woman. No wonder Ella considered her a role model. I was disappointed she saw no special meaning behind Ella's final words. Perhaps they weren't significant, after all.

I let Moe outside to patrol the backyard while I stepped into the shower. Planning ahead, I dressed in jeans and sneakers in case my stalker appeared, and I needed to make a quick getaway. Then I welcomed Moe back inside, careful to lock the door behind him.

"Take care of the house, boy." I gave him a final pat on the head. Feeling the effects of his restless night, the dog had already curled up on the floor—looking ever so much like a fluffy rug — and closed his eyes for a nap.

I smiled down at him and turned to exit through my kitchen door to the garage.

When I stepped through the threshold, I flipped the light switch by the door, but the bulb must have died. I could barely distinguish the shape of my car. I paused while my eyes adjusted to the dim interior then reached for my cell phone and swiped upward to use the flashlight app. It wouldn't be good to tumble down the steps in my own house.

The brilliant beam of light caught the outline of an object perched precariously on the top step. At first, I thought Moe had dropped one of his stuffed toys there. I knew Lamb Chop was in his toy basket where she belonged. This was larger than most of his toys. When I bent down to look, the small, dead creature sent shivers up my spine. I leaned even closer.

And then I screamed like a banshee.

Chapter Thirteen

Friday Mid-Morning

I t wasn't the dead opossum that made me scream but the note nailed to his poor little chest. It was written in bold block letters on a 4x6 note card, just like the ones stacked on my dining room table. The message was brief: **WATCH YOUR STEP.**

After my initial shock, I returned to my kitchen for a pair of latex gloves. I picked the opossum up by his tail and slid him into a large plastic bag, complete with the note nailed to his body. What began as fear turned to anger. Whoever had done this had been inside my garage. He had gone too far.

I laid the dead opossum gently in the trunk of my car and drove directly to the police station, all of my senses on high alert. Suddenly, my quiet little street had gone from charming to ominous. Where were all the cars? What if someone attacked me in broad daylight?

At the stop sign, I gulped huge breaths of air and rested my forehead on the steering wheel. Then I tried to rationalize my fear. I'd spent many years reporting crime stories in the big city without a panic attack. I lifted my head and studied my surroundings.

Primrose Lane was deserted. If an intruder had been lurking on our block, there was no sign of him now. Fall foliage painted the landscape in brilliant shades of crimson and gold. The vivid blue sky was clear as a bell. It was difficult to imagine any threat of evil on this serene October day.

Except I had just stowed a dead animal in the trunk of my car with a threatening note affixed to his chest. And the creature had been delivered sometime after I received a prank call from an anonymous robot.

Finally I understood. These things should not occur in a small town. Murder. Threatening phone calls and dead animals. Somehow, they were more frightening because they happened in this idyllic village. Ella's death wasn't a random killing like the crimes I'd covered as a reporter in the city. It was personal. I refused to let some guy with a robotic voice scare me away from investigating her murder.

Chief Marshall wasn't happy when I dropped the bagged opossum on his desk.

Instead of commending me for using latex gloves, he scolded me. "How would someone enter your garage? Didn't you lock your doors?"

I was a little embarrassed to admit I hadn't yet considered how the dead opossum landed on the step *inside* my garage. The realization that my stalker had boldly invaded my personal space hit with a vengeance. I clenched my hands together to stop them from shaking. "I don't know how—or when—this could have happened."

And then I had another thought. "Oh my gosh. The note card is identical to the ones I use. Could this guy have been *inside my cottage* while Moe and I went for our walk?"

I trailed behind Chief Marshall as he took the opossum into the station's evidence room and turned it over to a detective. "See if you can track the nail, or the note, or the handwriting. We need to know who delivered this message."

Then, he ushered me into his familiar little conference room. I was sure the half-empty coffee pot held the same burned beverage as it had on my last visit.

"Coffee?"

"No, thank you." I pulled out a chair and sat, looking up at him.

"Can't blame you." He walked to the pot and turned off the burner.

I clutched a thick folder with the notes from my interviews, but they were the least of the chief's worries now.

"Let's get to the bottom of this opossum business, shall we?"

"I'd like that."

The chief paced back and forth in front of the huge whiteboard on one wall of the conference room. "What time did you park your car in your garage yesterday?"

"Early. I only drove the car to the police station to meet you. That was before noon. Later, Moe and I took a walk in the park, but we were home by four."

"You never left the house again?"

"No. In fact, Harvey brought dinner to my house. I wasn't in the garage anytime yesterday afternoon or last night."

"You received the prank call at 10:27 p.m., because you called me immediately afterward."

"Yes, but this creature could have been planted on the step any time after I pulled into the garage around noon."

The chief glanced at his ever-present notepad as he spoke. Then, he wrote the time on the whiteboard: **Noon Thursday.**

"Think back, Josie. Was anyone around when you arrived home at noon?"

"No. I opened the garage door and drove inside."

"Did you lower the garage door from your remote control while you were still inside the car? Or did you wait until you were inside the house?"

"Uh-oh. I'm sure I hurried to get into the house first. I remember I walked up the two steps to my kitchen door, then turned to look back at my car before I pressed the pad on the wall to close the door. Could someone have slipped inside the garage during that short time?"

"It's possible he sneaked in as you entered the garage. Hid behind the car while you closed the door. Planted the opossum on your step. Then exited the side door into your yard. It would be simple enough to lock the door and pull it shut behind him."

I shook my head. "My neighbor across the street would have seen him. Mrs. Abernathy is always in her yard or watching from her windows."

The chief continued to pace. "Good point. It's more likely he came in after dark. Was the side door locked when you put away your computer and turned off the lights?"

"Maybe. I think so. I don't know. I don't use it often." I shivered. "This means someone was in my garage while I was getting ready for bed last night."

"We'll take a look around your house to see if we can discover any footprints. It has been dry for the past week, so I'm not optimistic."

I looked at the chief with a spark of hope. "Harvey planted a Golden Rain sapling on the side of my cottage a few days ago. It's near the side door to the garage. I water it each evening." For once, I was thankful I spent so much time nurturing the plants in my backyard.

"Good," the chief said. "If we're lucky, the intruder stepped into some soft earth and left us a clue."

Suddenly I had another thought. "Wait. Could this be the same guy who killed Ella?"

The chief stopped pacing. He clenched his jaw and set both of his hands squarely on the table in front of me. His broad ebony face creased with concern. "We're going to find out. Hand over your house keys and garage door opener. I'll send a patrol car to check the house."

"Surely no one is there now." I wrung my hands as I imagined an intruder skulking in my garage. "What about Moe? If this crazy man harms my sweet dog, I'll never forgive myself. I need to protect him."

Chief Marshall held his huge hands out, palms down. "Now, now. Let's not get carried away. The guy is probably long gone. He accomplished his purpose. Scared you enough to make you reconsider your involvement in this case. There's no reason he would hang around where he might be captured."

I cringed to think there might have been a murderer in my house and that he could still be lurking nearby. It was more important than ever to follow the clues and identify the killer. Taking a deep breath to calm myself, I asked the chief, "What do you think of the message?"

"It's well-worded." The chief paced again. "There's no actual threat in the words. In fact, 'watch your step' could be considered a common cautionary message."

"Except it was nailed to the chest of a dead animal," I said.

The chief gave me a grim smile. "Yes. That takes the meaning to a different level." He skewered me with his 'don't give me any trouble' look and said the words I expected. "Josie, it's time you walked away from this story."

"Never." I scowled back at him. "This makes me more determined to find out who murdered Ella."

"I was afraid you'd say that. The problem is your stubbornness could get you killed. And as much as I'd like to have your assistance, I don't want another murder to deal with."

"Did you just say you'd like my assistance?" I repeated the only part of the chief's words that really mattered.

"No." The chief sighed heavily. "I said your life is in danger."

"We can't worry about that right now. We have Ella's murder to solve."

The chief paced the room. Back and forth. And back again. After several minutes, he cleared his throat and glared at me. "Here's how it's going to be: You will agree to extra security precautions. You will limit your research to pre-approved subjects. You will report to me by phone every day."

I resisted my urge to ask questions. "Okay."

He raised an eyebrow. "No arguments?"

"No."

If he doubted my meek agreement to his terms, the chief didn't show it. We spent the next half-hour talking about the investigation. He summarized his conversations with Ella's father, brother, and ex-husband.

Then he handed me a typed sheet. "Review this list and let me know if anything jumps out at you."

The document was organized into three sections: HOW, WHY, and WHO. I skimmed the contents before I commented. "You're sure about how Ella was killed?"

"Pretty sure. Ella fell when one of the wooden steps on the ladder broke under her weight. However, I observed several rungs had been weakened in an unusual way. Someone used miniature tools to make nearly indiscernible cracks."

"Tools of a watchmaker." I recalled the small tools used by students at the Adler Minetti school.

"If her physician hadn't noticed the marks on Ella's temple and suspected foul play, we might have assumed it was an accident," the chief said.

"We still don't know what actually caused her death. Hopefully, the medical examiner will explain how Ella could have fallen onto an unidentified implement. Then, we will have to figure out what happened to that tool."

The chief scratched his head. "If someone removed it from the scene, we have to know *who*…and *why*."

I glanced at my watch. "But first I need to meet Sharon at Cozy Cups."

Chief Marshall walked with me to the door of the police station. "Don't forget what I told you. Don't go home until you've checked with me. I want to be sure it's safe."

"I couldn't get inside if I did. You have my keys."

"Good."

"Chief?" I paused with my hand on the door. "Could I ask a favor of the patrolman?"

"What did you have in mind?"

"I wonder if he would let Moe into the backyard for a few minutes for a potty break."

The chief rolled his eyes. "We aim to please. I'll tell Devon to let Moe outside while he checks your house."

"And could he text me so I know Moe is okay?"

I could see from the expression on his face that I was pushing my luck, but a smile tugged at the corner of his mouth. "Will there be anything else?"

"Ah, no sir. Thank you," I said as meekly as I knew how.

As I stepped into the bright sunlight, I'd almost forgotten about the dead opossum. My mind was focused on figuring out who murdered Ella. And on keeping the opossum incident to myself.

Chapter Fourteen

Friday Late Morning

Sharon waited for me at a corner table. I grabbed my own cup from the mismatched variety near the front door, filling it with the house blend and a concoction of flavored syrups.

"What are you having?" Sharon raised one eyebrow and nodded toward my steaming cup.

"Medium roast with oat milk and equal squirts of chocolate, caramel, and coconut." I grinned at her appalled expression. Sharon was a black coffee purist.

"Better ingredients for a candy bar than a coffee," she said.

"Lorene wouldn't offer them if they didn't sell." I toasted her with my mug.

Sharon tipped her cup to mine. "You've gotta love the Cozy Cups concept. Lorene may have stumbled upon the idea of self-service and mismatched cups out of necessity, but it works."

"I still can't believe she bought garage sale cups because she ran out of money."

"If you asked me, the woman spent her budget where it mattered most. "All you have to do is look at her state-of-the-art kitchen." Sharon's face took on a dreamy expression. "How I would love to bake my pies in her commercial oven!"

"Be careful what you wish for. Lorene might try to recruit you as a bakery chef."

We ordered a cinnamon roll to share. While we waited, Sharon pulled a small gold box out of her handbag. She placed it on the table and looked at me, eyes twinkling.

"What is this?" I lifted the box and turned it over in my hands.

"Just a little something I picked up at The Curiosity Shop." She took a sip of her coffee. "Go ahead. Open it."

I lifted the lid off the small box. Inside, I found an oddly shaped hollow brass cylinder with an ornate flat handle. I pulled the metal piece out of the box and turned back to Sharon. "It's beautiful," I said. "What is it?"

"It's a clock key!" My friend clapped her hands at my baffled reaction. "They call it a 'butterfly' because the handle resembles wings sticking out from the body. I'm told they use it to wind older clocks."

"That's news to me. I've never heard of a clock key."

"I thought it might bring you luck as you're searching for the key to this latest mystery. There's a gold chain beneath the cotton, so you can hang it around your neck," Sharon said.

"I can't accept this." I pushed the box across the table toward her. "It's probably an antique—far too expensive."

Sharon waved her hand, dismissing the thought. "Not at all. I noticed an entire bowl of them beside the cash register when Nellie and I visited the McGregors yesterday. Alex says they are fairly common. I guess there are a bunch of styles and sizes. He was so eager to get us out of there he insisted I take one as a gift. Now, I'm re-gifting it to *you*."

She threaded the key onto the gold chain. "I found the chain in a corner of my jewelry box."

"Well..." I cradled the key in my hand, "I could use the inspiration, if you're sure you don't want it."

"You never know when you'll need a clock key," Sharon said.

"Thank you." I slipped the necklace over my head. "Tell me more about your visit with the McGregors yesterday. Why would Alex be uneasy having you there?"

Compared to Nellie's business-like report, Sharon's was more animated. She described Alex's rumpled shirt and the way he wrung his hands when he talked. Both Ella's brother and her father struggled to hold back tears when they accepted the casserole from Nellie. Sharon believed Alex had nothing to hide. She was convinced Alex was on edge because he was grieving.

"You know Nellie can ask too many questions," Sharon reminded me. "In my opinion, Alex was nervous because Nellie cornered him against the display case and demanded answers about where he was when his sister fell. Alex just lost his sister, for goodness' sake. He's a quiet guy. He probably wanted to go in a corner somewhere and cry."

"You didn't think he seemed suspicious? He brought her the ladder. No one else was in the shop that morning."

"Maybe no one came *inside,* but the ladder was stored *outside.* Alex said they kept the ladder in an unlocked shed behind their shop. They used it only a couple of times a year to reach the highest storage shelves for inventory purposes. Anyone could have entered the shed to tamper with the rungs."

"Interesting." I rubbed the clock key between my fingers.

Suddenly, the smooth metal of the small key reminded me of the tubular shape the chief had drawn when he described Ella's injury to her temple. I stared at it, trying to discern whether *this* type of implement might have caused the markings if she had landed on it when she fell. I felt a surge of excitement at the possibility.

"Thank you. Thank you." I stood up from the table and leaned over to give my friend a huge hug.

She pulled away to study my face. "Wait. What did I do to deserve the hug?"

"You reminded me of an important clue."

She shrugged her shoulders. "Don't know what I said. Enlighten me."

"Sorry. Can't say yet. I have to go."

I laid some cash on the table and raced out to my car. Even though the chief had told me to stick to interviewing Ella's friends, I knew Harvey might shed some light on the variations of the butterfly clock key. Besides, tracking down tools couldn't possibly be dangerous.

I drove directly from the Cozy Cups Cafe to Harvey's hardware store and pulled Piper into the only open parking spot in front of the building. A forest green awning spanned the entire length of the storefront, creating an inviting curb appeal. Three long tables stood out front, loaded with sidewalk-sale items. A bright yellow watering can, and several colorful end-of-season patio pots caught my attention. Might be a good time to stock up for next spring, I thought.

Over the past couple of years, Harvey's improvements to his family's hardware store had paid off in a big way. The additional lighting and neatly arranged shelving units brightened the interior, but I was convinced Harvey's personality brought in more customers.

I entered the door to see a teenaged clerk at the cash register and Harvey near a display to the left of the store near the windows. Not surprisingly, he was engaged in animated conversation with a customer. The older gentleman was considerably shorter than Harvey. He stood slightly hunched over at the waist, a crooked walking cane in one hand. His wispy hair was snow white. I watched the two men compare bird feeders. They motioned from one option to another, putting their heads together to study the hangtag of a large hopper feeder like the one for cardinals in my backyard. It was obvious they were both knowledgeable on the subject.

Harvey caught my eye and waved for me to join them. "Josie Posey, I want you to meet Mr. Barleycorn. He lives in Clearwater, about twenty minutes from here."

I extended my hand. "It's nice to meet you, Mr. Barleycorn."

"Please, call me Jethro." A huge smile creased his face. Piercing blue eyes peered at me from beneath bushy white eyebrows. "Your friend Harvey was just telling me about you."

"Oh?"

Harvey cleared his throat. "Actually, we were talking about bird feeders. But, earlier, we had a great conversation about sundials. Which led us to an entire discussion of timekeeping and clocks."

I looked from Harvey to the old man and back again before I spoke. "I'm interested in clocks too."

"You are standing before a master clockmaker, Josie." Harvey gave a nod toward his customer. "Jethro Barleycorn was in the clock business on the East Coast for many years. He retired to Clearwater a few months ago."

"What a coincidence. I stopped in to see if you sell any common clock repair tools, Harvey. Thought I'd look around."

The old man motioned to the butterfly key hanging from my neck. "You're wearing one of the most essential tools," he said. "My wife favored them, as well. She had an entire collection."

"Used for winding clocks, right?" I asked.

"Yes, ma'am," he answered.

"You'll find a variety on Aisle seven," Harvey said. "But wait till you hear about Mr. Barleycorn's training."

Now, Harvey practically bounced on his feet with excitement. "He attended the same school as your friend, Ella."

The old man nodded. "I did, indeed. About five decades ahead of her."

I turned eagerly toward the old man. "Would you be willing to answer some of my questions about clocks? I'd be happy to buy you lunch at our local cafe."

Mr. Barleycorn turned to Harvey. "What do you say, young man? Your girlfriend just asked me for a date."

"I'd say you should accept," Harvey grinned. "I've been trying to get her to ask *me* out for a long time."

"Meet you at noon," I said to Mr. Barleycorn. "The Cozy Cups on Main Street."

While Harvey carried Mr. Barleycorn's purchases to his car, I perused the bottom shelf of aisle seven to discover several bins of clock keys. One held butterfly keys similar to the one I wore, though not as ornate. Another contained ornamental brass clock keys shaped more like a skeleton key. Toward the end of the row, I found double-ended clock keys in two styles— carriage and butterfly. At the final bin of the bottom row, I reached into a container marked 'Universal Spider Key.'

What I saw in the palm of my hand made my heart race.

It was a brass clock key featuring five tubular prongs emanating from a circular center plate. In my opinion, the tool resembled a starfish more than a spider, but I supposed someone could squint their eyes and see the formation of a spider web.

Hurriedly, I pulled the chief's sketch from my purse and compared the shape of Ella's injury to the tool. *Yes! Something similar to this implement could have caused the marks!*

If the spider key had spilled from Ella's toolkit, she could easily have landed on it, I thought.

I grabbed the spider key and paid the teenager at the cash register. Then, I rushed to the police station to share my discovery.

Chief Marshall greeted me with good news. "You're cleared to enter your cottage, Josie," he said. "Moe is a happy dog, and there are no criminals lurking in your closet." He handed me an envelope. "Your keys are inside."

"Thanks, Chief." I accepted the envelope and pulled the hardware store shopping bag from my purse. "I have something to give you, too. Could we use the conference room?"

He gave me a curious look but led the way down the short hall and turned into the familiar room.

I held the bag on my lap. "Do you think the indentations on Ella's temple would match a tool like this one?" I pulled out the spider key and displayed it on my palm.

The chief's eyes blazed. "Where did you get that?"

"At the hardware store. Sharon gave me this single clock key necklace as a gift this morning, and the tubular prong reminded me of your drawing—except the drawing showed more than one prong. When she said the clock key was a common tool, I decided to see if Harvey carried them at the hardware store."

"Give it to me," the chief said, "I don't want anyone to see you handling it. I'll have our lab compare the dimensions to Ella's X-rays."

I hefted the key in my hand as I turned it over to him. "This thing could easily have fallen from her toolkit."

The chief studied the tool. "It could just as easily have been used as a weapon. Like brass knuckles, but with hollow prongs protruding from the base," he said.

I stared at the shiny brass object. "If she fell on it, why didn't anyone find it at the scene?"

"I don't know." The chief returned the tool to the bag. "Maybe Alex picked up a few of her tools before the ambulance arrived. At that time, her fall appeared to be accidental, so there was no reason to keep everything in place."

"Are you going to ask him?"

"Not until the lab confirms this is a match." He shifted in his seat, and I could see he was debating whether to share something more or send me home.

"What is it?" I asked.

"We *did* get a match on the mystery caller." The chief paused to wait for my reaction.

"And?" I prompted.

"We've identified him as Samuel Ternberry. We talked by phone. Sam says he knew Ella and Jack Benjamin in college. Even attended their wedding. His story is that he ran into Jack last week, learned the couple had divorced, and decided to reach out to Ella. He wanted to ask her out for coffee."

"Do you believe him?"

Chief Marshall shrugged. "Yeah. The guy sounded genuinely distraught to learn about Ella. He claims he arrived at The Curiosity Shop late in the afternoon intending to pay a surprise visit. The place was closed, and a patrol car was stationed out front. Sam approached the officer and was told there had been an accident; he should check back later."

"Did your officer confirm that?"

"Devon recalled that several people approached him with questions. Unfortunately, he didn't take any names." The chief rubbed his hand through his cropped hair.

"What's next?"

"Mr. Ternberry is out of town on business, but he has agreed to come in and make a statement on Tuesday."

"Could I meet him? I'd like to hear his impressions of the relationship between Jack and Ella during college...for my article."

"Sure. I'll see that you get introduced."

Chief Marshall walked me to the door and repeated his admonition to be mindful of my surroundings.

I was so relieved I could go home again that I failed to ask if they'd figured out how the intruder had entered the garage. It didn't matter now. There was no way the guy would try the same thing twice. Not with my cottage under constant surveillance.

I drove back down Persimmon Lane and pulled into my garage, where I sat in the car shaking from a flashback of the skewered opossum on my step. I took several deep breaths to calm myself from the unexpected panic attack.

When I finally composed myself enough to walk inside my cottage, one thought echoed in my head: Ella's murderer was still on the loose in our little village.

Chapter Fifteen

Friday Noon

After a soothing cup of hot tea and a brief conversation with Moe, I felt almost normal again. Shortly before noon, I returned to Cozy Cups. Lorene waved as I entered. She accepted the fact that I treated her business as my ad-hoc office. No matter how often I occupied a table, Lorene welcomed me with coffee and a smile.

When I walked into the cafe with my notepad, my new friend Jethro waited at a sunny table near the window. I should have realized the elderly gentleman would arrive early. After all, he was a clockmaker like Ella. From what she had told me, all respectable graduates of Adler Minetti were punctual professionals.

"Thank you for agreeing to have lunch with me, Mr. Barleycorn." I took a seat across from him.

"I'm more than happy to do it, but you must call me Jethro." The old man folded his hands on the table in front of him. "It isn't often I meet someone genuinely interested in the craftsmanship of fine clocks."

We both ordered Lorene's daily special, and the old man launched into a story of watch and clock making while I tried to figure out how to broach the subject of Ella's deathbed statement.

"Did you know the best watchmakers in the world are not really from Switzerland?" His question brought me back from my musings.

I hated to argue with my new friend, but I couldn't believe my ears. "How can that be true, with so many fine watch companies based there?"

"They have immigrants to thank. The first influx of them happened during the religious persecutions of 1500 and 1600. Later, a large group of them had Jewish roots—and Switzerland was a sort of safe haven for them all. The majority of the watchmakers who have revolutionized the watchmaking industry were foreigners who moved to Switzerland to live and work."

Before I could comment, Jethro continued his history lesson.

"Most of the technical innovations in horology came from outside Switzerland. Many were from England and France." The old man's eyes lit up as he warmed to his subject. "The English watchmakers were far superior to Swiss in the early years. Watches from Switzerland were considered as second or third behind them."

I nibbled on a homemade potato chip and tried to think of a way to interrupt him. All of this was fascinating, but I wanted to fast-forward a few centuries. When our waitress set a muffuletta sandwich in front of Jethro, he paused to taste it, and I jumped into the conversation. "I'd like to hear more about the industry, but first, may I share what led to my interest in the subject?"

Jethro proved to be a good listener. I told him about my writing assignment for *The Village Gazette*, which led to an interview with Ella McGregor. "We had barely covered her education and a few of her accomplishments. Naturally, when she died the very next day, I wanted to know more."

He set his sandwich on the plate. "I didn't know Ella, but I do know a few things about clocks. How can I help you, Josie?"

Taking care to avoid any mention of my role in a potential murder investigation, I leaned toward him. "Jethro, I wonder if you could explain the economics of clock making. Why would anyone kill a young woman who had barely begun her career? Could there be money involved?"

His bright blue eyes drilled into mine. "An excellent question. You might find my answer surprising."

After a brief tutorial on more recent developments, including the impact of digital watches on the industry, Jethro circled into the point. "Everyone thought craftsmanship would be replaced by mass manufacturing. Instead, a strange thing happened: the demand for beautifully hand-built watches grew even more. And their prices soared."

"What do these watches sell for?"

"The most expensive timepiece ever sold at auction was an Adler Minetti pocket watch." Jethro Barleycorn must have had a flair for the dramatic because he paused before he delivered the punchline.

"It sold for twenty-eight million dollars."

I had raised a glass of iced tea to my lips and nearly choked when I heard the number. "American dollars?"

"Yes."

I returned my tea glass to the table. "Why would anyone pay so much for a watch?"

"It was a beautiful piece with twenty-two complications, including a map of New York City's constellations, a triple calendar display, and an alarm that replicates the chimes from the George Delacorte Musical Clock outside the Central Park Zoo. I can assure you it was worth every penny."

I froze for a moment, unable to speak. "Could you repeat that part, please?"

"What part?"

"The thing you said about it being complicated."

"In horology, we refer to each different function as a 'complication,'" Jethro explained. "The more complications included in a watch, or a clock, the more value it has for a buyer."

I paused while my brain absorbed the information. Though I couldn't tell him about Ella's dying statement, I desperately wanted the old man's interpretation of her words. The chief's voice echoed in my head, telling me not to mention the deathbed statement. I ignored it and plunged ahead. "Jethro, Ella said something that made no sense to me. If I told you those words, could you help me decipher the meaning as it relates to clocks?"

"I'll try."

"There were three things." I watched his eyes as I recited the words from Ella's physician. "The number *32*. The word *complicated*. And, *long clock*."

Jethro's eyes widened. His mouth moved, but no sound emerged. He tried again, and the words came in a whisper. "Oh my…"

"What is it, Jethro?"

"Is it possible your friend said the word *complications* instead of *complicated*?"

I considered the circumstances. Although Dr. Grant noted Ella's words on her pad, she might have misunderstood the ending of the word.

"Yes. It's possible. Would that change the meaning?"

The old man looked at me intently before he spoke. "I suppose it could mean more than one thing, so we shouldn't jump to conclusions." He clasped his hands together and placed them firmly on the table. Then he leaned forward, and I saw excitement in his eyes. "However, speaking as a clockmaker, I'd say Ella may have come upon a long clock—or a design for a long clock—incorporating thirty-two complications."

"Would that make it valuable?"

"Very valuable indeed."

"Where would I begin to search for it?"

"If Ella had a workshop somewhere, the clock might be hidden in plain sight. It isn't unusual for a clockmaker to develop new functionality in a private workspace. The truth is, something this rare should have been stored under lock and key."

"What if Ella had drawn the plans for this clock and not yet built it?"

"The diagrams would still be extremely valuable. Unfortunately, they could be hidden anywhere. Clock drawings are similar to an architect's work. They require careful measurements and attention to detail. Printed documents are easily rolled and stored in a tube. Digital designs might be locked on a computer, a thumb drive, or somewhere in 'The Cloud.'"

"This sounds hopeless."

"Not necessarily, my dear." Jethro spoke kindly, and I saw compassion in his eyes. "All you need to do is shift your focus."

"I don't understand."

"Don't try to find the clock. Try to find the person who will claim credit for creating it. This is a small industry, with only a few very wealthy individuals or companies capable of purchasing such an item."

I nodded with comprehension. "They shouldn't be difficult to find. I can reach out to locate a potential buyer with inquiries to pique their interest in a new, highly complicated long clock."

"Be cautious, my friend," Jethro said. "Remember, someone wanted it badly enough to kill for it. They won't give it up easily."

My mind reeled from the information the old clockmaker had shared over lunch. I raced home to document our conversation while it was still fresh in my mind. Long ago, I had learned my handwritten notes were best deciphered the same day I wrote them.

It didn't help that I occasionally reverted to shorthand during interviews. It was an old habit from my days as a news reporter. Oddly, I often switched back and forth between longhand and shorthand—sometimes within the same sentence. The system saved time on the front end, but could cause excruciating delays during the transcription of those same notes. If I waited until tomorrow, the notes would be cold, and I would struggle to capture all of the words correctly.

Besides, Nellie's tasting party tonight left me no wiggle room for investigative work. I couldn't wait to summarize Jethro Barleycorn's thoughts and share them with the chief.

All those good intentions flew out of my mind when sweet Moe greeted me at the door, his leash in his mouth. My heart melted when I saw him. "Okay, boy. You win. But only to the park and back. I have work to do."

I set my purse and notebook on the kitchen counter, tucked my phone and keys in the pocket of my jeans, and took off with Moe down the sidewalk. A brisk walk on this clear October day was exactly what we both needed. Except I didn't anticipate our brief afternoon walk would end the way it did.

We had just completed the familiar turn to circle the gazebo when Moe stopped in his tracks beside a towering old walnut tree. He sniffed. Whined. Sniffed again. Probably another tennis ball.

I tugged at his leash and urged him forward. "Come on, Moe. We don't have time to dig in the leaves today."

He ignored my plea, shoved the pile of leaves aside with his paws, and plunged his face into the dirt.

"Please, Moe." I wrapped my arms around his neck and attempted to pull him away from the tree. Moe reacted by spinning his body around to face me, which knocked me off my feet. I landed on my rear in the wet leaves with Moe sitting on my lap.

The fluffy dog licked my face with his muddy tongue. Yuck!

I scrambled to stand and brushed the dirt from my pants. That's when I noticed my phone and keys had fallen from my pocket. I glanced around the deserted park. Good! There was no one to witness my romp in the leaves.

With no other recourse, I dropped to the ground, dived into the pile, and searched for the lost items. I felt the smooth surface of my cell phone first. Grabbed it and raised it into the air.

"Got it!" I waved the phone at Moe and shoved it back into my pocket.

Of course, Moe thought the whole escapade was a game, so he started digging alongside me. Seconds later, he raised his head, keys dangling from his mouth.

I held out my hand. Moe dropped the prize into my palm, and I saw the shiny object that most likely had attracted his attention in the first place. The hairs raised on the back of my neck. It was Ella's beautiful sundial pendant.

I plopped onto my rear and leaned against the tree. Moe stretched out beside me and rested his head on my lap while I retrieved my cell phone and hit the speed dial for Chief Marshall.

By the time we walked home, the chief had already arrived. Mrs. Abernathy stood in her front yard watering flowers, and Moe's tongue hung tiredly from the side of his mouth. I sighed. Unlocked the door for the chief. Waved at my neighbor across the street.

Inside, I filled Moe's water bowl and sat across from the chief at my kitchen island.

"You said nothing had been stolen." I placed the small pendant into the chief's hand. He lifted the gold chain to study the diamond and emerald sundial.

"I didn't know." The chief laid the necklace onto the cool surface of the counter between us. "Ella's family took a full inventory of the clocks. They must not have noticed she wore the necklace that day."

"Can't believe Moe found it."

"You understand this puts you squarely on the suspect list." Chief Marshall motioned to the necklace.

"What? You think I killed Ella to steal her necklace?" I threw my hands in the air. "That's ridiculous."

"You were the last person to talk to her. Now you have discovered an expensive necklace no one else even realized was missing. If you didn't take it, who did?"

"Obviously the killer stole it. But why would he bury such a valuable item? Why not keep it? Or sell it?"

"Maybe he lost it. Or hid it until he could retrieve it." The chief raised one eyebrow.

I closed my eyes and rubbed my temples. "Now you're suggesting I took the necklace. Hid it. Pretended to find it. And called you to report it?"

"What I'm suggesting is that this discovery puts you in greater danger. If Ella's murderer learns you found the necklace, he won't be happy."

"What shall I do?"

"Do your job as a reporter, and I'll do mine. You stay out of the investigation. Don't tell anyone about the necklace. Not even the mavens." His fierce look might have frightened the daylights out of any normal criminal. I refused to be intimidated.

I raised my head and glared back at him. "Humph. I met a gentleman today who attended the same school as Ella did. He explained some things I think you'll want to hear."

Now, it was the chief's turn to back down. He planted both palms on the counter and growled at me. "You'll continue digging unless I lock you into a jail cell, won't you?"

I stared at him without flinching. "Somebody has to find the murderer so I can clear my name off your suspect list."

Chief Marshall sighed so loudly Moe lifted his muddy face to look at him.

"My office. Tomorrow morning at nine-thirty sharp. Can you be there?"

"Wouldn't miss it."

I walked with Chief Marshall to his car. "Don't forget what I've told you about diligence," he said. "Pay attention to everything around you. If anything—or anyone—seems out of place, let me know."

"I will." I answered the chief with confidence. But that was before I saw the UPS delivery van turn onto Primrose twenty minutes later. Who would suspect a guy with a clipboard?

Chapter Sixteen

Friday Afternoon

W hen the UPS driver knocked on my door, I opened it wide.
"Josephine Posey?"
"Yes."

"I have several packages for you. If you sign for them, I'll carry them to the porch for you."

I'd moved three packages to my kitchen island before I realized I should have been more cautious. The stranger could have been a killer! Lucky for me, he was simply what he appeared to be: a guy in a brown uniform representing one of the biggest delivery companies in the country. The box labels were written in clear, round handwriting with a return address from Lucy Buttons in New York, NY.

With the necklace safely in the chief's hands and a couple of hours remaining before Nellie's tasting party, I couldn't resist the boxes. Just a peek. Then, I would transcribe the Barleycorn interview notes and look at the chief's typed suspect list.

I sliced the exterior packing tape of the smallest box and tore it open. Inside, I found a small journal, a packet of letters wrapped with ribbon, and a prescription bottle from a New York pharmacy. I couldn't wait to explore the contents, but I knew it would take longer to investigate than I could devote to it this evening. So, instead of further unpacking the boxes, I set everything in my hall closet and closed the door.

The transcription of the Jethro Barleycorn interview turned out to be quick and easy. In less than thirty minutes, I completed the task and filed the notes into the folder I would share with the chief. I also made a note to call Logan Lavender again to get her reaction to Mr. Barleycorn's thoughts on the meaning of Ella's last words. Hopefully, she could also suggest names of potential buyers for a valuable clock design, if one existed.

Before I considered my next move, my phone pinged with a text from Leslie Anderson with a cryptic reminder. "The clock is ticking," she wrote. "I NEED your article."

I responded with a "thumbs up" emoji and hoped I could hit her deadline tomorrow morning. Could be a long night ahead.

Harvey and I planned to attend the early evening tasting party together, then go to dinner at the Philbrook. I was relieved he had offered to drive, especially since I now felt queasy at the thought of entering my own garage. I hadn't told anyone but the chief about the dead opossum. Not even Harvey. Chief Marshall had assured me they would find my intruder quickly. I wanted to shove the incident from my mind.

With an hour to spare before the party, I had a decision to make. Ella's journal beckoned to me, but the chief's suspect list was shorter. I opted to review the chief's information first and save Ella's journal till later.

I pulled his list from my purse and settled into my favorite reading chair with pen in hand to see whether his suspect names matched mine. First up, the "WHO" column.

The chief's list was disappointing, to say the least. He had included both Thomas and Alex McGregor, with notations beside them: "Pinochle alibi." Others on his list were Jack Benjamin, ex-husband, and Samuel Ternberry, the mystery caller now identified. Four in total.

Yikes. I had more ideas for suspects than the chief did. My own list included Ella's Lover and my Unknown Stalker.

The only encouraging thing about the list was that my own name wasn't on it. We had a lot of work ahead of us.

Since the suspect list was a total bust, I wasn't optimistic about the motives. Under the "WHY" column, the chief had simply included broad categories:

Love. Revenge. Money. Again, I was disappointed. Anyone who'd watched an episode of *Murder She Wrote* could have come up with those. No wonder the chief was willing to accept my help.

I set his list aside and retrieved the box that contained Ella's journal. Perhaps the victim's words would provide better insight into who might have taken her life and why. There was a note from Lucy Buttons inside.

> *Ms. Posey,*
>
> *I have sent several items at Ella's request. These include her journal, a picture that hung on her wall, and a few other items.*
>
> *Most were odds and ends I found while cleaning her bathroom, dresser, and closet. I hope you don't mind delivering them to the appropriate people.*
>
> *I didn't want to dispose of anything here, although I'm certain some of the clothing will simply go to a charity or the waste bin. Please let me know when a memorial service is planned. Ella was a very special young lady. I will miss her.*
>
> *With regards,*
> *Lucy Buttons*

After I read the note, I knew to pay special attention to the journal, the letters, and the framed picture. I was also curious about the prescription bottle. The clothing could wait until last.

I picked up her journal and ran my hand over the leather cover. Inside, Ella's name was printed neatly in the upper right corner. This first entry was dated just six months earlier. I wondered how long she had kept a journal and whether this one would tell me what I needed to know. There was only one way to find out.

Her handwriting was small and precise. Very small. I supposed it made sense, given her occupation. She was accustomed to working with microscopic watchmaking tools. Clearly, she was comfortable with tiny lettering. Her side notes were miniature by any standard. I pulled out my magnifying glass to enlarge the script. The larger print helped, but my eyes tired easily. I plowed through, determined to read everything I could about the last weeks of her life.

While she was quiet and reserved in person, Ella expressed her thoughts in an organized and entertaining style. I smiled at her self-deprecating comments as I scanned the content for an overview of Ella's life. She had poured her innermost thoughts onto the pages, one sentence flowing after another. She wrote mostly about her career, her ideas spinning from words into diagrams and drawings. Occasionally, she mentioned a partner—someone who shared her joy of clockmaking.

It was clear to me Ella was deeply in love. What wasn't clear was the name of her suitor. She referred to him with terms of endearment rather than a name: my *beloved*, my *love*, my *soulmate*. Reading Ella's journal was almost like traveling into an earlier, more romantic era.

I marked several passages by slipping thin paper between the pages, but I also made notes as I read to capture pertinent dates and comments. I hoped the random pieces might somehow lead me to conclusions related to her murder. Resisting the urge to skip to the end of the journal, I forced myself to return to the beginning and read her entries in chronological order. My eyes began to burn with the effort. I was only a few pages into the journal when tears streamed down my face from the strain. Ella's belongings would be time-consuming to sort through—especially with her microscopic handwriting.

Since Harvey was due to arrive in twenty minutes, I reluctantly set the book aside. I showered and changed into comfortable palazzo pants, a soft V-neck T-shirt, and my go-to denim jacket. The pants always made me feel a little taller—something I had wished for my entire adult life.

When Moe heard Harvey's truck pull into the drive, he bounded toward the front door. I took his collar in my left hand and directed him to "sit." He gave me his sad-eyes look but obeyed the command. Then, I swung the door open for Harvey. Moe squirmed with excitement but he stayed in place until I released my hold on his collar.

Harvey stood on the porch, a brown shipping box in his hands. He tucked it under one arm and called out to Moe. "Good to see you, boy."

He walked into the kitchen and set the box on the floor by the coat rack. Moe raced to his side, wagging his entire body in an enthusiastic welcome. Harvey held out one closed fist, and Moe sat obediently. Then, Harvey opened his hand to give Moe a treat as he did every time he'd come.

I'd known from the first time we met that Harvey loved dogs. But it had taken weeks for me to realize he always kept a dog biscuit in his jacket pocket. Now, the routine was so familiar that Moe had come to anticipate a treat whenever he saw Harvey. No wonder he adored the man.

"What's in the box?" I nodded toward the package as I hurried to fill Moe's water bowl before we left for the evening.

Harvey shrugged. "It was on your front porch. I figured it was the UPS delivery you expected."

"Hmm. I signed for the boxes earlier this afternoon. The delivery guy must have placed another on the step after I carried the first ones inside. Just put it with the others in my hall closet, please."

While Harvey stowed the box, I returned Moe's bowl to its proper place. Then, I took one final glance to see if I'd forgotten anything. Satisfied that all was well, I picked up my purse and walked out of the cottage, careful to lock the door behind me before we headed toward Harvey's truck.

We arrived early to find Nellie and Sharon outside, lighting candles at the center of each table. Sharon waved for me to join them. "They're citronella." She motioned to the candles. "We shouldn't have mosquitoes this time of year, but it's good to be prepared."

"Candles are always a nice touch," I said.

While the two ladies worked around me, I stood at the center point and turned in a slow 360-degree circle to absorb the beauty of Nellie's backyard. It was an imaginative combination of flowers and light. Music flowed softly from speakers hidden somewhere in the lush gardens; water bubbled gently on the patio.

"Don't you love it?" Nellie bounced on her toes with excitement. "Tim added the lights and speakers this afternoon."

True to form, Nellie's husband, Tim, had transformed an already lovely space into something magical. The base of each tree was wrapped with tiny white lights, giving the effect of an enchanted forest in a fairy tale. From the overhanging branches, Tim draped dozens of hanging globe lights above the patio. Finally, he used Edison-style string lights to decorate delicate trellis walls around the outside rim of the patio. The strings arched upward into a center ring suspended from their huge walnut tree. The result was a canopy of light that twinkled above the patio like a sky filled with fireflies.

"Oh. My. Goodness!" I stretched my arms upward. "This is so beautiful."

"It is, isn't it?" Nellie swept her gaze across the outdoor space. Her eyes landed on the serving tables where she and Sharon had placed their baked snacks for the art show volunteers to enjoy prior to the main event. "Now I wish we had invited everyone to the tasting."

"No worries. I'm sure all the volunteers will appreciate the effort," I said. "Especially since we will be working while our guests eat the appetizers on Sunday."

"Why are you here so early?" Sharon asked. "We wanted to have everything on the tables to surprise you."

"We couldn't wait to see it," I said. "And, I *am* surprised. So, mission accomplished. Harvey and I are going to the Philbrook for a light dinner afterward."

"Thought we'd make it an early evening before the big weekend," Harvey said. He waved to Tim across the patio. "If you ladies will excuse me, I want to congratulate Tim on the decorating job." He left us to circle the fountain and stride toward Nellie's husband.

Sharon sighed. "He's perfect for you, Josie."

I couldn't help admiring my lanky blacksmith friend as he walked away. He made blue jeans and a chambray shirt look like a trendy casual ensemble straight out of a high-fashion magazine. When he turned back and caught me watching him, Harvey gave me a lopsided smile.

I rolled my eyes, but I couldn't stop the butterflies that danced in my stomach. Fortunately, Nellie provided a new distraction.

She clasped her hands in front of her and claimed my attention. "I have another surprise for you, Josie."

"What?"

"One of the judges for the event stopped by today to introduce herself."

"Do I know her?"

"She was a college friend of Ella's. While our hometown girl was making a name for herself in the watchmaking industry, her college roommate was a rising star in the art world."

"She must be good if she's a judge for the art show."

"Her name is Maria Paige. *Forbes Magazine* selected her as one of their "Top 30 Artists Under the Age of 30." She's been in town all week, partly so she could visit with Ella."

"I have to meet her!"

"Here's a better idea," Nellie said. "The volunteer who was supposed to escort Maria tomorrow can't do it. She cracked a tooth this afternoon and has an emergency appointment with the dentist in the morning. Want to take her place?"

"What time, and where?"

"She's staying at the Philbrook Inn," Nellie said. "Pick her up at ten thirty and take her to the art museum. Gallery A. Then join her later for the city tour and tea. You'll be with her till mid-afternoon."

"Great! You're a genius, Nellie. I owe you for this one."

The evening went by quickly. Thirty-five volunteers mingled in what I had secretly named "Nellie's Tinkerbelle Garden." They marveled over the decorations, tasted the delicious appetizers, and picked up their official packets for the weekend. By seven thirty, only the Mahjong Mavens remained.

"Thanks for a wonderful event." Sharon hugged Nellie as she prepared to leave.

"Thank *you* for the ever-appropriate napkins and tableware. I've never seen those before."

"I kept it simple," Sharon said. "Everyone agreed we could describe your treats with one word." She picked up a napkin from the table and waved it at Nellie. It was bright green with the word "YUM" printed in huge letters across the center.

We worked together to clear the party supplies from the patio. Kate gathered remaining foods, placing the leftovers into containers. Nellie blew out the candles and packed them into their original boxes. I folded tablecloths and stacked the extra chairs against the patio wall near the garage.

Everyone was prepped and ready for the weekend.

"See you tomorrow."

As we headed toward Harvey's truck, fatigue from a long day settled into my bones. I looked forward to an early dinner and a quiet night. If only it had gone that way.

Chapter Seventeen

Friday Night

The waitress led us to my favorite table near the front window. Harvey knew I enjoyed sitting where we could see guests inside the dining room and others strolling outside.

"Shall we order wine?" he asked.

"I would love a glass. This has been a busy day."

"How's the murder investigation?"

I leaned back in my chair and picked up the menu. "I'm starving. Let's order first and talk later."

We talked easily as we enjoyed our meal. It felt good to have Harvey lead the conversation. He told me interesting stories about his day at the hardware store, and I laughed at his descriptions.

"One poor guy came in three times…for a gasket." Harvey shook his head, remembering the scene. "He tried twice to buy the right size on his own. The third time, I sold him a rubber O-rings kit with an assortment of universal sizes. It probably cost less than the gas he used driving back and forth to the hardware store. Now he has what he needs for most any simple leak repair."

"Did he appreciate your advice?"

"No." Harvey sighed. "He was upset because I didn't suggest it earlier."

"The customer is always right."

"That's why I didn't try to interfere when he checked out the first two times," Harvey said. "Some guys don't like a suggestion. They come into the store, buy what they need, and go home happy. Others could benefit from a little guidance."

Chief Marshall and Lorene entered the restaurant as we ordered dessert. I was struck again by the physical differences between them. The chief was tall and broad, an all-star football player in college. Beside him, Lorene appeared to be child-size. When she was at the coffee shop, serving customers, she was a tiny whirlwind of energy—clearly in charge of her domain. But here, standing beside her husband, her four foot eleven height took the top of her head level with his shoulder. Tonight, she looked even younger, in a deep magenta tunic over black leggings. She had a flawless complexion. When I had once asked her secret formula for beautiful skin, she pooh-poohed the question. "It's hereditary. I come from a long line of Asian women."

Now, the handsome couple crossed the dining room to be seated near our table. Lorene stopped to chat.

"Hey, Josie. It's good to see you."

"Like twice in one day wasn't enough?" I referenced my back-to-back meetings at her cafe earlier in the day.

Lorene winked. "We are happy to serve you anytime."

The chief held Lorene's chair for her, then returned to our table. "Do you mind if I interrupt for a moment? I know this is your dinner hour, but I'd like to share some news with Josie."

"What is it?" I asked, truly surprised because the chief rarely mixed business with pleasure.

"Two things," he said. "First, we identified a unique shoe print from the side of your house. It's the same size and brand our detective found near the storage shed at The Curiosity Shop."

Harvey shot me a look. "You've had a prowler?"

"Not exactly." I avoided Harvey's eyes and looked at the chief instead. "What kind of shoe was it?"

"Crocs."

"Crocs?"

"The plastic clog people often wear for gardening. They have the name stamped in on the bottom of the shoe, so it was easy to identify." He turned to Harvey. "Did you wear Crocs when you planted the tree?"

"No sir," Harvey answered. "I don't own a pair."

I was puzzled by the information. "I don't remember seeing anyone in Crocs."

Chief Marshall agreed. "Me either. Let's be on the lookout."

"What is your other news?" Harvey asked.

"I got a tip that an expensive prototype of a watch was stolen from the Adler Minetti factory in Geneva. Someone substituted a relatively convincing mock-up."

"Is it related to our case?" I asked.

"Don't know. But it involves Adler Minetti Timepieces. I'll email you the details."

"Where did you get the tip?"

The chief gave me one of his rare smiles. "I have my sources."

Which, of course, made me start thinking about the murder case all over again. Since the chief had already spilled the beans to Harvey, I spent several minutes reciting a watered-down version of my prank call and the ensuing opossum incident.

Harvey wasn't buying it. "If this prank caller of yours is the same person who tampered with Ella's ladder, he's capable of murder."

I nodded like one of those bobblehead dashboard ornaments while he told me to be more careful. Then he paid our tab and escorted me to his truck for a quiet drive home. At my door, Harvey took my hands in his.

"Look. I know you're a strong, independent, capable woman. Just remember that there's safety in numbers. Try not to go anywhere by yourself until the chief has your Crocs-wearing stalker apprehended."

I promised to follow his advice. "This weekend is filled with art show activities. I'll be surrounded by people."

He waited on the porch until he heard the click of my door lock from the inside. I watched from the window as his truck pulled away. Then I turned to the new question swirling through my head.

Crocs? I tried to remember the last time I'd seen a pair. They were a popular brand. Inexpensive to buy. Why would a murderer wear a shoe style so distinctive? This case was driving me crazy.

Harvey had urged me to lock the doors and get some rest, but it was impossible. I was too deep into the murder investigation to let it go.

Instead, I changed into pajamas, filled a glass with icewater, and returned to my workspace at Grandma Molly's expansive table. Moe stretched out at my feet.

Determined to make sense of the seemingly unrelated clues, I re-stacked my note cards, placed Ella's journal beside them, and opened my laptop. Instantly, I saw the chief's email with details about the missing prototype. He, too, worked late tonight.

Pasted into his email was an article from a Reuters World News brief datelined Switzerland.

RARE WATCH PROTOTYPE STOLEN
FROM ADLER MINETTI FACTORY

Authorities announced today a rare prototype of the Galaxy Blue has been stolen from Adler Minetti's factory, where it had been on exhibit in recent months.

The company declined to comment, but an anonymous highly placed source confirmed the watch was the third most complicated ever made by Adler Minetti Timepieces. It ranked only behind the Cosmic 1000 and the Supernova Plus.

Launched in 2000, complete with twenty-one complications, the Galaxy Blue was noted not only for its complexity but also for its ease of use. The perpetual calendar synced automatically with the equation of time, sunrise, and sunset. All date displays auto-corrected upon use, and the watch played Westminster chimes on the quarter hour.

The prototype was an early and unfinished version of one of the most famous and lauded Minetti's of all time. It was valued at more than

$15 million US dollars but has been declared "priceless" by the Adler Minetti CEO. Police request anyone with information about the missing prototype call the hotline listed at the end of this article.

I picked up Ella's journal to flip through it again. The theft was big news in her industry, but I had no idea how it might be related to her murder. From what I remembered, she barely mentioned visiting the factory to see the prototype.

Though I had bookmarked important passages in Ella's journal with tissue-paper inserts, it would take time to find any comments related to her Geneva trip. I strained to read the journal, even with my magnifying glass.

As much as I wanted to find the reference to the prototype, it would have to wait until the weekend. My eyes were too tired to read her cramped writing. Instead, I pulled out the second box from Lucy Buttons. Time to see what other surprises the landlady had sent me.

I cut through layers of packing tape before I could loosen the cardboard flaps. The large box was stuffed with Styrofoam peanuts cushioning another wrapped package. Lucy had outdone herself to protect whatever was inside. The item was about 24" x 30", wrapped in heavy brown kraft paper and tied with knotted string. I used my scissors to clip the knots, then cut away the edges of the paper wrapping. Inside, I discovered another wrapping of lightweight foam. At last, I removed the foam to reveal a framed painting. I carried it to my kitchen island, where the light was brighter. What I saw made my heart race with excitement.

This was not a photo of Ella or her friends. It was an oil painting of the inner workings of a clock. My eyes moved quickly to the artist's signature: Maria Paige. No wonder Lucy Buttons had wrapped the package so thoroughly. This was a valuable painting. I admired the intricacy of the piece for several minutes before I turned it over to see the backside.

A glossy photo had been slipped into a clear envelope and pasted to the lower right corner. I studied the two young coeds in the picture. Maria was on the left, tall and lithe, with her long blond hair and wide smile. She had her arm around Ella, who stood six inches shorter, dark curls wildly springing out from her perfect heart-shaped face. Both girls stood on the front steps of a stately limestone building with huge columns, most likely from their university days. I pulled the photo from its protective sleeve and turned it over. Maria had written a note on the back:

"32 Complications" by Maria Paige
I dedicate this painting to Ella, my best friend in the whole world.
May our lives never be as complicated as this clock.

I gasped. This must be the message Ella conveyed to her physician in the last hours of her life. She had referred directly to Maria's painting when she said "thirty-two" and "complicated." And, if the clock parts were representative of a "long clock," my deduction would be confirmed. I propped the painting against the backsplash of my kitchen wall and snapped a photo of it. I couldn't wait to see Maria at breakfast. Surely, Ella's friend could decipher the hidden meaning of the painting. After all, she had painted it.

I was so pumped I felt like dancing on the countertop in my pj's. If it hadn't been past midnight, I would have dialed the chief to share the good news. This was too significant to send as a text or email. I wanted to hear the excitement in his voice. Instead, I settled for telling Moe.

"We did it, boy. We found the clue Ella wanted us to see."

Moe's reaction was a disappointment. He raised his head to acknowledge he had heard my voice. He stood and stretched. Then he ambled to my side and nudged his face against my knee.

I walked with him to the back door and stepped outside. "Be quick, boy."

The broad expanse of lawn was eerily dark. The former gardener's cottage at the rear of my property was barely visible this moonless night. I glanced toward the garage side of the house to see the spindly limbs of the Golden Rain tree Harvey had planted. When I peered into the darkness, I imagined the shadow of a man. Was someone staring back at me? I shivered and stepped back into the house. I clapped my hands twice, and Moe bounded toward me, his ears flapping like happy wings.

Safely inside, I locked the doors and shook off my fears. Moe would have barked, if a stranger lurked near the cottage. It was late, but I was so excited by the painting breakthrough I couldn't resist another look at the treasures from Lucy Buttons. I returned to the original box and sorted through its contents. The prescription bottle caught my eye first. The label indicated a physician named Patricia Rosenberg had prescribed propranolol for Ella. Columbia Pharmacy filled the order. It allowed for no refills.

I didn't recognize the name of the drug. It wasn't a common prescription for blood pressure or cholesterol, or anything else familiar to me. Moe and I returned to the dining room table, and I opened my laptop again. I navigated directly to Google, in search of the doctor.

"Patricia Rosenberg, New York physician," I typed.

Google didn't disappoint. The doctor's impressive background included several degrees and a specialty in neurology. She practiced at Columbia Medical Center. I read her brief bio, struck by the significance of a single paragraph:

> Dr. Rosenberg is a lifelong resident of New York, currently serving as Chief of Clinical Practice and Services in the Division of Movement Disorders. She has been involved in research on the genetics of Parkinson's disease and the treatment of this disorder. Dr. Rosenberg is the first to hold the Daniel K. and Myrna L. Bergmann Chair in Neurology. She has been named one of New York Magazine's Best Doctors.

The neurologist had prescribed a high-powered drug for Ella. I wondered what symptoms the talented young watchmaker exhibited to warrant the treatment. She hadn't mentioned an illness when I interviewed her. Another thing to explore with the chief. A neurological disease could have made Ella unsteady on the ladder, even without the tampered rungs.

Now, both my eyes and my brain felt blurry. Moe raised his sleepy head to look up at me, and I leaned down to rub his head. "It's bedtime," I told him.

Seconds before I drifted off to sleep, I remembered the additional unopened UPS box. Too tired to climb back out of bed, I snuggled deeper into the covers. The box would wait.

How was I supposed to know the package wasn't from UPS?

Chapter Eighteen

Early Saturday Morning

Early Saturday morning, I lay perfectly still with my head on the pillow, not quite ready to be awake. Finally, I sensed someone's steady breathing next to me. I opened my eyes to discover Moe's nose inches away from my own. I never understood how a one-hundred-pound dog could climb onto my bed without awakening me. Yet, here he was, stretched on top of the covers, snoring comfortably.

"Moe," I said quietly. His eyes opened to look directly into mine. "What are you doing on the bed?"

He jumped up and launched himself onto the floor.

"That's better." I sat up and swung my legs to the floor so I could pet his fluffy head. "Let's get some breakfast."

By seven, I had strewn my various notepads and pens across Grandma Molly's antique table. Moe settled underneath my feet, where he nuzzled his favorite Lamb Chop toy while I sorted through a dozen stacks of paper and a pile of note cards. With the mess organized and a mug of coffee beside me, I wanted to see what I could learn about Maria Paige before I met her in person.

I flipped open my laptop to search her name. Google didn't let me down. Miss Paige was featured prominently in the *Forbes* "Art & Style" edition. The young artist was already well known for her contemporary art featuring social activism. I read the profile aloud so Moe could hear it.

"This young artist is turning heads by creating new and unexpected pieces that often incorporate recycled materials. Even when the subject matter has a deeper meaning, her work is cheerful and uplifting. Ms. Paige's art combines a surrealistic aesthetic within a minimalist essence. Interestingly, her multimedia paintings feature an abundant use of negative space. The emptiness around the central image allows the picture to grow figuratively. It is simultaneously inspiring and thought-provoking. We are awed by her maturity and her unique style."

Moe yawned, but I was impressed. "Now I have three reasons to meet Ella's friend: her friendship with Ella, the *32 Complications* painting, and her own beautiful work," I told him.

I set aside my notes and finished my breakfast deep in thought. It seemed I had more loose ends than ever. The call with Professor Davis was incomplete. I hadn't attempted to reach Ella's former classmate, Carlos. And the chief had provided no additional information about his conversations with Ella's father and brother. I'd slipped the sympathy note under the door at The Curiosity Shop but had received no reaction from Thomas or Alex. In this case, I considered it good news.

As I cleared away the breakfast dishes, I planned for a busy day. First, I would meet with the chief and share my latest discovery. Afterward, I would chauffeur Maria Paige to the art show and accompany her on Kate's tour of the village. If we had an opportunity to talk privately, I wanted to ask Maria about Ella's marriage to Jack. Her college roommate should be able to describe those early years. By late afternoon I would be free to read more of Ella's journal.

I let Moe outside while I stepped into the shower. Then I dressed in navy slacks, a starched white blouse, and a patterned red, white, and navy mesh cardigan jacket. It was a bit dressier than my normal attire, yet comfortable enough for the walking I intended to do. I slipped into a pair of navy flats and grabbed the spider key from the nightstand. Then, I returned to the kitchen to retrieve my notes and handbag.

When I glanced out the kitchen window, I noticed the drooping flowers in my front porch patio pot. I filled a watering can and stepped outside, intending to splash a little water on them before I started out for the day.

Mrs. Abernathy called to me from her driveway. "Did you see the package the young man delivered yesterday?"

"What young man?"

"The jogger. He raced up Persimmon Street, deposited a box on your front porch, then ran back the way he came. Odd way to deliver a package, if you asked me. Made me wonder where it was from."

"Are you sure it wasn't from the UPS truck?"

"Not unless they switched from brown shorts to red sweatsuits."

"Thanks for the heads-up, Mrs. Abernathy. I'll take a closer look at the package before I open it."

Great. Now I had a strange package in my living room from an unknown jogger.

I heaved a sigh and called the chief. "Want the good news first, or the bad?"

"Are you bleeding?"

"No."

"Then give me the good news."

I described the painting I'd received from Lucy Buttons. When I told him the title was *32 Complications* the chief was almost as excited as I had been, though I'm pretty sure the word "excited" isn't in his vocabulary. He approved my plan to ask Maria about it. Which was a good thing, since I hadn't yet mentioned I'd be spending most of the day with her.

"As the original artist, she should be able to identify any tweaks to the painting. This could be a major breakthrough. Good job, Josie. Go ahead and call her."

"Thank you."

"What's the bad news?"

"I might have brought a dangerous package into my house."

"Might have?"

"Don't know whether it's actually dangerous. But it's definitely inside my house. My neighbor said a jogger delivered it yesterday after the UPS guy stopped by."

"You let the UPS guy into your house?"

"Well, yeah. But he wore brown and carried a clipboard. I figured he was legitimate. Anyway, he's the one who brought the packages from Lucy Button."

The chief groaned over the phone. "Remember when I told you to be diligent?"

"*Yessss.*" I drew the word out to a long hissing sound so he would know I didn't appreciate being treated like a ten-year-old kid.

"Do *not* open the package. Bring it to the station this morning. I'll have our bomb guy check it out."

I did an exaggerated eye roll the chief would never see. "If it was a bomb, it would have exploded already."

"Unless it's rigged to go off when opened."

I stared at the brown box by the doorway. "You'll have it in ten minutes."

I placed the mystery box into my ice cooler like it would protect me from an unexpected explosion and drove to the police station. Slow and steady. No sudden bumps or turns. Grateful the work crew had patched our tiny pothole earlier in the week.

When I arrived, the chief sent Devon to carry the cooler inside. He raised his eyebrows when he saw the precaution I'd taken, but wisely kept his mouth shut.

We talked for a few minutes about the other items I'd received from Lucy Buttons. Then the chief told me The Curiosity Shop would remain closed through the weekend while his team finished processing the crime scene. I figured this was as good a time as any to let him know I was submitting a news article to *The Village Gazette*.

"Leslie Anderson needs an update on the crime story ASAP." I looked at the blank notepad on the scarred table in front of me.

"She'll have to wait," the chief said. "We can't release details. The coroner hasn't officially verified her cause of death."

"Does that mean you won't give me a statement?"

"You're writing it?"

"I already have. It's due today, with or without your comment."

Chief Marshall gave an exaggerated sigh. "My comment is 'no comment'—and you can quote me on that," he said with more than a hint of sarcasm.

"Got it." I made the notation on my pad.

"And don't release details." He glared at me as I made another note.

"No worries, Chief. I kept it simple. Ella's fall has been determined 'suspicious' in nature. Despite rumors to the contrary, no 'foreign object' was found at the scene. Police have several leads and are investigating. Her family appreciates everyone's concern. The Curiosity Shop will be closed for the next several days."

"That's it?"

"I filled in with some of Ella's bio and quotes from her friends. By the next issue, we can announce the arrest of whoever is responsible for her death."

Chief Marshall grumbled under his breath, but turned to his whiteboard to change the subject. In bold letters, he wrote:

"Method: strike to the head. Weapon: Spider Key (to be confirmed)." He turned back to face me. "I hoped the murder weapon might point us to the killer, but since you purchased one at our local hardware store, anyone could get their hands on one."

"Sharon said they have an assortment of the single butterfly keys at The Curiosity Shop. I suppose they have the spider style for sale, as well."

The chief nodded. "Most likely, it was a weapon of convenience. The killer grabbed it from Ella's toolkit or the floor. Ella didn't fall on the spider key, Josie. The markings would have been different if she'd fallen on it."

"It isn't heavy. Makes me believe whoever did this put some force behind the blow. Probably a man."

"I'll be interested to see what the coroner thinks," the chief said. "All of this is speculation until he confirms it."

I glanced at my watch. "We know how she died, even if we can't announce it yet. Now, we have to figure out who could have done it. And why. But first I need to report to Nellie at the art show. She's got me scheduled for volunteer work."

Chief Marshall cocked his head. "Wouldn't want your volunteer commitments to be delayed by a murder investigation."

I ignored his sarcastic comment. "Is it okay if I stop by again later? I'm due at the Philbrook to pick up Maria Paige. Ella's college roommate is judging our art show."

The chief chuckled. "You are driving the artist who painted *32 Complications?*"

I looked him in the eye. "Yes, Chief."

"How did you manage to land this assignment?"

"I got lucky. Another volunteer had to cancel. When Nellie realized Maria was Ella's former roommate, she assigned me the task. I will escort Maria to the judging venue."

"Might have known one of your mavens would be involved. I suppose you intend to ask her a few questions along the way?"

I grinned at him. "Great suggestion, Chief. I'll see what I can learn."

The chief's face turned serious. "Get acquainted with this artist before you quiz her on the painting. Give me time to check her itinerary to see when she arrived in town. Rule her out as a suspect."

"Surely you don't think…" I stopped mid-sentence at the chief's look. "Got it. Nothing about the painting until you okay it."

The artist waited on a bench outside the Philbrook Inn and I was immediately struck by her grace. She wore a bright red dress. Short. The flared skirt whirled around her long legs when she walked. A thin gold belt circled her waist. The girl stood to greet me as I pulled into the drive.

"I was told to watch for a little red convertible." She extended her hand in greeting. "I'm Maria Paige."

"Josie Posey," I said. "And the convertible is named Piper. Happy to meet you."

I observed her as she climbed into the passenger seat beside me. Everything about this lovely young woman gave me a sense of calm. I have never before used the word "willowy" to describe anyone, but this girl was the definition of "willowy." She was tall and slender, and she swayed ever-so-slightly as she moved, long blond hair swinging across her back. It was as though she had a gentle breeze flowing through every motion. Her skin was tanned and healthy, her eyes a deep hazel, her smile a bright flash between two deep dimples. She settled gracefully into the passenger seat, fastening the safety belt in one smooth click.

"It's not far." I turned to face her. "Okay, if I leave the top down?"

"I hoped you would." She clasped her seatbelt. "Piper's an interesting name for a car. Mind if I ask how you chose it?"

"Most people ask why I named the car at all." I shifted into first gear. "Piper is from a childhood memory. Sure you want to hear it?"

"Yes, please."

We pulled away from the curb, and I told her of my idyllic life as a young girl in a small aviation town where almost every family had someone working at an airplane manufacturing plant nearby. The dads talked about planes all day long. Many were licensed pilots.

"My best friend was a little girl who lived just down the street from me on Van Arsdale. We loved to ride our bikes. We rode as fast as we could, arms outstretched, pretending to fly. In my imagination, my bike was actually a Cessna Piper Cub, one of the sweetest two-seater planes ever built. Driving this little car takes me back to that same wind-in-the-hair freedom I felt back then."

Maria trailed her hand over the side of the car to feel the breeze. "That's a beautiful story. And Piper is a perfect name."

"You don't think it's silly to name a vehicle."

"Absolutely not. I don't own a car in the city. When I move to the suburbs, I intend to buy one. Her name will be Betsy."

"Because?"

"She was my first baby doll, and I loved her dearly."

I smiled. This young woman had heart. I could not imagine her as a killer.

We drove the remaining distance to the art museum in companionable silence, each of us enjoying the fall afternoon. As we turned into the parking lot, I pulled to a stop under the shade of an ancient walnut tree.

"We are a few minutes early, so I thought I'd share one of my favorite spots.

Sometimes, I drive across town to park under this tree. I lean my head back and study its branches against the blue of the sky."

She turned her eyes toward the treetop, nodding her head. "I can see why. Too bad I don't have a sketching pad with me. I'd love to draw the tree from this angle someday. Mind if I take a few photos?"

While Maria snapped several shots on her cell phone, I took the opportunity to ask her about Ella. "I understand you and Ella were roommates in college. I'm really sorry for the loss of your friend."

"Yes." Maria returned her cell phone to her purse. "We were close. I talked to her almost every week."

"A friendship like that is rare. You must have known her before she married Jack."

"I still remember the night she met him. They went on a blind date, which is something Ella never did."

"Date? Or date someone she'd never met?"

Maria smiled. "She rarely had time to date. And a blind date? Never."

"What changed her mind?"

"Some guy in her science lab introduced them. Jack invited Ella out for coffee after class. Ella always said coffee was a necessity, not a date. It turned out she and Jack were both so passionate about the micro-science of watchmaking they stayed up all night talking about it. The coffee shop kicked them out at midnight."

I explained I had interviewed Ella for a story in our local newspaper the day before she died. "She was a talented young woman. It's not surprising you were friends."

"Why is that?" Maria asked.

I studied her face before I answered. "You came from two different disciplines, but you were both artists."

"You are quite observant," Maria said. "Most people saw us as total opposites."

"Your physical appearance is the opposite of hers, of course. Ella was much shorter, and she had those saucy dark curls. And your personalities were different. You are outgoing and poised; Ella was more reserved. But, when it came to your careers, you both had curious minds that craved answers."

"How do you know?"

"From the way you asked about Piper's name. And the way you photographed the tree limbs." I grinned at her puzzled expression. "It's easy to spot a curious mind in others because I have one, too. I was lucky enough to land a career that rewards curiosity. I apply it to learning about people so I can tell their stories."

Maria leaned toward me and spoke more softly. "I'm told you also help solve crimes. Is it true?"

"Not officially. I dabbled at amateur crime-solving when I was a news reporter in the city. I'm retired now. But sometimes, an outside observer can see things others miss. I try to help Chief Marshall when I can."

"Will you help him find Ella's murderer?"

"I hope so."

"She was my closest friend, and someone needs to pay for taking her away from me. Please let me know how I can help."

"Could you answer some of my questions about Ella? I want to trace her movements over the past few weeks. I need to know more about her relationship with Jack. And, I've uncovered a few secrets Ella was keeping. Maybe she shared them with you?"

Maria sighed. "We were close, but there were many things she kept to herself."

"How about brunch tomorrow morning? I can ask all of my questions, and you can give me guidance on where to look for answers."

"Okay." She wrote her cell phone number on a business card and handed it to me. "Text me the details later."

I escorted the young artist into the museum's main gallery, leaving her there to score the entries displayed there. While she focused on judging, I had time to return to the police station to check the status of my mystery box.

Chief Marshall greeted me at the door.

Chapter Nineteen

Saturday Midday

C hief Marshall's face was grim when he broke the news. "No fingerprints. No distinguishing wrapping. No bomb."

A wave of relief washed over me as I realized the mystery box was never intended to harm me. "Another scare tactic? Did it warn me to watch my step?"

"Not this time." The chief led me into the conference room and closed the door behind us. My cooler sat in the center of the table. I glanced toward it.

"What was it? Why send a box instead of sliding a note under my door or an envelope in my car?" The stalker's strategy made no sense to me.

"Looks like he decided to switch directions. Instead of another warning to drop your investigation, he delivered a clue."

The chief removed the box from the cooler and set it in front of me.

"Shall I open it?"

Chief Marshall shoved it closer. "It's safe. We've cleared it and photographed it. After you've seen it, I'll lock it in our evidence room.

I lifted the lid of the cardboard box and pulled out a colorful tin box. Immediately, I recognized the classic child's toy with the hand crank protruding from one side. "A jack-in-the-box?"

"Seems your stalker has a sense of humor."

I turned the crank and hummed along with the familiar music until the crescendo, "Pop, goes the weasel." The lid popped open, and a smiling clown jumped from the box. In his outstretched arms, he held a note: "Look at me."

The chief grimaced. "Turns child's play into something more ominous, doesn't it?"

I studied the box. "Any idea where it came from? Did you call the local toy shop?"

Chief Marshall read from his spiral pad. "Three sold in the past month. One yesterday. All went to matronly grandmother types. Nothing suspicious. All paid cash. We figure whoever did this bought it somewhere else. Maybe in one of the big box stores in Wichita. It's a popular toy. Difficult to trace."

I closed the lid and returned the toy to the cardboard box. "The message is clear."

The chief nodded. "Someone wants us to take a closer look at Jack Benjamin."

"Which makes me think he is *not* the murderer, but a potential scapegoat."

"Or, he *is* the murderer, and someone knows it. The tipster wants Jack to pay for Ella's death."

As always, the chief and I differed in our interpretation of the clues.

After my visit with the chief, I returned to the art gallery. It was time to accompany Maria on the city tour set to depart from Cozy Cups Cafe. Maria talked nonstop from the gallery to the cafe. She gushed about the level of the entries in the competition. "This was truly enjoyable. I look forward to seeing which artists win top honors."

Startled, I turned to question her. "Don't you know? As a judge?"

"No." Her blond hair tossed in the wind. "Every judge completed a separate scorecard on each of the paintings. The committee totals the scores of all the judges and then announces the winners. I know who I chose, but the other judges may have scored someone else higher."

"So, you will be just as surprised as the artists when winners are announced."

"Yes! The committee will place ribbons beside each winner. The judges will see those the same time everyone else does."

She explained the system was a common method to help ensure balanced judging. "Generally, the best art rises to the top. It's rare for judges to disagree on the overall winner. The surprises happen at the lower levels—second and third place winners and honorable mentions."

As she talked about surprises, my hands grasped Piper's steering wheel a little tighter. I hoped the surprises surrounding Ella's murder were behind me. The jack-in-the-box delivery had rattled me. It would have been far too easy for my stalker to plant an explosive in the package instead of an innocuous note.

We pulled up to the cafe in time to see the Philbrook carriage turn onto Main Street. *Clip clop, clip clop.* The sound of horses' hooves echoed on the cobblestones. A team of four Clydesdales pulled the wooden carriage with its bright red and white awning. The driver wore blue jeans and a bright red Western-style shirt with white fringe dangling from the front and black yokes. A black cowboy hat sat squarely on his head. With a gentle "whoa" to the horses, he pulled slightly on the reins, and they came to a stop directly in front of us.

Maria turned to me with wide eyes. "I've never ridden in a carriage before."

"Not even in Central Park?"

"No. I always wanted to go but felt a little foolish about riding by myself. The men I've dated didn't seem interested."

"You're dating the wrong men," I said.

Our driver introduced himself as Roy Mayfield. "I'm a Kansas cowboy, born and bred. Retired from herding cattle long ago, but this carriage business still keeps me near the horses."

He set a wooden stool beside the carriage and held out his hand to assist us in boarding. "Watch your step."

As soon as he said the words, an image of the dead opossum flashed before my eyes, and I stood like a ninny, frozen to the spot.

"You okay, ma'am?"

"Er. Yes." I collected myself and took his hand to climb into the carriage.

The tour began just as Kate had planned. She sat up front with Roy while the rest of us found seats on the rows of benches behind them. Surprisingly, the springboard seats were quite comfortable. We bounced along on the padded seats, taking a slow but steady pace down Main Street and onto the country lane just a few blocks outside of town. Serving as the tour guide, Kate turned to face the passengers.

"You're about to see the most beautiful views of English Village," she said. "Feel free to ask questions or take pictures along the way. Our first stop will be a lovely covered bridge called The Palladian. It's a replica of a famous bridge of the same name, located in Bath, England."

We enjoyed the gentle rocking of the carriage as the horses continued down the winding lane. The trees arched above us were a mixture of reds, oranges, golds, and yellows.

Maria bounced alongside me, camera raised to photograph the scenery.

"This is so beautiful. Usually, after I judge an art show, the remaining activities are excruciatingly dull. Art lovers can be a bit stuffy."

"The ride is a nice break in activities, but we still have the winners' announcement this afternoon and a reception at the gallery tomorrow afternoon," I reminded her. "Those may not be as exciting."

She snapped another photo of the scenery. "I know. But every day has included a unique experience here. Most art shows are focused entirely on art. We spend hours judging, then more hours standing in the gallery."

I was surprised. "Don't you go out for dinner or tour the city?"

She shook her head. "We judge. We stand around. We chat over wine and cheese. And then we go back to our hotel rooms."

"That does sound boring. Kate was concerned you judges would be disappointed because we didn't have a major attraction to share with you."

Maria spread her arms wide, motioning to the lush countryside surrounding us. "*This* is a major attraction."

When we arrived at The Palladian, Cowboy Mayfield slowed the horses to trot across the single-lane stone bridge. About one hundred feet beyond the bridge, he urged the team to a halt at the side of the road.

"First stop, Palladian Bridge and the Hidden Waterfall," he called out. We stepped down from the carriage and gathered around Kate.

"As you see, this bridge is modeled after one designed by Andrea Palladio, an eighteenth-century Venetian architect." Kate pointed to the carved stone. "The style was influenced by ancient Greek and Roman structures, so it's quite ornate. The one in Bath, England, is located inside Prior Park Landscape Garden. It was constructed in 1755 and was the last of three of its kind built in England. This is the only replica in North America, built here shortly after the town was founded."

Maria and the other judges studied the beautiful bridge. They admired its intricate stone structure and read the brass plaque posted nearby. Most took photographs of the bridge, framed by the riotous colors of our fall foliage. After a few minutes, Kate gathered everyone near her again.

"It is my pleasure to share this bridge with you," she said. "We're proud of our connection to the Cotswold area of England, as I'm sure you have noticed from the architecture of our many cottages...and this bridge."

Several of the judges asked questions about the origin of English Village, and Kate assured them our tour would include an introduction to the village namesake. "First, I want to show you a sight we reserve for very special guests. It isn't something most visitors ever notice because it is tucked away from view."

She led the group along a pathway of stepping stones, walking ahead of us twenty feet into the center of a grove of trees. We could hear the water before we turned the corner to see what lay ahead. Kate motioned the judges forward. "This, my friends, is The Hidden Waterfall of English Village."

We stood in awe of the secluded waterfall. I had stopped by last week, but today, I was struck anew by the beauty of this place. Lush foliage circled three sides of the waterfall, forming a natural cove protected from the winds that normally blew across our rolling plains. Only the babbling waters broke the silence. Monarch butterflies fluttered happily from tree to tree. "This is migration season for the butterflies," Kate noted. "Our fields and groves are dotted with their bright orange wings."

The judges snapped selfies with the waterfall until Kate finally insisted it was time to move to the next leg of the tour.

I nudged Kate before reboarding the carriage. "Maybe we should have saved this part for the last. The waterfall is a crowd-pleaser."

She shook her head. "Wait till they see the view from the church tower."

The English Village Chapel was built of native white limestone and sat in the center of green lawns and gardens. When visitors first saw the tall steeple and heard the chimes from the bell tower, they were entranced. Those who took the time to climb the tower were treated to a spectacular view of the village.

Our little group rode in hushed silence along the quiet country lane. They relaxed into a state of contentment, becoming animated only when we passed the wildflower fields and Crystal Pond. When the Clydesdales pulled up to the chapel at precisely eleven thirty, it was evident Kate's tour was already a success. Each of us basked in a happy state of mind, calmed by nature's relaxing effect.

Pastor Pinkerton greeted us at the end of the sidewalk. After the cowboy helped each guest alight from the carriage, the pastor welcomed our group into the front courtyard of the chapel. He smiled broadly at everyone, hands folded across his wide girth in the way preachers do.

"We will serve tea in the gardens today. First, please feel free to freshen up. Restrooms are in the narthex as you enter to your left."

I stepped into the line with the other ladies, but Pastor Pinkerton had other plans. He grabbed ahold of my arm and jerked me into an alcove while the others walked toward the chapel. "Could we talk?"

His voice sounded so urgent I assumed there was a problem with the tea arrangements. "What is it? Does Jill need help in the kitchen?"

"No, no. The tea is all set. I've been in a tizzy waiting for you. I am relieved to see you arrived safely."

"We rode in a carriage, pastor. Not on the backs of wild stallions. Nothing to worry about."

The preacher's round face creased with concern. "This is a serious matter, Josie. About ten minutes ago, I received an odd phone call. A man asked to speak with you."

"And?"

"And he disguised his voice with some sort of robot contraption. When I told him you had not yet arrived, he asked a rather odd question."

136

"What was it?"

The pastor hesitated as one of the judges passed by the bench we had taken. He leaned toward me and spoke softly. "The man asked if you would be climbing to the bell tower."

"What?" The uneasy feeling I had pushed away just returned with a vengeance.

"That's how I responded." The pastor patted my hand. "I said I didn't know."

"And, what did he say next?"

"He gave me a message for you. Then he ended the call."

"The message?"

"Watch your step."

I felt a flush of heat flood my face. "This has got to stop!"

"I hope you don't mind, but I called Chief Marshall immediately. He is on his way here. He's asked that you wait for him."

"I'm glad you did." I shivered to think a murderer might be stalking my every move. "Even though this is most likely only meant to scare me, it will be good to have the chief inspect the stairway to the tower before anyone goes up there."

I glanced up to see Maria walking toward us in search of me. "Could we keep this between us?" I said to the pastor.

He gave me a wink. "Confidentiality is my specialty."

"Please ask Kate to announce the tower tour will take place after the tea. Chief Marshall will have assured everyone's safety by then."

To my ears, my voice sounded normal. I hoped Pastor Pinkerton couldn't sense the fear pounding through my veins.

Chapter Twenty

Saturday Afternoon

Jill Pinkerton had outdone herself on the tea. We sat in the midst of the park-like garden a few steps from the chapel. White linen tablecloths and colorful bouquets decorated the tables. An intricate trellis twined with Woodbine honeysuckle provided both shade and a sweet, heady fragrance. I breathed in the floral perfume and shoved thoughts of a creepy stalker from my mind.

As we completed our salad and prepared for dessert, I noticed Chief Marshall and Pastor Pinkerton near the entry to the garden. The pastor shook the chief's hand before turning to walk toward our table.

"Ladies, I see you have nearly completed your lunch," Pastor Pinkerton announced. "Is anyone interested in climbing up to see the view from our bell tower?"

I caught his eye, and he nodded to acknowledge the steps had been examined.

"A lift will take you most of the way, but there are about thirty steps beyond that point you must climb to reach the top. I assure you the view is worth the effort if you are so inclined."

The judges and their hosts chattered among themselves, and Maria was the first to respond. "I would love to see the village from the tower. Where do we begin?"

"When you've finished your desserts, join me by the fountain on the edge of the garden." The pastor indicated a sidewalk toward the fountain. "We'll start the tour in about ten minutes."

As Jill cleared our dishes, about half of the guests opted to do the tour. Others preferred to walk through the gardens on their own. I offered to help Jill with the cleanup and encouraged Maria to go ahead to the tower. "We'll meet back in the narthex when you're ready." Although the chief had declared the tower steps were safe, I wasn't ready to risk it.

Kate and I carried the remainder of the dishes to the kitchen. "I think it's going well, don't you?"

"Yes." I set a stack of used dessert plates on the counter. "Just one more stop before we take them to the art show. We need to leave soon to stay on your schedule."

"You head for the carriage. I'll gather our guests from the gardens and meet you out front in fifteen minutes."

Kate headed toward the gardens at a brisk pace. I watched her turn the corner behind a tall hedge. Seconds later, she flew out from the same hedge, running like she'd just poked a hornet's nest. Her gray curls bounced in every direction.

"He's here! Call the chief! Call the chief!"

"Who, Kate? Who's here?"

"The guy." Kate was out of breath from racing across the expansive lawn. "The one wearing Crocs. He's in the gardens. I saw him."

I picked up my phone and pressed the speed dial number for Chief Marshall. He answered immediately. "What is it now, Josie?"

"It's Kate. She saw a man in the garden. He's wearing Crocs." My voice quivered when I realized my stalker might be only a few feet away, behind the hedge.

Kate grabbed the phone and lowered her voice to speak calmly to the chief. "Chief Marshall, you need to come and arrest him."

I heard only half of the conversation as she continued. "No, of course, I didn't confront him." Kate sounded insulted. "I saw his feet, and I came inside to warn Josie and to call you."

She paused, listening. Then she ended the call. "Yes, sir!"

"Well?" I looked up at her. "What do we do now?"

Kate sighed. "You stay close to me and get away from here. We are to finish our tour as though nothing happened. The chief will send an officer to look through the gardens. If the guy is still around, he will approach him. Chief Marshall said he can't arrest someone just for wearing Crocs."

"That makes sense." I tried to sound brave, but I couldn't help turning my head around to see if anyone was lurking nearby. "What did he look like?"

Kate's face turned red. "I don't know! I was so astonished to notice his shoes I forgot about being observant. I'm sorry, Josie. He might have been five-foot-seven with dark hair?"

"Anything else? Think harder, Kate."

"He wore a Kansas City Chiefs ball cap!"

"Great! I will text your description to the chief. I'm sure he will find him."

Kate's brow creased with worry. "Jill told me about the call Pastor Pinkerton received. The guy threatened you. I don't want him near you."

"Me either. Let's take our guests and get out of here." I shot a sidelong glance toward the front of the church, where part of the group had already reassembled. A few had witnessed Kate race from the garden, screaming bloody murder. Now, they clustered around Pastor Pinkerton, bombarding him with questions while waving their arms toward the pillar where Kate and I stood with our heads together, plotting how to get everyone to safety.

"We better go," I said, taking her arm to move urgently toward the distraught group.

Kate took a breath, straightened her posture, and marched toward the visitors. "My apologies if I caused you any concern," she said with a measure of aplomb. "I'm terrified of wasps and thought I'd stumbled over a hornet's nest. As it turns out, I was mistaken. There's nothing to worry about."

Pastor Pinkerton chuckled, assured the visitors they were in good hands, and hustled the group to our waiting carriage. Soon, everyone was aboard, and we were on our way, the incident of Kate's panicked race from the gardens forgotten—except by Kate and me. The two of us continued to watch the road behind us, leery of being pursued by the Crocs-wearing stranger.

Maria sat beside me, chattering as we rode. "What an incredible sight. I wanted to stay longer, to enjoy the birds-eye view of English Village."

"Then you might miss the real highlight of our tour."

"I can't do that." Maria looked back at the idyllic church. "I'll find a way to return another day."

Refreshed after their brief rest, the Clydesdales had an extra spring in their step. They trotted along the country lane past several rural cottages.

I snapped a few photos. "There's something quite lovely about the combination of yellow limestone structures against the lush green of the lawns."

Maria bowed her head. "I don't understand why someone dared to spoil this beauty by murdering my best friend." She raised her eyes to challenge me. "You have to find him, Josie."

I didn't have the heart to tell her I had made no progress on the case. Everyone loved Ella Benjamin. Her dad and brother. Her mentor. Her professor. Her landlady. Even her ex-husband. By all accounts, she was talented, with a bright future ahead of her. My best hope was that Maria's painting held a clue to Ella's dying words.

Suddenly, it occurred to me that Maria might have known Sam Ternberry, the young man who had left a phone message at The Curiosity Shop on the day Ella fell. I leaned toward her and lowered my voice so the others could not overhear our conversation. "Maria, you may be able to help with the investigation."

"What do you need to know?"

"Do you recall a college student named Sam who hung out with Jack?"

"Uh-huh. Sam Ternberry! He was Jack's friend, but he was infatuated with Ella."

"What if I told you he was in town that day?"

Maria gazed at me, her clear blue eyes unwavering. "I'd say there's *no way* Sam was involved in Ella's fall. Sam was a great guy. Sweet and funny. He would never harm Ella."

"Okay. I believe you," I said. "I'm meeting with him in a couple of days. Good to know that he's someone you trust."

We curtailed our conversation to listen to Kate's commentary as we turned into the historic district and came to a stop alongside the Blacksmith Shop. Kate stood at the front again to share a brief history. "Our blacksmithery is one of only three working blacksmith shops in the Midwest." She handed each person a brochure and continued her commentary.

"Three talented blacksmiths share the space. They began this venture as a hobby, but it has turned into a popular tourist spot and a profitable sales center. All three of these artists have other jobs. They work here in the evenings or on weekends. Occasionally, they open the shop for the public to watch."

As our visitors took photos of the historic building, they exclaimed over the quaint storefront and signage. Kate led them toward the front door. "We have a special treat for you today. Harvey Jacobs, a blacksmith artist and owner of our local hardware store, has agreed to share some of his work."

With perfect timing, Harvey walked out the front door onto the sidewalk. When the judges saw the tall, gangly man wearing a protective leather apron, they burst into applause. I did a mental eye roll. Harvey had a flair for the dramatic, yet he was oblivious to the impression he made on his audience.

Harvey grinned at Kate. "You gonna talk all day? Or can I invite these visitors to step inside?"

And just like that, my handsome friend Harvey charmed everyone into joining him for a tour of the blacksmith shop. They "oohed and aahed" over his wrought iron creations, and I smiled at the thought of Harvey's handcrafted first gift to me before we began dating.

The judges took their time exploring the shop. Several purchased personal items to take home with them. Harvey had already set aside small trivets for each of the judges, wrapped in brown kraft paper with raffia ribbon. They accepted them graciously; two asked for his business card.

When a couple of the women asked him to pose with them for photos, Harvey suggested a group picture instead. He gathered the entourage in front of the blacksmith shop for a selfie and managed to pull me close to his side. Again, with the butterflies. I felt like a swooning teenager.

Our final stop was a short walk across the park to the Hank English statue.

Kate read the plaque aloud:

> *"Henry Nolan 'Hank' English was born July 5, 1883, and died March 31, 1919. He was the son of a Welsh father and a French mother, an artist in the Welsh Movement, and a prominent soldier in World War I."*

"Is it true this man never visited the community that bears his name?" Maria asked.

"That's correct." Kate stood beside the statue. "It is a wonderful love story if you'd like to hear it."

I listened as my friend shared the tale.

"Hank's wife, Elizabeth, was from America. In 1908, at the age of eighteen, she traveled from New York to Liverpool aboard the Cunard liner *Mauretania* to visit her grandmother for an extended holiday. While there, she met Henry and fell madly in love. He was both an artist and a soldier. They married, settled in Wales, and had two children."

"What happened to them?" Maria asked.

"The children remained in Europe their entire lives."

"I still don't understand why the town was named English Village," one of the judges said.

Kate gestured back to the statue. "After Hank died in World War I, Elizabeth returned to the U.S. to settle her father's affairs. The wealthy farmer died during the 1918 influenza pandemic, leaving all his land to Elizabeth. She offered to give a large parcel to the local township on the condition they name their fledgling city after her husband and honor him in their city park."

Kate smiled at our guests. "So, you see, Hank was an artist, like you. Our art show honors his memory. And now we must hurry. We have only a few minutes before the gallery opens. Winners will be announced at two this afternoon."

With her words echoing in our minds, we returned to the carriage.

The rest of the afternoon flew by. Kate's painting took second place in the amateur category. The artists were excited to see all the winners. I was relieved my role for the day was over. My final responsibility would be to drive Maria back to the inn.

I paced the lobby as I waited for a photographer to take group photos of the winners and judges. My attention wandered, and I walked outside to sit on a bench. The quiet plaza would offer respite from the whirlwind of the day's events and space to consider how I would spend the rest of my day. I wanted to return to my cottage to check on Moe. And I hoped to study the remaining materials from Lucy Buttons.

Inevitably, I thought about the man in Crocs at the chapel garden. Was he my stalker? Suddenly, a stranger in blue jeans and a plaid shirt appeared from the sculpture garden and speed-walked toward me. I jumped to my feet, prepared to scream, but he only nodded and raced beyond me into the gallery. I collapsed on the bench again, shaking.

I felt foolish for being so jumpy. This stalker thing was enough to put anyone on edge. Just as I decided to return to the safety of the crowded gallery, my cell phone rang loudly in my purse.

I fumbled to grab it, swiping the screen to answer. "This is Josie."

It wasn't until I heard the chief's familiar voice that I realized I held the phone in a tight grip of fear. I relaxed only slightly as he spoke.

"We've got him, Josie," he said.

Chapter Twenty-One

Saturday Night

At home in my cottage, I replayed the chief's call in my mind.

"We've got him, Josie," he said.

My initial sense of relief faded when he shared details of the arrest. "The guy hasn't confessed to anything, but he ran when we approached him."

The chief chuckled as he described the chase. "I don't know what he was thinking when he tried to run in those Crocs. They aren't made for sprinting."

The man in custody was named Carlos Perez, a trained clockmaker who attended the same elite school as Ella. Most likely, this was the same "Carlos" Ella had listed as a friend in her phone numbers—the one I hadn't yet called. Although Carlos admitted knowing Ella, the chief said he denied having any role in her murder.

Chief Marshall detained Mr. Perez for additional questioning. "We can only keep him for a few hours. Unless we uncover evidence to connect him to the murder, we will have to let him go tomorrow."

I felt slightly better, knowing a suspect was off the streets. I hoped Chief Marshall would find additional evidence quickly. Maybe Mr. Perez would confess?

With my art show responsibilities completed for the day, I changed into jeans and grabbed Moe's leash.

"Let's take a walk, boy."

We headed briskly to the corner before turning toward the park. I talked as we walked. Moe trotted along beside me, a willing listener. The fresh air was good for both of us. By the time we circled the gazebo and retraced our path back to the cottage, my head was clear. Hindsight was a wonderful thing. If I had known Carlos might be involved in this mess, I would have called to interview him earlier. Somehow, it never occurred to me that Ella's former classmate might be a suspect. The others on my list were much closer to Ella.

I filled Moe's bowl and pulled some of Harvey's leftover Santa Fe Casserole out of my refrigerator for dinner. It was good to be alone for a few hours. I wanted to think about next steps for the investigation. If Carlos confessed, the murder would be solved. Somehow, it seemed unlikely. We still had no motive for the murder, and Carlos wasn't talking.

I hadn't yet wrapped my head around the Carlos connection when my phone rang with an unexpected call from Alex McGregor. I flipped on the recorder and answered.

"Ms. Posey, this is Alex. Ella's brother."

"Yes?"

"I wanted to thank you for the note you sent us. My father and I appreciated your kindness."

"I'm truly sorry for your loss," I said.

"It doesn't seem real, you understand? That she's gone."

"I know."

"What you said in the note. The part about her legacy—"

"Yes?"

"Ella and I argued after she came home. She was always the 'perfect child' when we were growing up. Getting all the attention. Sometimes, I ragged her about it. But I loved her."

"I'm sure you did," I said.

"That ladder. It was broken. I feel responsible for her death. I want to make it right somehow. Telling her story is a good idea. Let me know how I

146

can help."

I listened for a hidden meaning in his words, but his voice was filled with genuine remorse.

"Thank you, Alex. I'll reach out after Chief Marshall concludes his investigation."

"And, Ms. Posey?"

"Yes?"

"Write something about Ella that tells the world how special she was."

"I'll do my best."

After the conversation with Alex, I was more confused than ever. Could he have found his sister unconscious and struck her in the head? He was jealous of his sister. He had the opportunity to kill her. He admitted he felt responsible for her death. But he didn't confess to her murder. I would share the recorded conversation with the chief at our next meeting. But first, I wanted to read Ella's journal.

Hoping to discover additional clues, I settled into my reading chair with my laptop, Ella's letters, her journal, and my magnifying glass. The first journal entry mentioned Logan Lavender:

"My friend Logan called today to encourage me. I'm so excited to be very close to a breakthrough. Logan couldn't be happier for me."

I pondered the entry. Ella shared something important with Ms. Lavender, meaning the woman knew more about Ella's work than she had admitted in our call. Deciding to try again to reach her, I picked up my phone. The call went directly to voicemail. I listened to the rich, warm voice of Ella's friend in the outgoing message before hanging up.

I started a new list of questions to be answered. Number One: Is Logan Lavender intentionally avoiding my calls? She was a wealthy woman with many responsibilities. Perhaps she was exceptionally busy this week.

Chief Marshall must have been on the same wavelength because as I laid my phone on the chair beside me, he called.

"Josie, I have news about Logan Lavender."

"That's funny. I tried to call her just now."

The chief's deep chuckle rippled through the phone. "You won't be able to reach her for a while. Ms. Lavender has been arrested in London."

"What?"

"The missing Minetti prototype turned up in her possession. She was apprehended as she went through customs at Heathrow Airport yesterday."

"How do you know this so quickly?"

"I told you I have my sources."

"Yes, but in London?"

I could almost see him wink at me as he shared his secret source. "If you must know, I'm signed into Google Alerts for any news about clockmaking, Adler Minetti, Logan Lavender, and a few other pertinent names and topics."

He was so proud of himself I had to laugh. "You're getting reliable information from around the world, delivered to your cell phone? I wish I'd thought of that."

The chief never failed to surprise me. He might be a small-town officer, but he was smart and resourceful.

"Why would she steal the prototype?" I asked him.

"Sometimes people want what they can't have," the chief answered wisely.

"Seems like a risk not worth taking. Do you think it's related to Ella's death?"

"Don't know, but I'm not ruling out anything."

"Me either. Every time I find an interesting lead, it takes me nowhere."

"I have good news on the artist," the chief said. "She arrived here after Ella's fall. You can pursue your questions about the painting."

"Thanks, Chief." Before we ended the call, I asked one more question. "By the way, did Ella's family mention an illness when you interviewed them?"

"No. Was she sick?"

"She had a prescription from a neurologist in her medicine cabinet. Maria Page said Ella feared contracting the same disease that plagued her mother. It would have ended her career."

"I don't know how a medical diagnosis would be connected to her murder, but details are important. Let me know if you uncover something."

Since reading Ella's journal strained my eyes, I decided to set it aside in favor of researching Essential Tremor. Sometimes fate smiles on our efforts, and this was one of them. The first article I clicked gave me the insights I needed. It quoted Dr. Martin Solomon of Kansas University Medical Center.

"More than 85% of patients with Essential Tremor report significant functional impairment. Tremor frequency can range from 2.5 Hz to 12 Hz. Most experience ranges between 5 Hz and 5.7 Hz Higher frequencies are easier to treat. In some patients, tremor frequency decreases with time."

I was interested to see the physician's explanation in the very next sentence:

"It causes trouble for both the patient and the treating neurologist because medications become less effective."

Skipping to the paragraph about treatments, I read:

"Although several therapies are available, Essential Tremor is not easy to treat. Only one medication, propranolol, is supported by Class I evidence. Other off-label brands are often used, with varying degrees of success."

How frightening it must have been for Ella to face this diagnosis on her own, I thought. I read further into the story:

"Medication helps approximately half of patients, but half have no discernible improvement. Side effects of the medication may include drowsiness and cognitive difficulties that limit the dose a patient can tolerate. Sometimes, the treatment is worse than the disease."

The significance of the diagnosis was undeniable. I imagined Ella, learning her hands, would no longer be able to perform the work she loved most in the world. Was this the news she had intended to share with her ex? Was it the reason she chose to return home to the family business? The answers to these questions might be found in the pages of Ella's journal. Sighing, I rubbed my eyes and picked up the pages again.

Before I could decipher the next passage, Nellie called. Grateful for the interruption, I picked up on the first ring. "How's the Queen of the Art Show?"

"I'm calling to say thank you," Nellie said. "The judges couldn't stop talking about the fantastic tour you and Kate gave them this afternoon."

"We enjoyed it too." I leaned back in my chair. "Is everything else going as you planned?"

"So far, so good," Nellie answered. "We still have tomorrow afternoon's reception to get through. You and Harvey are helping, right?"

"Count on us. We will arrive early, if you need anything."

"I hope you're taking a break tonight." I heard the concern in my friend's voice. "You've had several stressful days."

"Actually, I'm trying to read Ella's journal, and it's making me cry."

"Oh, no! Is it that bad?"

"The problem isn't the content," I explained. "It's the size of her handwriting. Even with a magnifying glass, it's taking me forever to read each page."

"That's crazy!" Nellie exclaimed. "Bring it here. Tim has a huge scanner. He can place the journal pages against the glass and it will print out copies at whatever size you want. Then you can read more quickly and save your eyesight."

"Can he really do that?"

"Of course. Come over right now. It won't take long."

I grabbed my keys and drove to Nellie's.

Chapter Twenty-Two

Late Saturday Night

T hanks to Nellie and Tim, I returned to my cottage with a legible stack of pages from Ella's journal. The duplicates were enlarged to triple their original size, making them easy to read without a magnifying glass. Once again, my practical friend had offered a simple solution to save me hours of time. Plus, since the pages were copies, I could make notations or highlight passages directly on the entries. I couldn't wait to complete the journal.

I decided to make an all-nighter out of the project. In preparation, I made a huge bowl of buttered popcorn and filled a glass with iced Coca-Cola. Caffeine and snacks were essential to any in-depth investigation.

Moe nudged me with his sleepy-eyed look. "Sorry, boy. We can't go to bed. I have work to do." If dogs could roll their eyes, Moe would have. Instead, he stretched out in front of the sofa and tucked his head between his paws, deep in sleep within minutes.

With renewed energy, I spread the pages over my dining room table. What a difference the large print made! I grabbed a couple of Sharpies and a yellow highlighter, poised to scour the pages. Reading the journal entries, I felt as though I had walked alongside Ella during the last few months of her life.

Quickly, I determined Ella had written three threads of notations intertwined through the pages. The first centered around her health. I tracked a timeline from the days when she first noticed her hands were trembling until she set an appointment with the neurologist and, finally, her trip to see the physician. The most interesting notes on her disease came near the end of the journal. Despite the fact Ella's doctor had prescribed medication for Essential Tremor, she remained hopeful she could continue her work. In fact, her physician had encouraged her to research an experimental treatment if the medication failed to cure her symptoms.

"Things have changed since my mother was diagnosed with ET," Ella wrote in an early entry. *"There is much greater success with propranolol than with earlier treatments. I'm so excited to begin this medication. If it isn't successful, my doctor has recommended a promising experimental procedure."*

Later, she remarked: *"I have studied the Calmevegus treatment. It looks like a wonderful option if my medication begins to fail. It is still in the clinical study phase, but I feel sure I would qualify."*

And, toward the end of the journal, she had more praise for the experimental treatment. *"It is incisionless, treating ET from its source in the brain. I can't believe the cure for this disease could be as simple as applying soundwaves to my brain. It's an outpatient procedure. I'm not afraid of the side effects if this ultrasound could provide relief from my tremors forever. I could work again!"*

After I read Ella's comments, I Googled the treatment to read more details on the company's website:

> *Calmevegus uses targeted ultrasound waves to treat the small spot in the brain considered to be responsible for causing tremor. No incisions or permanent implants are needed for the treatment, and it is performed using focused ultrasound and an MRI scanner.*

More than three thousand patients had received the treatment, and the site listed several benefits. It promised no scars as found in traditional surgeries. No overnight hospital stays. Minimal side effects. Immediate results. No wonder Ella was excited at the possibility. This treatment was FDA-approved and clinically tested. But it wasn't without risks.

The treatment could be uncomfortable for patients, who might experience nausea or pain during the ultrasound procedure. Additionally, the website warned a small percentage of patients developed temporary or permanent numbness/tingling, imbalance, unsteadiness, gait disturbance, and muscle weakness.

From what I read in her journal, Ella believed her illness could be controlled. She planned to begin the medication after a pharmacogenetic test to determine probable side effects from the drug. Perhaps that was why she had not yet worried her father and brother with the news.

In preparation for my meeting with Chief Marshall I summarized Ella's health notations into a series of note cards. Diagnosis. Treatment Plan. Hopeful Outcomes.

Moe snored and rolled onto his back in a not-so-subtle reminder it was now hours past my bedtime. I stood to stretch my legs and refilled my glass for another shot of caffeine before I returned to the journal.

The second thread of Ella's entries focused on her career. She was determined to develop a clock with more "complications" than anyone else before her. Judging by her notations, she was confident of her ability to accomplish the goal.

"Seeing the prototype in Geneva gave me new ideas," she wrote. *"I am closer than ever to visualizing the dream clock I want to create."*

And in a later entry, *"I've got it! I know what 32 complications I will incorporate into my clock. It will take time (ha!), but I started the drawings tonight."*

Finally, near the final pages of the journal, she wrote: *"My clock is designed! It will make my father so proud. This one will be a new world treasure. I'm hiding the drawings until I can secure a sponsor and a workshop."*

For this subject, I had only two note cards: "32 complications accomplished" and "Designs hidden."

The final topic interwoven through her journal was romance. Ella wrote lovingly of her "soulmate" and her "new love." Although she was straightforward when she wrote about her health and career, she was secretive about naming her lover.

"I can't wait to tell him how I feel," Ella wrote in the early pages of her journal. *"He is my soulmate. I sense he shares my feelings, but the words remain unspoken."*

Midway through the journal, I found another reference to the mystery man in Ella's life: *"He loves me! He must! We share the same passion, and he sees how good we could be together."*

And toward the final pages of her journal, Ella confided: *"I will tell him this week. I can't contain myself any longer. His letters reassure me we can, and will, spend our lives together. But first, I must tell Jack."*

On the topic of romance, I needed only one card: "Ella is in love."

I set aside the journal to read the letters. My expectations were low. Ella and her friends were likely to communicate with each other through email and texts, not handwritten letters. When I first glanced through the box, most of the correspondence appeared to be from her father. Now, I saw the envelopes were bundled into several smaller groups. The largest stack was from Mr. McGregor, but a few were from her school. There were two from Jack and one from an insurance company.

I scanned the letters from her father first. Not surprisingly, most of them were loving notes to congratulate her on her graduation and to say he was proud of her accomplishments. The most recent letter invited her to return home and join the family business.

"You may not be ready yet," her father wrote, *"but we would love to have you join us at The Curiosity Shop if you ever decide to return home. Please know your brother and I love you. The family business will be half yours when I am no longer here. Let's talk soon about your plans."*

Next, I read the two brief notes from her ex-husband, Jack. They expressed regret, but also a hint of something else—perhaps anger or jealousy.

"My dear Ella," Jack wrote. *"You know I will always love you. I have so many regrets. I wish we could try again. Would that ever be possible?"*

And, later: *"You have always been a stubborn woman. Your strong will—and your incredible talent—are two of the things I love most about you. Since you have made your choice, I will not ask again. But I will forever wish things could have turned out differently."*

Both were signed, *"Forever yours, Jack."*

The envelope from the insurance company contained a copy of Ella's life insurance policy. I gasped when I realized she was heavily insured. The policy would pay the beneficiary $1 million upon her death. Unless Ella had made changes after purchasing it, Jack Benjamin was named her beneficiary. I tucked it into my purse to take to the chief on Monday. The policy may have been changed. If not, I wondered whether Jack was aware of his windfall.

It was past midnight, but I decided to plow through the Minetti school letters to complete my task. I fully expected they would contain routine information about her schedules or perhaps a recommendation from her professor. Instead, I found the most important correspondence of all.

All three letters were from Professor Daniel Davis. They were written on the school's letterhead, but the content and tone were personal in nature. All were postmarked within the last month. I handled them with care:

> *"Dear Ella,"* the first letter began. *"Thank you for sharing your dreams and your life with me. I am honored you have requested my help in pursuing your career. Within a week, I will be in touch with you about locating a sponsor to fund your project."*

He included a few more details before closing with a loving message: *"I trust you know how very special you are to me. Highest regards, Daniel."*

The second letter was more openly affectionate:

> *"My Dear Ella,"* he wrote. *"We share a passion like no other. You are a beautiful woman with a magnificent mind. I have no doubt your dream will come true. Might I dare to hope we could work on it together? I would do everything in my power to assure you a lifetime of happiness. Most sincerely, Daniel."*

The final letter was both loving and insistent:

> *"My Dearest,"* the professor began. *"I cannot deny my feelings any longer. I will fly there to meet your family during our October mid-term break. I have exciting news to share and a proposal to make. I cannot wait to see you. My darling, brilliant love. Wait for me. Yours, Daniel."*

"Woohoo!" I jumped from my chair and danced around the room with the letter in my hand like I'd just won the Pulitzer Prize. Moe, awakened by the commotion, scrambled to join the celebration. He bounced behind me, fluffy ears flying in a happy trot of his own.

When I'd calmed myself enough to resume my work, I considered the content of the letters and pondered their meaning. Without a doubt, Daniel Davis lied to me. The sixty-year-old professor was in a relationship with his young protégé. I reread the letters from beginning to end, searching for subtleties in the wording. Although the professor was old enough to be her father, he was most certainly the soulmate Ella mentioned in her journal.

My mind raced with new questions. I scribbled onto note cards:
Why did Professor Davis lie to me about his relationship with Ella?
Were the feelings he professed in the letters sincere? Or had he also lied to Ella?
Did he know where Ella had hidden her dream-clock drawings?
Was he in love with his student? Or wooing her to have access to her talent?

Judging from the details in his final letter, the professor was scheduled to arrive in English Village soon. Did he still intend to visit? I checked my watch. Only seven hours to wait before our scheduled phone call.

I hoped Daniel Davis would keep our phone appointment on Monday morning. The professor had some explaining to do.

Chapter Twenty-Three

Sunday Morning

I woke abruptly when Moe pushed his cold nose against my face. Clearly, I was past the age where I could work all night and still "rise and shine" at my normal hour. My brain felt fuzzy, and my eyes were nearly swollen shut. I had slept so late I nearly missed the morning service.

Pastor Pinkerton greeted me with a warm handshake as I hurried up the steps. If he noticed I hadn't showered, he was kind enough to keep any judgment to himself. Kate was already seated in our pew. She raised an eyebrow to acknowledge my ponytailed hair and tardiness. "Late night?" she whispered.

"I'm exhausted from using my brain all night. Remind me not to do that again."

Kate chuckled. "I hope it was worth it. We are still committed to one more event for the art show this afternoon."

"I know." I groaned and pulled a hymnal from the rack in front of me. "I'll take a nap before then."

As we stood for the opening hymn, the beauty of the world washed over me. Even though my mind drifted from Pastor Pinkerton's words, the service had a calming effect. I relaxed and allowed my senses to go with the flow.

I was aware of the music, the sunlight bursting through stained glass, the shifting of worshippers in their seats, but I could not concentrate on the words booming out from the pulpit. In a daze, I went through the motions.

157

Kate nudged me to stand again for the closing blessing. I heard the pastor's comforting voice, reciting the King James version of my favorite benediction:

"The Lord bless you and keep you;
The Lord make His face shine upon you,
And be gracious to you;
The Lord lift up His countenance upon you,
And give you peace."

I could use a little peace right now, I thought.

There was something to be said for traditions like this one, where the faithful attendance to a weekly worship service brought a familiar sense of calm. I could not have repeated the theme of Pastor Pinkerton's sermon, and yet my spirit was still refreshed for having been present in the pew. I felt more energetic than when I'd arrived. It wasn't until we walked out of the chapel and onto the lawn that Kate frantically pulled me aside.

"Did you see him?" she whispered urgently.

"Who?"

"The guy in the Crocs. He was here. Sitting in the back row as we took our seats after Communion. He slipped out before the blessing."

"No!" I exclaimed. "The chief told me he would release him, but I didn't know it would be so soon."

"Now what?" Kate's worried look put me on edge again.

"I don't know." My mind was too weary to function. "This guy shows up wherever we go. I'm getting sick and tired of his shenanigans. Time to give him a piece of my mind."

Kate pumped her fist. "That's my girl!" she exclaimed. "He won't know what hit him."

"Yeah. Right after I meet with Maria."

Though I'd rushed around like a whirlwind, Maria arrived at the café before I did. She was dressed in yellow and looked like a bright ray of sunshine at her table near the window. I grabbed one of my favorite cups from the shelves near the coffee pots. Squirted a bit of vanilla syrup into the brew and waved at Lorene from across the room.

Maria looked up from her menu as I approached the table. "I'd suggest the Savory Crepe special." I pointed to the promotional card clipped to the menu. "It's new, and I'm told it is excellent."

"Thanks. I couldn't decide what to choose. Everything here looks delicious."

Lorene appeared at our table. "Good morning ladies."

"Two Savory Crepes," I said.

"Good choice. Let me know what you think of it afterward."

As Lorene walked away, Maria sighed. "You have a good life here. I envy you the small-town atmosphere."

"That's one of the reasons I moved here." I sipped my flavored coffee. "You have almost the same thing in the city—just within neighborhoods instead of the whole town."

"True," Maria said. "I have my favorite deli, and I know my hairdresser. But they don't really know me back. Here, everyone knows everyone. It's different."

"Which can be a problem." I waved to my friend Kate, who'd just arrived. She took a seat across the room where she could see our table. "Every now and then, it would be nice to be anonymous. It's hard to hide in a village this size. If I take Moe to the vet, I'm likely to get a call from someone later, asking if he is okay."

"At least they care enough to check on you. I could be missing for several days before anyone would think to give me a call."

"Still, you have a big career in the city."

Maria nodded. "For now. I balance my time between painting and wooing art galleries to sell my work. It's easier to do in the city. Maybe in a couple of years, I'll paint wherever I want, and the galleries will knock at my door to buy them."

"When you're ready, come join us here. We would love to have you."

Maria leaned toward me, a serious expression on her young face. "Have you found anything I can help you with?"

I took several minutes to tell her about my efforts to learn more about Ella's life and the various people I had contacted. When I explained that Chief Marshall had asked me not to visit with her family or her ex-husband, Maria nodded. "I can understand that. It's only been a few days, and you can't interview everyone."

"Right," I said. "But it would help if I knew more about her relationships with them."

"I can tell you about Jack." Maria's voice held a tone of disgust. "I knew him before Ella met him. He was in my English Literature class at the university. All the college girls thought he was a catch. But I wasn't so sure."

"What made you doubt them?"

"He was smart enough to do the work, but he tried to get by on his charm instead."

"Was there anything specific?"

She hesitated. "Nothing I can prove. There was a rumor he plagiarized one of his papers. His professor allowed him to rewrite it."

"How did Ella feel about it?"

"I never told her," Maria said. "She was head-over-heels after their first date. I didn't want to ruin her joy for something that might not be true."

"Did they marry before they went to horology school?"

"Yes. I was her maid of honor. It was a small wedding, with just the two families. Jack's parents died a year before the wedding. He had only one brother, James, who was his best man. I questioned Ella before the wedding to confirm she wanted to marry him."

"Why wouldn't she?" I asked.

Maria hesitated. "Because he cheated on her while they were engaged. Ella knew about the affair. She forgave him. She always put her whole heart into everything—her friendships, her career, her marriage. I admired that about her, but I also worried she would get hurt."

I understood her concern. "It must have been difficult for you to watch."

"The first six months, they seemed happy," Maria said. "After a while, Jack began to resent Ella's success. She was clearly a superstar. He didn't like being in her shadow. They lasted two years. Both of them handled the divorce well. They were able to remain good friends."

I told Maria about my attempt to read Ella's journal, and she burst out laughing. "Her handwriting was always microscopic. Even the notes she left for me at the dorm were so small I could barely read them."

"Did she ever mention a new man in her life?"

"No, but I suspected there might be someone. She seemed lighter, happier, on our phone calls the last few months."

Recalling Ella's references to her "beloved," I gave Maria several examples from the journal. "She never includes his name, but she definitely cared deeply about the mystery man she referenced."

As Lorene cleared our dishes, I still had two important questions for Maria. I pulled my phone from my purse and swiped it open to the photograph of her painting.

"Look what Lucy Buttons sent me." I shared the screen with her.

Maria gazed at the photograph with tears in her eyes. "This brings back wonderful memories," she said. "I completed the painting my senior year in college. Ella suggested the topic, as you might guess. I told her she could make three wishes, and I would build them into the painting."

"What were her three requests?"

Maria smiled. "She wanted it to represent the inside of a clock, her dream number of 32, and her favorite animal, the turtle."

I laughed at the odd combination.

"That's how I reacted," Maria added with a smile. "I told her I preferred minimalist paintings."

"And how did she respond?"

"She looked at me quite calmly and said: 'This will expand your horizons.'"

Sitting across from me in the café, the young artist explained the number 32 was Ella's dream goal: she wanted to be the first to create a clock with thirty-two complications. To represent the number, Maria had incorporated thirty-two microscopic turtles into the painting.

"You'd never know it. They are inside some of the cogs of the clockworks," Maria said. "It was an inside joke, just between us. A nod to the fact that we felt time was moving too slowly for us back then. Even my professor didn't notice the turtles—they were our secret. I never felt it was my best work, but she loved it."

"Who named the painting?"

"We named it together. It was supposed to represent the complicated nature of life and the passing of time."

Laying my hand over Maria's on the table, I spoke quietly to her. "I have to tell you something about Ella's final words before she died."

Maria clasped her hands on the table in front of her.

"She said three words to her doctor. The number 32. The word *complicated*. And, *long clock.*"

Stunned, Maria looked again at the photograph on my cell phone. "She referred to the painting. I'm positive. What else could it be?"

"That's what I thought when I saw it last night. Somehow, the painting must contain a clue Ella wanted us to find. I hoped you might know what it was."

"Was there any note or marking on the painting?" Maria asked.

"Only a photo of the two of you, pasted on the back."

"Nothing more?"

"Not that I could see. I wonder if you would take a look tonight or tomorrow? Perhaps you will be able to notice whether something has been added to the painting."

"Yes. I can swing by before I leave town. I'm here for a few more days."

Time was short, but I had one last question for Maria before we ended our breakfast. "I found one other troubling item in the package Lucy sent me. It was a prescription from a neurologist."

"For Ella?"

"Yes. Do you know whether she had been diagnosed with an illness recently? Something a neurologist would treat?"

Maria thought for a moment before she answered. "Ella didn't mention anything. But she always feared she would have the same problems her mother did."

"And what was that?"

"Essential Tremor," Maria said. "The disease could mean the end of Ella's career as a clockmaker."

Chapter Twenty-Four

Sunday Afternoon

After brunch with Maria I went straight home, slipped off my shoes and padded into the bedroom. As soon as I closed the drapes, the cool darkness of the room worked its magic. My head had barely touched the pillow when I fell into a deep sleep. Two hours later the ringing of my cell phone dragged me from my nap. It was the chief.

"H-hello." My tongue felt dry in my mouth.

"Josie?"

"Yes." I covered a yawn with my hand.

"Did I wake you?"

"Yes." I glanced at my bedside clock, startled at the time. "But thank you, Chief. I need to dress for the art show reception."

"I heard you'd been burning the midnight oil again. Did you find anything interesting?"

"Several things." I recalled the recorded call from Alex McGregor and the stacks of note cards I'd written during the binge reading from the night before, as well as the information from Maria Page. "But I'm tied up in art show stuff today."

"Let's meet at the station around eleven tomorrow," the chief said. "And Josie...we had to release Carlos, but he's still a suspect. Be careful out there."

"Did he admit to anything?"

"He claimed Crocs are popular footwear," the chief said. "His alibi checks out for the day Ella fell from the ladder. He was still in Switzerland. He arrived here the day after."

"What's he doing here?" I asked.

"Apparently, he and Jack are friends. All three of them—Jack, Ella, and Carlos—were in the same class at school. Carlos said Jack invited him to visit."

"Did Jack confirm it?"

"According to Jack, the invitation was accurate, but the timing was a surprise. Carlos was to arrive next week, but he caught an earlier flight."

"And what did Carlos say?"

"Carlos said Jack phoned and asked him to get here sooner."

My head was spinning with more questions, but it was time to change my clothes for the reception. "We have a lot to talk about."

"Bring your notes tomorrow." The chief's firm voice calmed my fears. "Both these men are rattled. They know more than they're telling us. We must be close to a breakthrough."

I hoped the chief was right. It was time to end this roller-coaster ride.

The brief nap had helped restore my energy, and I was ready to attend the art show reception when Harvey arrived at my door. He was handsome in casual khaki pants and a pale blue button-down shirt. No tie. A tailored tweed sports coat stretched across his broad shoulders and narrowed at his waist.

My eyes hurt to look at him, and the butterflies launched in my stomach again. My voice froze in my throat, but I had the good sense to open the door and let him in.

"You are beautiful," he said, displaying his lopsided smile. I felt a flush of heat move up my face.

The dating thing was still new for me, and I wasn't used to genuine compliments. I wore a simple floral dress that brushed my ankles and a soft plum-colored silk jacket. My hair was damp from the shower, so it fell in curls around my face.

"Thank you." I draped my purse over my shoulder. "I've been flustered all day, so it's good to know I look acceptable."

"You're beautiful," he repeated. "No one will want to look at the art when you're in the room."

This time, I laughed. "Now you've gone too far. But, thank you, just the same."

Harvey took my hand when we arrived at the art gallery, and we walked toward the registration table together.

Sharon greeted us. "Welcome. Here are your nametags. The two of you are responsible for the double doors over there." She motioned us to a side door that served as an entry from the parking lot.

Our job was a simple one: Greet guests as they arrived. Point them toward the registration table. I felt my shoulders relax as Harvey and I chatted between the arrivals. He entertained me with colorful stories about his hardware store customers, and we shared jokes about Crocs shoes.

He laughed when I insisted Crocs had become a fashion statement in English Village.

"I hadn't noticed." Harvey pointed to his plain brown dress shoes. "I should buy a pair."

I lowered my voice so the visitors entering the gallery wouldn't hear me. "You might want to wait until after the chief solves this murder."

The words were barely out of my mouth when Kate and Sharon rushed toward us.

"Get out of here," Kate stage-whispered as she tugged at my arm.

I pulled back, but the retired Marine was still strong enough to flip me onto my derrière if she tired of my resistance.

"You two need to leave," Kate insisted. "Sharon and I will take your place."

"What happened?" Harvey's calm demeanor had no impact on the mavens.

Sharon waved her arms in the air, looking like a mother hen in distress. "We saw two men wearing Crocs. They signed in for the reception but walked immediately outside to the sculpture gallery. You might be in danger."

I straightened my shoulders. My mahjong friends were so protective I could hardly breathe. If I always followed their advice, I'd never leave my cottage.

"Ladies, I'm sure we're safe." I gazed over the beautiful gardens. "This is a public place, and I can't run from everyone wearing Crocs. Besides, the chief has already talked to a couple of people about their shoes. Until we find out whether the markings on the soles of their Crocs match the ones at the crime scene, there's nothing we can do."

Harvey flashed me his "get serious" look, and I realized he wanted to confront the two men face-to-face.

Kate had grasped my hand to pull me toward the exit, but Harvey grabbed the opposite hand to drag me into the gardens. I stood between them like a human wishbone until Harvey shooed Kate away.

"I've got this, Kate," he said.

I paused, unsure what to do.

He tugged at my hand again. "Let's go, Josie. I'm tired of running from everyone in Crocs while we wait for a lead on your stalker. We'll look around. If we see anyone suspicious, we'll call Chief Marshall."

Astonished, I looked up at him. "Are you the same guy who always tells me to be more cautious?"

"Yep. But in this case, I think we should check it out. We're in a public place in broad daylight. Ella's killer was a coward who seized the moment when she was vulnerable. He isn't likely to pull out a gun in an art gallery. It won't hurt anything to stroll through the sculpture garden."

I shrugged. "Fine with me."

Kate and Sharon made another attempt to dissuade us, but Harvey held firm. We left the mavens behind and sauntered toward the outdoor gallery.

Harvey had made a good point about Ella's murderer. He had attacked her when she was alone. I doubted he would assault me in the middle of a crowded garden. Still I had to ask Harvey the question: "You don't really think we're in danger, do you?"

"Not a bit," he answered. "The guy who killed Ella didn't have enough courage to do it face-to-face. He won't pull a stunt in front of this many people."

"Unless he feels cornered," I said under my breath.

Harvey squeezed my hand a little tighter. "Let's see what we can find."

The sculpture gallery was dappled with shade. Huge trees formed a canopy overhead and filtered the sunlight through their leafy boughs. At the fork, we took the sidewalk to our right. I noticed a man seated on a bench. For a heartbeat, I thought he was real. Then I realized it was a new bronze sculpture on loan from the British artist Richard Austin. The plaque beside it read: *Sir Malcolm Arnold*. Harvey and I commented on the fine detail of the piece.

Throughout the exhibit, life-size sculptures of various people stood at every turn. I saw a woman with her skirt and hair blowing in the breeze and two gentlemen playing checkers. All cast in bronze.

I was so intrigued by the pieces I almost forgot why we'd entered the garden. "This makes the gallery come to life in a totally new way," I said.

Harvey agreed. "The last time I was here, the sculpture garden was filled with contemporary pieces. It was thought-provoking, but this exhibit feels more personal."

We stepped around a bronze gathering of three women standing at a bistro table that caught my eye. "Look at this one! They remind me of the Mahjong Mavens sharing gossip at a garden party."

Near the center of the meandering walkway, I spied two visitors ahead of us. They had stopped to admire a sculpture of a businessman who appeared to be wading across a puddle. His hands grasped his bronze pant legs, pulling them up to show bare feet. The expression on his face made me laugh, but the chuckle caught in my throat when my eyes swooped downward to the two guests' Crocs-wearing feet!

Chapter Twenty-Five

Sunday Evening

My heart beat faster as Harvey led me toward the sculpture. I wondered whether he had failed to notice the men's footwear. Glancing sideways to study his face, I saw by the set of his jaw that he was determined to speak with them.

I studied the two men as we approached. They didn't look like murderers. Both were young-ish, around thirty. They read the plaque beside the artwork and talked to each other like ordinary art lovers. With Harvey by my side, I summoned an extra measure of courage. There was no reason to be nervous, I decided. Still, I scoured the landscape for a quick escape path if I needed to bolt. The hedges were too high. My only recourse was to run pell-mell back the path we had just walked.

When I pulled back a little, Harvey stepped forward. He called out to the men in a friendly voice. "Hey there. What do you think of the exhibit so far?" I marveled at how calm he sounded.

My own voice froze inside my throat. The two men had turned to face us. There was no turning back now.

They stopped their own conversation mid-sentence and stood staring at us. The taller one stuck his hands in his pockets. I nearly jumped from my skin. Did he have a gun?

Neither of them spoke, so Harvey continued. "We're volunteers for the art show." My handsome friend was so smooth I could have hugged him on the spot. "Part of our job is to gather feedback."

Startled, the shorter one glanced at me before he answered Harvey. I caught a flash of awareness in his eyes. "We like it very much. This piece reminds me of a man I saw in New York last year. He rolled up his trousers and splashed in the puddles at Central Park." He spoke with a trace of a Brazilian accent, and I knew this must be Carlos Perez.

Harvey extended his hand and introduced himself. "Harvey Jacobs. And you?"

The taller man answered first. He was handsome, I supposed, in a rakish sort of way. He squinted his eyes and blinked as he smiled at me. "Jack Benjamin," he said, and I hoped he didn't notice the small gasp that escaped from my lips.

Harvey waved his hand toward me. "This is my friend, Josie."

My voice cracked as I tried to smile. "Josie Posey."

Both men had the poise to acknowledge they recognized my name. "Oh, yes," Jack said. "Ella mentioned you. The reporter, right?"

Carlos added. "We've heard so much about you." His phrasing was stilted, but he seemed genuine. I searched his dark eyes but saw no hint of danger.

We stood for a few minutes admiring the sculpture on a Sunday afternoon. It was an odd sensation, given the fact one of them might have been lurking around my home in the very Crocs he was wearing.

The thought flitted across my mind, but it didn't stop me from boldly asking the question: "Aren't you the guy Chief Marshall arrested for wearing Crocs?" I blurted out.

Harvey did a double take and shook his head, laughing. "Josie, that may not be an appropriate question."

But Jack's companion laughed, too. "I can't say I blame you for asking. Yes. I'm Carlos Perez." His accent was charming, and I couldn't imagine him as a killer.

Jack shrugged. "It was obviously a mistake, or he wouldn't have released Carlos."

"Would the two of you like to join us inside for refreshments?" Harvey suggested. "Maybe we can sort this out together. I'm certain Josie has more questions. She *always* has more questions."

I thought Kate's head would spin off her neck; she swiveled it so fast when we walked through the reception area together. I smiled and waved as the four of us found a table near the appetizers. Sharon hovered nearby, refilling platters and making certain the tasty treats were fresh and hot. I suspected she also hoped to catch the drift of our conversation.

When we were seated with our small plates in front of us, I turned to Jack. "Ella said very nice things about you."

He blinked at me and rubbed his eyes; I wondered whether he was going to break into tears at the mention of his ex-wife. "That was kind of her," he said simply. "Thank you for telling me."

"Could I ask you a few questions about her?"

Jack gulped his drink before he squinted up at me. "I don't mind. She told me you were writing a story about her. People were always doing that."

"Writing about her?"

"Yes." Jack smirked. "Ella was a rising star, you know."

"Did it make you uncomfortable?"

He sneered at the question. "What do *you* think? Her career ruined our marriage."

"That must have been painful."

"You sound like my shrink. Yes. It was painful." He squeezed his eyes tight and ducked his head. Then he took a deep breath and nudged Carlos.

"This guy helped me through it."

Carlos grinned back at him. "That is friendship, correct?"

I decided to try one more question, before I changed the subject. "One of your wife's mentors told me Ella had a secret. Do you know what it might have been?

"My *ex*-wife," he corrected. "She no longer shared secrets with me."

"She said nothing about a special clock, or an illness, or a new relationship?"

His eyes flashed, and his voice was firm. "I told you: I don't know anything."

"Okay." I raised my hands in surrender. "I had to ask."

When he blinked his eyes again, I wondered whether his belligerence hid a broken heart. "I hope I haven't upset you with my questions," I said.

Jack rolled his eyes. "It's nothing. I have new prescription eye drops, and they don't work."

Sharon caught Harvey's eye, and he left the table for a few minutes. He returned with a full tray of fresh appetizers. I eyed the pecan tarts but clasped my hands tightly under the table.

"She said we weren't eating enough," Harvey nodded toward Sharon. "We've been instructed to finish all of this before we leave the reception area."

Jack and Carlos heaped the finger foods onto their plates. Carlos popped a crispy polenta bite into his mouth.

"I'll do my part," Jack waved a cheese straw in the air. "This is excellent."

"You have great taste in food and art," I said to the two men. "What do you know about fashion?"

They both looked at me like I'd just stepped off an alien planet.

I directed my attention to Carlos. "Tell us about these Crocs."

He glanced down to his feet. "Like I explained to the chief, these are popular shoes. Jack wears them, too."

"We all did," Jack said.

"All?"

"The students."

My mind went blank. "The students?"

"Yes." Jack leaned forward and repeated the words. "The students. At the Adler Minetti School. We were required to wear white Crocs when we entered the classroom. It was a science laboratory. They insisted we wear the shoes to help maintain a sterile environment."

My jaw dropped as his words registered in my brain.

"It's true," Carlos said. "After a while, we all appreciated the comfortable fit of the Crocs and wore them outside of the classroom as well."

Harvey interjected. "Literally *everyone* who studied at Adler Minetti wore Crocs?"

"Everyone." Jack took another lemon tart from the tray. "Even the instructors."

Harvey gave me a slight headshake, and I stopped asking questions. Instead,

172

we excused ourselves to tour the exhibits. I was pleased to see Kate standing beside her painting with a bright red ribbon signifying her second-place prize. I appreciated the inside story behind her choice. Not many would see the "naked lady" Belladonna Blossom as a murder reference. I grinned at the title: *Drop Dead Beautiful.*

As the reception drew to a close, Harvey and I returned to the kitchen to help the Mahjong Mavens with clean-up duty. I whispered the new information about the shoes to my friends, who expressed a healthy dose of disbelief.

"I'd say the entire story is a *Crock*!" Sharon announced. The woman had a pun for nearly every situation.

Harvey and I walked to his truck when the reception concluded. "You okay?"

"Tired and confused," I said. "If their story is true, it changes everything."

"Not necessarily." Harvey opened the passenger door so I could climb inside. "Those two are the only students from Ella's class here in English Village. As friendly as they appeared, one of those men is probably your stalker."

"I'll let the chief know," I said, as a small shiver of fear sent goosebumps up my arms.

Harvey took the wheel and maneuvered the old pickup out of the parking lot.

I relaxed into my seat as he drove down the familiar streets toward my cottage. At the corner, my phone rang. I grabbed it to check the caller ID and heaved a sigh of relief. It was my editor.

Giving Harvey an apologetic look, I answered. "Hi, Leslie. What's up?"

"That's what our readers want to know," she said. "When will you finish your story about the watchmaker?"

"I'm working on it."

"You said the same thing yesterday."

"I could send you a 300-word story with the facts as we know them."

Leslie moaned into my ear. "The whole village already knows the girl fell from a ladder and died. I need a full feature story. Preferably with a conclusion to confirm whether her death was an accident or a murder."

"Give me another two days, Les. You'll have an article as soon as the chief allows me to release it." My head throbbed from the tension between news reporting and murder investigating.

At home on my laptop with Moe at my feet, I turned to Google for confirmation of the Jack-and-Carlos Crocs story. What I read surprised me.

At the Adler Minetti workshop, where the most sought-after expensive watches in the world are created, the craftsmen all wear one of the least expensive of shoes—white Crocs. A dozen pairs of the plastic footwear line the shelf at the entry to the lab. Everyone in the facility, including instructors and supervisors, is mandated to wear the unfashionable shoes. The reasoning behind the requirement? Sanitation. The timepiece company is serious about maintaining a pristine environment where quality cannot be compromised by a speck of dust.

"Good grief!" Moe raised his head at my exclamation. "How could I have missed this in my earlier research of the school?"

Moe nudged my knee, but his sympathy could not erase my oversight. Suddenly, our cast of suspects had multiplied. *Anyone* associated with Adler Minetti might be the murderer.

On a hunch, I pulled the last of Ella's boxes out of my closet: the one marked "Clothing and Miscellaneous." Inside, I opened a shoebox and discovered a pair of white Crocs in Ella's size. Next to the shoes was a framed snapshot. I peered at the photo. It was a group shot of her entire class inside the Adler Minetti laboratory. All of the students wore white Crocs.

I was tempted to dial Chief Marshall with an update on the popularity of the shoes among Ella's classmates, but it was already nine at night, and the news weakened our case instead of strengthening it. Besides, the mess of cards and photos currently spread across the entire surface of my dining room table would not impress the chief. He preferred a brief list of conclusions supported by solid facts. This would wait until morning.

Sighing, I pulled out my laptop again. If I wanted to have my notes organized before the meeting, I'd better get started.

Chapter Twenty-Six

Monday Morning

After a late night, I awoke rested and refreshed. I ate a leisurely breakfast, read the paper, and tied my unruly hair into a messy ponytail. My notes for Chief Marshall were typed and organized into dozens of note cards filled with bullet points. I had separated them into folders.

One contained information about Ella's career, the references on *32 Complications,* and notes on the history of a long clock. Another focused on the people who might have wanted Ella dead. A third folder contained unresolved questions I hoped the chief could help answer.

While I still had no idea who might have caused her death, I sensed we were closer to connecting the dots. As soon as I completed my call to Professor Davis, I would drive to the police station. Hopefully, Chief Marshall had new information to share.

To his credit, the professor was ready and waiting for my call.

"Good morning, Ms. Posey. It's so nice when someone is prompt these days."

"Journalists always have deadlines. We're trained for punctuality." I turned on my recorder to capture our conversation. "If you're ready, we can get right into my questions."

"Fire away," he said.

"First, tell me more about your impressions of Ella as a student."

"As I said before, she was outstanding." Professor Davis spoke with a warmth he had not exhibited earlier. "Her work was impeccable, but her mind was her greatest asset. She had the imagination required to be innovative, yet she was also practical."

"Would you say she was superior to the other students in her class, Professor?"

"Please, call me Daniel." His offer was out of character. I wondered why he felt inclined to befriend me now, when our previous conversation had been contentious.

He continued as though he were determined to be helpful. "I would say Ella was superior to all my students. Not just the ones in her class. But all the young people I have taught in my lifetime. She was that rare."

"What kind of a relationship did you have outside the classroom?"

"W-why would you ask?" *Aha.* His startled tone indicated I had touched on a more sensitive subject.

"Ella obviously stayed in touch after she completed your class. Would you say you were in a student-to-teacher relationship, a professional peer-to-peer relationship, or something else?"

The professor danced around his answer. "We were close. We both shared a deep passion for our trade. We talked for hours about the future of clocks and how we might influence the way they were made. I would say we were like partners—equals with many of the same goals."

"Peers, then?"

"Yes. In all ways except our age."

"Did you see her often?"

"Not in person. We communicated by phone or email. When she was no longer my student, we were free to have an occasional coffee or dinner."

"Were you aware of any secrets Ella might have been keeping?

"Who said she had secrets?" The professor jumped on the question faster than I could have said "lickety-split" and with far greater anxiety.

"Logan Lavender." I decided to reveal my source since Ms. Lavender had indicated she and the professor often worked together on patron events for the school. Perhaps he would feel inclined to verify his peer's observations of Ella. "She told me Ella was hard at work on a secret project. She also said Ella was moody in recent months."

"What would Logan know?" Professor Davis scoffed at my comment. "The woman has always been jealous of Ella."

"How long have you known Logan?"

"We go *waaaay* back." The professor elongated the word. "We met in college, before she married her wealthy philanthropist and began traveling in the high-altitude circles of the rich and famous."

"Yet you remained friends."

"Yes. We reconnected after her husband died. Logan wanted to spend his money, and I needed patrons for the school. It was the perfect match."

"I understand she met Ella at a watchmaking competition?"

"Yes. Ella won the Marco DeLuca Watchmaking Competition, and Logan insisted on meeting her. She arranged a celebratory dinner."

"When we spoke, Ms. Lavender described Ella as a friend."

The professor coughed. "Logan Lavender was jealous of Ella. I wouldn't put too much stock into anything she told you. The woman had nothing to offer but her money. She loved being a patron because she wanted to be seen with talented young people. Ella was one of them."

"I believe their relationship was stronger than you indicate. Ella considered Logan a close friend and mentor. She wrote fondly of Ms. Lavender in her journal."

"Ella had a journal?"

"Yes," I said. "I must say her handwriting was extraordinary."

Professor Davis burst into laughter. "Try grading her assignments. I insisted she type all of her answers. A man could go blind reading her letters."

"Did she write letters to you?" I asked innocently.

He brushed aside the question. "I wasn't speaking from experience."

"Did she ever tell you of a secret project, possibly a very special clock?"

The professor hesitated before he answered. "She dreamed of making a clock with many more complications than the world had ever seen. She had been working on the designs for months. Whether she completed them, I don't know. She didn't confide in me."

I paused, trying to think of the best way to ask the next question. Finally, I blurted it out. "Daniel, were you dating Ella?"

"No!" he answered emphatically. "I'm nearly old enough to be her father."

"Could she have believed you were in love with her?"

"Did she write *that* in her journal?" he shot back.

"She wrote of a soulmate. I thought it might be you."

"I was an admirer of Ella's. Nothing more. Was there anything else? I really must go."

"Oh, I almost forgot. Logan Lavender was arrested in London this weekend. Did you know?"

"What?" I couldn't detect whether he was surprised at Ms. Lavender's arrest, or surprised that I knew of it.

"Yes. They've charged her with the theft of the Galaxy Blue prototype from the Adler Minetti factory."

I heard a sigh of resignation in his reply. "I have just returned from a trip. I didn't know of her arrest, but I'm sure I will hear from the school. She is still one of our patrons. It's likely they will ask me to help clear up any confusion."

"Does it surprise you that she would have the prototype in her possession?"

"Logan is a woman of constant surprises." The professor circumvented my question. "She has great wealth and a burning desire to own the world's finest collection of artifacts on watches and clocks. This time, she may have gone too far."

I ended the call and stared at the phone. My own impression of Logan Lavender didn't mesh with the woman Professor Davis described. Somehow, I needed to reconcile the two. Surely, her arrest was the result of a huge misunderstanding.

Still puzzled over the call, I turned to see that Moe was sound asleep on the cool kitchen tiles. I set my phone on the counter and walked to the back door of my cottage.

"Time to go outside, Moe," I called. He raised his sleepy head, scrambled to his feet, and sauntered to my side.

I had always appreciated Old English Sheepdogs as a breed, but Moe was far more than a household pet. Watching him chase a rabbit across the yard, I realized how much joy he added to my life. He followed the bunny all the way under my lilac bush, then stopped with his nose to the ground and his bottom wagging in the air. His silly antics made me laugh out loud.

"Come on in, Moe," I called. "He beat you this time."

It was nearly time to meet the chief at the station, so I packed my folders into a tote bag and gathered the additional items he might want to see. I included Ella's journal, the insurance policy, and her letters from Professor Davis. Deciding the painting was too large to carry, I returned it to the safety of my closet. Finally, I bent to pick up the photograph of Ella's classmates wearing their Crocs.

I glanced at the photo again, searched their smiling faces for any sign of conflict between them. Carlos was on one end of the picture with Jack beside him. They sat on a lower step and crossed their legs in an identical pose. As I studied them more carefully, something new caught my eye. Heart racing, I grabbed my magnifying glass to take a closer look.

"Yes! This photo might include important evidence."

At the last moment, I tossed the magnifying glass in with the rest of my notes and loaded the entire mess into my car.

Chapter Twenty-Seven

Monday Midday

C hief Marshall arrived late for our meeting. Had it been anyone else, I would not have worried. The chief was never late. He planned his schedule to the finest detail. A poster on his office wall declared his mantra:

EARLY IS ON TIME

ON TIME IS LATE

LATE IS UNACCEPTABLE

New officers sometimes learned this policy the hard way, drawing extra work hours to make up for tardy arrivals. On the rare occasions when the chief was detained by official business, he called or texted to let me know. This was a courtesy he extended to everyone equally—from his wife to his co-workers to his refrigerator repairman. Truly. The Chief Was Never Late.

I fidgeted in the small conference room that had become as familiar to me as my own dining room. The bare metal table carried scratches from years of wear. I imagined it as a living thing that had borne the abuse of thousands of clipboards and cell phones, coffee mugs, and briefcases without complaint. The smell of burnt coffee emanated from the corner, where a glass pot simmered on the burner. In the way of cops and office workers everywhere, the pot still held a sliver of liquid. No one wanted to take the last pour and be responsible for making a new pot.

A whiteboard hung on the wall at one end of the long table. I watched as the clock above it ticked its way to 11:15. Checked my phone again. No message from Chief Marshall. I paced the floor of the tiny room. Then, I sorted through my note cards and wrote several key points on the whiteboard.

Had the chief told me to be here at 11:30? I reviewed my calendar for the third time. When the minute hand crept toward 11:17, I could contain myself no longer. I walked briskly to the front office, where one young officer filed reports and a clerk stood talking to a woman about her lost dog.

"Excuse me," I said to no one in particular, "has anyone seen Chief Marshall?"

As the young officer turned toward me, I heard a buzzer from the rear door.

"Ms. Posey?" The officer gulped and blurted an apology. "I'm so sorry. The chief told me to let you know he would be late for your meeting."

I almost—but not quite—felt sorry for the kid. He continued to stammer while I stared at his discomfort. "He called a little before eleven. It was just after you arrived. And then I took another call. And, well..." The officer looked nervously over my shoulder as he spoke, "I guess I forgot."

"What was it you forgot, Walker?" the chief's voice boomed from behind me, and I turned to see him glowering at the rookie. I can't say I've ever described anyone as "glowering" before, but Chief Marshall had a scowl on his face that left no room for misinterpretation. He lowered his eyebrows and delivered a piercing look that zapped the officer like a bolt of electricity.

Walker snapped to attention. "Sir. Your message, sir. I forgot to give Ms. Posey your message."

The chief motioned toward the file cabinets. "Get back to your work, Officer Walker." He glared at the quaking patrolman. "Don't let it happen again."

Then he turned to apologize to me. "I am sorry, Josie. I was detained in a meeting with the forensics scientist over in Lindsborg. Walker was told to let you know I would be late."

Relieved, I smiled at his serious face.

"If you're okay, I'm okay. I have to admit I was a little concerned about your safety. You are *never* late to a meeting."

"I do my best." The chief hiked up his pants and smiled back at me. "Let's get to work."

We spread our papers across the conference room table, and the chief outlined his plans. "I hope you don't mind, but Lorene is bringing lunch. It was the least I could do after wasting your time waiting on me."

"A working lunch sounds good." I motioned toward the paperwork stacked in front of us. "We have a lot to cover."

The chief began by sharing the forensic scientist's report. "The lab confirmed the cuts to the ladder were done with micro tools like those used for clock repairs. We suspected that would be the case."

"It's good to have confirmation," I said. "Most likely the offender had his own tools, or access to the tools through The Curiosity Shop."

"According to the experts, the work was meticulous. Our experts said the pattern was similar to termite damage. Apparently, the perpetrator wanted investigators to think the old wooden ladder was infested."

"Was there anything else?"

"One important detail." He pointed to a section of the report. "Whoever did this was left-handed."

The news surprised me. "They can tell from microscopic marks in wood?"

"Yes. Assuming the person who tampered with the ladder is the same guy who struck Ella's head, our killer was left-handed. At the very least, he or she was ambidextrous."

"Do we have any left-handed suspects?"

"I don't know." The chief raised one eyebrow. "Do we?"

Lorene soon arrived with lunch from the Cozy Cups Café as I stood to study our suspect list on the whiteboard. I paused for a few delicious bites of her chicken potpie before I reviewed the latest list with Chief Marshall. I had included Ella's brother, her ex-husband, the mystery caller, her classmate, her mentor, and her professor.

"It's a long list." I sipped my latte and returned the cup to the table. "Maybe we can narrow it down by discovering who is left-handed."

The chief took the marker from my hand and placed check marks beside three names. "I'd say these are our top candidates."

✓ Jack Benjamin (ex-husband)

✓ Alexander "Alex" McGregor (brother)

✓ Carlos Perez (classmate/friend)

"What about the mystery caller?" I asked.

"Sam Ternberry appears to be in the clear, based on my phone interview with him," the chief said. "However, let's leave him on the list until we've taken his official statement tomorrow. We know he was in town the day Ella fell."

"And the other two?" I pointed to the remaining names of Logan Lavender and Daniel Davis.

"I doubt we can tie Ms. Lavender or Daniel Davis to the murder. Neither of them was in the country when it happened. They had no opportunity to tamper with the ladder."

I nodded my agreement. "Her mentor and professor both wanted access to Ella's talent, but I don't know how they would have killed her. They were too far away."

"When I interviewed Alex, he admitted he hoped to assume full control of the family business someday. He claims he was happy when Ella decided to return home. He welcomed her help. I tend to believe him." He drew a line through the name.

I cleared my throat and looked down at my hands.

"What?" Chief Marshall stood with the marker in his hand.

"It's nothing, really." I stammered to explain that Alex McGregor had called to thank me for the sympathy note I'd sent.

"He called you?"

"Yes."

"And?" The chief's dark eyes drilled into mine.

"And he sort-of admitted he felt responsible for Ella's death. But I agree with you that he's probably not guilty of killing his sister. Maybe you should listen to the call before we mark him off the list."

I played the call for the chief. We listened to it a couple of times before we decided to leave Alex's name on the suspect list until the chief could question him again.

CHAPTER TWENTY-SEVEN

"Still three names on the board," I said.

Chief Marshall drew a circle around Carlos Perez. "This guy keeps rising to the top. We know he owns Crocs. The only stumbling block is his airline schedule. The flight manifest confirms he arrived here the day after Ella fell from the ladder. Unless he has friends with the airline who faked his itinerary."

"Let's talk about the Crocs," I said. "Remember when Carlos told you everyone wore them?"

The chief nodded. "He said they were a popular shoe, and it wasn't a crime to wear them."

"You're not going to believe what I learned."

Quickly, I told the chief about confronting both Carlos and Jack at the art show. He listened as I described Kate's panic at the sight of two men in Crocs lurking in the garden. When I explained Harvey, and I followed them into the sculpture exhibit, the chief interrupted my story.

"How many times have I told you to be cautious?" He towered over me and pointed his finger in my face. "If these two men murdered Ella, you put your own life at risk."

"I had Harvey with me." I spread my arms wide. "And they seemed harmless."

The chief sighed. "I thought Harvey had more common sense. What if something had happened to you?"

"Sorry, Chief." I ducked my head to avoid his stare.

He crossed his arms over his chest. "You may as well tell me what you learned in this escapade."

"This!" I shoved the photo across the table to him. "The Crocs weren't just popular. They were required footwear for everyone at the Adler Minetti school!"

"Carlos said the school laboratories were off-limits to street shoes. Students all wore Crocs to maintain a sterile environment. Then I found this class photo in Ella's belongings. It verified his claim."

The chief held the photo up, looking intently at the faces of the bright young students. "Well, look at that! Every single one of them is wearing a pair of Crocs."

Excited to share my additional discovery, I handed him the magnifying glass. "Now, look at the front row students who have their legs crossed with the bottom soles of their shoes visible. What do you see?"

Chief Marshall peered into the glass, moving it methodically to study the bottoms of the shoes visible in the photo. "They are all alike. But they are not identical."

"I believe some of the students personalized their shoes. Carlos has an additional 'C' on his, and Jack has carved a 'J' below the logo."

The chief stood and paced the floor. "This is important, Josie. Whether they did it to tell their shoes apart or simply to make a personal statement, the carvings in the soles of their shoes may lead us to a killer."

"At least we can look at more than a shoe size," I said.

Chief Marshall set the photo on top of his case file. "Let's review the rest of your notes before we bring Jack and Carlos in for additional questioning. I will also have our detective take another look at the footprint he pulled from the soft dirt in your yard. Once we saw the Crocs logo, we didn't study it for the subtle carvings I see in this photo."

We made quick work of my additional notes. I shared the note cards I had prepared with the relevant bullet points. The first card referenced Maria's painting.

"Maria created a special painting for Ella titled *32 Complications*. It's a long clock with thirty-two turtles hidden in the gears. She painted it at Ella's request. At the time, it was a joke between them. Now, I'm sure it's a clue to Ella's final words. If Ella has hidden a message in the painting, Maria will find it. She will search for it before she leaves town."

The chief's face broke into a broad smile. "It would be good to understand what her final words meant. The name of the painting fits. Let me know what Maria discovers."

My next card contained potential motives. "Everyone on our suspect list wanted something from Ella. Logan Lavender and Professor Davis both wanted her plans for the extraordinary clock. Her brother wanted sole ownership of The Curiosity Shop. And her ex-husband was her beneficiary in an insurance policy."

I handed the insurance papers from Ella's collection to the chief.

"I'll have my detective reach out to the insurance company to confirm whether the policy is active."

"The only person without a motive is Carlos. Yet he's our number one suspect. We must be missing something."

The chief jotted notes onto his spiral pad. "Let's see which pair of Crocs matches the prints at The Curiosity Shop and on your lawn before we dig further into motives."

The final note cards summarized my findings from Ella's journal and letters. I read them to the chief:

"First, Ella was recently diagnosed with Essential Tremor. She felt hopeful about a new medication.

"And second, Ella was in love with someone. I suspect it was Daniel Davis. His letters prove he was in a relationship with her, but he denies it was a romantic one."

Chapter Twenty-Eight

Monday Evening

The mouthwatering aroma of grilled steaks drifted out of the blacksmith shop in a thin blue line of smoke as I approached the historic district. I followed my nose to the huge open barn doors, where the sound of laughter spilled into the evening air.

Impromptu cookouts had become a favorite activity for our mahjong friends. Most often, we gathered on the weekend. Harvey had made an exception when he invited everyone for a Monday night barbecue.

"We worked all weekend on the art show. Now it's time to relax," he said.

Earlier this summer, Harvey and the other blacksmiths built a cooking grill to the side of their blast furnace, using an old charcoal forge as a base. They added a stainless steel workspace large enough to convert into a table for up to twelve guests. Sharon and Nellie designed two portable counters to slide into place as a serving center. The result was both beautiful and functional, transforming the little shop into a casual chef's kitchen at a moment's notice.

As I stepped inside, Sharon handed me a chilled glass of white wine. "Try this Chardonnay. It's from the new little wine shop next to The Garden Cart." She practically danced on her tiptoes as she waited for me to taste it. Her short stature and impish smile gave her the appearance of an eager young woman, not a senior citizen in her late sixties.

I lifted the glass to my lips for a small sip, then gave her an appreciative nod. "It's nice."

"Harvey grilled jumbo shrimp as an appetizer, so this is a starter." Sharon lifted the bottle to pour another glass. "I brought a Merlot to go with the steak."

"Not for me. I'll fall asleep if I have more than one glass."

Sharon wasn't surprised by my comment. Though she and the other mavens were a decade older, they all had a higher tolerance for adult beverages than I did. She patted my hand. "You're such a party girl."

"Always have been." I toasted her with my wine glass.

Everyone gathered around the new grill to watch Harvey cook. The rest of us had contributed side dishes, but his steaks were the main attraction. Kate supplied the shrimp. Nellie brought baked potatoes and the ingredients for toppings. Sharon provided dessert.

I hovered over her apple pies, breathing in their sweet fragrance. "How did you find time to bake pies when you cooked all weekend for the art show?"

"It was easy." Sharon leaned over to whisper in my ear. "I had the pie in my freezer, ready and waiting."

"I bought Caesar salad from Lorene's café," I admitted.

"That's as good as homemade," Kate assured me. "Besides, you've had too much going on to worry about cooking."

Content to let the conversation swirl around me, I sat back and watched my friends interact with each other. Sharon and her husband Terry sat at the grill, chatting with Nellie and Tim. They all listened as Harvey explained his "secret seasoning" recipe. I knew this story by heart, so I waited to hear their reaction to Harvey's punchline.

"Last but not least, I massage it with dark roast coffee."

"I've never heard of using coffee as a steak spice," Nellie said dubiously. "Why would you do that?"

Harvey grinned his lopsided smile. "It's guaranteed to *perk up* the flavor."

Sharon groaned. "Sounds like a story I would tell."

"But you really do use coffee?" Terry asked.

"Yep," Harvey nodded. "It's the most important ingredient."

To my right, the remaining guests gathered around the appetizers Lorene had arranged atop a huge wooden keg covered with a tablecloth. Kate and

Lorene were engaged in an animated conversation. Chief Marshall stood to the side, grinning from ear to ear. Curious about their topic, I walked closer.

All eyes were centered on Lorene. The tiny woman gestured with her arms spread wide. "He didn't have a chance." She shrugged and smiled up at her husband.

The chief's booming laughter filled the room. "That's not the way I remember it."

Kate pulled me into their circle. "Lorene just told the story of how she and the chief first met. There is a difference of opinion about which of them initiated their relationship."

I picked up an appetizer and took a small bite. "I don't have to hear the story to know I'm with Lorene on this."

The chief reacted with a belly laugh. "I surrender. I know when I'm outnumbered."

Harvey rang the wrought iron dinner bell, and we hustled to fill our plates. The room grew quiet while we savored the tender beef.

Lorene pointed her fork at Harvey. "I need your recipe."

"I'd be willing to do a trade." He winked at her.

She laughed at the hopeful expression on his face. "You know I never share my recipes."

This was a conversation the two of them repeated whenever we enjoyed a meal together. Harvey often requested Lorene's recipes from her Cozy Cups menu. She always refused.

Kate waved at me from the end of the table. "Speaking of secrets, Josie, what can you tell us about the murder investigation?"

"Maybe the chief should answer." I nodded in his direction.

Chief Marshall shoved his chair back from the table and turned his penetrating gaze on Kate with a twinkle in his eye. "You understand this is an active investigation?"

"I do." Kate returned his level stare.

The chief raised his eyebrow and studied the faces around him. "I can't give you any details we haven't made public." He paused dramatically before he continued. "But, if y'all want to help, I'll pose a couple of puzzling rhetorical questions."

"You mean like a party game?" Tim asked.

Chief Marshall shrugged. "More of a riddle. Josie tells me you mavens are good at answering *hypothetical* questions. We could use a new perspective on two situations we haven't been able to crack."

"Let's do it over dessert," Terry said. "How about if we separate into two teams? You set up the situation, and we'll see who solves it first."

"Men against women?" Tim suggested.

"That works," the chief said.

We cleared the dinner dishes, and Sharon sliced her apple pie. I scooped a dollop of vanilla ice cream on top, and Kate helped carry the plates to the table. When everyone had been served, the chief stood at the head of the table where we could see him clearly. The three men—Tim, Terry, and Harvey—sat along one side of the huge table. I took my place with Nellie, Sharon, Kate, and Lorene opposite them.

Tim motioned a time-out signal with his hands in the air. "Wait. The guys have a smaller team."

Nellie shrugged. "You're the one who proposed it."

Chief Marshall stood and addressed the gathering like a master storyteller. He cleared his throat and waited until he had our undivided attention.

"Suppose a suspect left his footprints in two locations," the chief began. "The prints look the same. One man's shoes match the footprints, but he was not in our city the night the first prints were made. Our detective confirmed the suspect arrived the day after we collected the first footprint."

Chief Marshall raised his hand and held one finger in the air. "Question number one: How could a man leave his footprints in the ground before he arrived in our city?"

We groaned. The question seemed impossible to answer. The chief shrugged. "Want another one?"

A chorus of voices shouted: "Yes!"

The chief cocked his head to one side. "Ready?"

We nodded in unison.

"Let's assume an exceedingly wealthy woman was arrested with a valuable stolen object in her possession. The item was a prototype of a famous watch." The chief raised his hand again. This time, he held two fingers high in the air.

"Question number two: Why would a woman who could afford to purchase the real thing risk her reputation and her freedom to steal a prototype?"

The chief directed us to separate into groups and bring back our answers in ten minutes. Our group of women moved to the large round appetizer table in the corner and bent our heads together to whisper ideas.

Kate, our poised retired U.S. Marine, already had a pad of paper and a pen in her hand and volunteered to lead our team. "Okay, ladies, what have we got for the question on the footprints?"

Nellie answered first. "Obviously, he couldn't have made the prints if he wasn't here."

"But the footprints match," Sharon said. "And his shoes match the footprints."

We wrestled with the options for a few minutes without success. Finally, Kate said, "What if his shoes were already here, and someone else wore them the first day?" Everybody laughed.

Sharon chimed in. "It would be the first time somebody's luggage arrived before they did, but it's as good an answer as any of the others we've considered."

On the second question, our team was even more confused. "It makes no sense to steal a fake—especially a valuable fake—if you have enough money to buy the real thing," Nellie said. "Somebody must have planted it."

"That's it!" I exclaimed. "She was arrested, but she hasn't been found guilty. Maybe she didn't take it."

We felt confident of our answers as the chief called everyone back together. "Ladies, first."

Kate explained our answers, and the men laughed at our conclusions.

"Seriously?" Tim pointed to his wife, Nellie. "You think someone else borrowed the guy's shoes, and the woman was framed?"

The chief raised his hands for silence. "Men, do you have something better?"

"Of course we do," Terry declared. "We believe the guy snuck into the country earlier than he claimed. He made his own footprints, then faked a later arrival time."

Harvey took the last bite of his pie and waved his fork in the air. "He might have doctored his receipt to change the day. Or, he could have returned to the airport and picked up a flight ticket somebody tossed in the trash."

"Interesting." Chief Marshall jotted notes onto a napkin. "What about the rich woman who stole a fake watch?"

"That's an easy one," Terry reported. "She did it for love. Women always follow their hearts."

Our side of the room erupted in protest. We groaned about their sexist comment until the chief called the party back to order. "Good job, everyone."

"Did we solve it?" Sharon asked.

The chief scratched his head. "Not yet, but you gave me something to think about. Tomorrow, we will explore these possibilities."

Nellie tucked her perfect salt and pepper bob behind her right ear. "That reminds me. Mr. McGregor called to invite us to his shop tomorrow afternoon. Ella's professor will be in town. He wants to see the shop and visit with Ella's friends and family."

"That's odd." I rested my chin on my fist. "I talked to the professor this morning, and he didn't mention he was on his way here."

The chief caught my eye. "Another question without an answer."

Chapter Twenty-Nine

Tuesday Morning

Tuesday morning, my phone started ringing at seven and didn't stop until nearly nine. First, Nellie called.

"I hope I didn't wake you," she began.

"I'm up." I lifted my mug to take a sip of fresh coffee.

"I wanted to thank you again for your help with the art show."

"Don't be silly. I didn't do much."

"You did more than you know." Nellie rustled papers on her end of the phone. "I have the numbers in front of me. The event was a huge success. Can't wait to report to the art foundation board next month."

"That's wonderful." I pictured my friend at her kitchen table with a calculator. "I'm glad you were able to hit your goals."

"We did more than that." Nellie's voice was an octave higher than usual as she rattled off the numbers.

"We exceeded our ticket sales by one hundred guests. We made 30 percent more profit than we projected. And we attracted photographers from two national art magazines."

"Be careful, Nellie." I poured myself another cup of coffee. "The board will put you in charge every year."

"There's one more thing." Nellie shared her biggest news in a rush of words so fast I could barely understand them. "An anonymous donor contributed $ 100,000 a year for the next ten years for an endowment to fund the show.

Can you believe it?"

"Fantastic!" No wonder Nellie was excited. "Can you tell me who it was?"

"No, but you might be able to guess."

"The only person I can think of is Maria Paige."

"I really couldn't say." Nellie hedged her reply. "You could ask her."

Minutes later, I answered my phone to hear Maria's warm voice. "I hope I didn't wake you."

"No, I'm up." I popped an English muffin into the toaster.

"Could I come by this morning to see the painting?"

"Your timing couldn't be better. I need to be at the police station by eleven. Sam Ternberry will be there to make his statement, and I'd like to meet him before the chief, and I talk about the evidence I've gathered. Could you come here around nine-thirty?"

"See you then."

I had taken the first bite of my muffin when my cell phone rang again at eight. I swiped to answer. "This is Josie."

"Josie, this is Daniel. I hope I didn't wake you." The professor sounded winded, and I heard PA announcements in the background.

"No, I'm up."

"I'm flying to English Village today, and I'd like to meet in person, if you have time."

"I'm available later this afternoon." I paused a beat. "When did you decide to visit?"

"Actually, Ella's father invited me when I called last week, but I couldn't get a flight confirmed until after I talked to you yesterday."

"I see," I said, though I doubted his story.

"I wonder…" The professor hesitated before he stated the real reason for his call. "Would you be willing to let me see some of Ella's things? I still can't believe she is gone."

"By the time you arrive, Chief Marshall will have her journal and letters. They may be used as evidence in her murder."

"There were letters too?"

"Yes." I could almost hear his brain scrambling to figure out whether I'd read his letters to Ella.

"What about her other personal things?"

"Ella had moved many of her belongings into an apartment. Jack helped her with the boxes. I imagine they are still there."

"Josie?"

"Yes."

The professor spoke in a rush: "I lied to you earlier.

I allowed myself an eye roll he would never see. *"Did* you?"

"Yes. When I denied having a relationship with Ella."

I turned on my phone recorder to capture his confession. "Are you prepared to tell me the truth now, Professor Davis?"

His voice caught in a sob. "Yes. The truth is, I was deeply in love with Ella. She is—was—an old soul. She didn't care about the age difference between us."

"But you did?

"Ella was ready to share our relationship with the world. I was worried about what people might think."

"What people?"

"My colleagues. Her father. Our patrons. Horologists worldwide."

"That's a big list."

"People can be cruel. I was afraid of the whispering."

"And Ella?"

"She was fearless. For her, nothing mattered but love and her career. She couldn't wait for us to marry and begin working together."

The professor sounded sincere, but I sensed he wasn't telling me everything. "Did you know about Ella's diagnosis?"

"Ella shared everything with me. She felt confident her medication would work. Nothing could stop her from becoming one of the world's greatest clockmakers."

"Almost nothing," I corrected.

"True." His voice cracked, and I almost felt sorry for the pompous man.

Before we ended the call, I asked one final question. "Daniel, who would do this to Ella?"

He answered bitterly. "Someone so jealous of her work they would kill her in order to steal her designs."

I stepped into the shower and lathered my hair with shampoo. The professor's words swirled in my head. Daniel Davis was sixty. He was well-established in his career. I understood why he felt others might judge him for dating his former student. But I couldn't help wondering whether he had other reasons for keeping his relationship with Ella a secret. Was he trying to protect her? Or himself?

Promptly at nine-thirty, Maria Paige knocked on my door. I welcomed her inside and offered coffee. She accepted the steaming cup and perched on a stool at my kitchen island.

The young painter looked beautiful, as always. She wore a one-piece aqua jumpsuit with a silver cord tied around her slender waist; tassels dangled from the ends. Her straight blond hair framed her face and fell perfectly into place. I shook my head in wonder.

"Maria, if I wore that outfit, I would look like a giant Gumby. But you look spectacular."

She laughed. "I try to keep my clothing as simple as I can. I'm so thin I can't wear florals or prints. I turn into a pale face, lost behind a heavily patterned wallpaper."

"Really?" I had never considered a slender figure as a challenge when it came to selecting a wardrobe. "I wouldn't have guessed."

"It's true." Maria took another sip of the hot coffee. "It can get a little boring, but I always wear solid colors."

I thanked her for participating in the English Village International Art Show. "Nellie called this morning to tell me the show was a huge success. The event created positive awareness for our community and exceeded their financial goals."

Maria returned her mug to the counter. "I'm not surprised. Next year, it is likely to attract artists from a wider region. Talented people are drawn to a well-organized show."

"Nellie said someone made a significant contribution to establish an endowment for the show." I gazed at her. "You wouldn't know anything about that, would you?"

Maria smiled. "You got me," she said. "I wanted to do something special to support Ella's community. This seemed like the perfect opportunity. Please don't tell anyone. I prefer to keep a low profile when it comes to donations."

"Your secret is safe with me." I steepled my hands and changed the subject. "Speaking of secrets, shall we look at your painting now?"

I removed the artwork from my closet and laid it atop the kitchen island. "The light is probably best here."

Maria gazed fondly at the painting. "This brings back so many memories. Did you know my instructor gave me a C+ when he graded the project?"

I shook my head. "I hope you have reminded him of that now that your art is selling for many thousands of dollars."

She stroked the frame of the artwork. "I haven't. Ella wanted me to go back and protest the grade. She loved this piece from the beginning. But, of course, it was a clock—and it was her idea."

I handed Maria the magnifying glass and a small laser pointer flashlight. "I studied the back myself. It looks like a typical professional finish, with double-faced tape holding kraft paper in place. The photo of the two of you was tucked inside the corner of the frame."

Maria stretched a pair of thin white nylon gloves over her hands. Gently, she turned the painting over to see the back side. She bent toward the frame. Studied the edges.

"This has been reframed since I gave it to Ella," she said quickly.

"Are you sure?"

"Positive."

"It doesn't look like anyone has disturbed it."

"That's how I can tell it has been reframed." Maria repositioned the painting between us so she could point to the discrepancies.

"I was still in college when I framed it. Ella and I were always short of money. I spent everything I had on art supplies. But I saved on framing materials. I made my own double-faced tape, rolling strips of Scotch tape to create a cheaper substitute. It worked but wasn't quite as precise as the real thing. The kraft paper I used was a little heavier than this art paper." She motioned to the brown paper backing.

"I borrowed packing paper from the meat market. The butcher there loved to help starving artists. Art paper and supplies were far too expensive."

I was surprised by her revelation. "So, Ella had it reframed?"

"Or she redid the back of the artwork herself." Maria spread her palms up to emphasize her words. "Don't forget, Ella was a perfectionist who could easily have replaced the paper. She watched me do it many times."

"Do you think she hid her clock design inside the frame?"

"Yes. Knowing her final words, this is the most logical hiding place."

"Do you want to open it?"

Maria shook her head. "Let's take it to Chief Marshall. He can check for fingerprints to ensure no one else helped frame it. He can arrange for an expert to retrieve her design from the inside. Knowing Ella, the clock mechanisms may be drawn on a thin tissue paper in a series of microscopic sketches for each of the thirty-two complications."

"I'll deliver it to him later this morning."

"Josie?" Maria looked at me with concern in her eyes.

"Yes?"

"Someone else wants this painting enough to kill for it. Take care to conceal it when you take it to the chief. And watch your step."

Her words sent shivers up my spine.

Chapter Thirty

Tuesday Afternoon

I arrived at the police station with a box of Ella's things for Chief Marshall. He sent Officer Walker to carry the carton into the conference room. By the time the chief entered, I had spread my gifts onto the table. Ella's journal sprouted twenty bright ribbon markers that corresponded with the printed notes I had already provided. The painting rested face-down on a square linen tablecloth I used to cover the scratched metal table. Next to those, I set Ella's white Crocs. Three stacks of letters were arranged beside the shoes.

"Well, well, well. What do we have here?" The chief beamed when he saw the treasures. "My birthday isn't until next month."

"I thought you would prefer to have originals in your possession. Clearly, they have become important to the investigation. I don't know which of these you might need as evidence, so I brought everything."

"Everything?"

"Everything relative to the case." I handed him a list of the additional items at my home. "There are a few small articles in a box of clothing, but nothing struck me as valuable."

Handing the chief Ella's letters, I told him about my morning phone call with Daniel Davis. "Based on these letters and her journal, I'm positive Ella was in love with Daniel."

"What about the professor?

"He claims he loved her, too." I handed the chief my cell phone. "I recorded our conversation so you can hear it for yourself."

"You have doubts?"

"I can't put my finger on it, but something doesn't feel right." I shook my head. "I'd like to believe him."

"Let's talk to him at the McGregors' this afternoon. Face-to-face conversations are always better."

The chief turned to the artwork on the table. "Is this our famous painting?"

"It is titled *32 Complications.*" I slid the framed piece toward him. "Maria looked at it this morning. She said the paper covering the back has been replaced."

The chief lifted the painting to study the backside. When he turned it over to view the artwork, he gave an appreciative nod. "Finally...the long clock Ella wanted us to find."

"Maria thinks Ella hid the plans for her dream clock inside this frame. She wanted you to have it. The drawings could be worth millions."

"We will take good care of it." Chief Marshall returned the painting gently to the table. "I have an archivist standing by. He will determine the best way to disassemble the piece while protecting the contents."

I motioned to the remaining possessions on the table. "I brought Ella's Crocs and her personal journal as well. The Crocs have her initials etched into the bottom."

The chief called his detective into the room, instructing her to tag the items and store them in an evidence locker. "Make sure they are in our temperature-controlled lockers."

Over lunch, we discussed the evidence and planned our strategy for the afternoon. "I have Jack and Carlos coming in soon. It's time to get answers about those footprints."

We agreed to separate the two of them. The chief would interview Jack while I spoke to Carlos in my role as a reporter.

"I'll set you up in our testing room," the chief said. "We have a two-way mirror there. Detective Cooper will observe. I believe Carlos will be more relaxed talking to you, especially since you and Harvey shared a table with him at the art show reception. You can ask about the Crocs in the context of the Minetti School as a detail to include in your feature about Ella."

"You want me to put him at ease before you interrogate him?" I held back a smile.

"The last time we questioned him, we didn't have lab results. I have more evidence now."

"What did the lab report show?"

"As we anticipated, all of the footprints came from Crocs shoes with an extra 'C' carved into them," the chief said. "Our dilemma is that Carlos didn't arrive here until the afternoon after Ella fell from the ladder. We hope he can explain how that could happen. It's possible he is innocent, as he claims. Someone else may have worn his shoes or carved a 'C' in another pair to frame Carlos in both locations—near the shed at The Curiosity Shop and at your home."

"Do you think Carlos is the one who harassed me?" I had mixed feelings about confronting a confirmed stalker without an officer in the room. Especially one who had repeatedly attempted to terrify me.

The chief shrugged. "All we know is the responsible party wore shoes identical to Carlos's Crocs."

"If the shoe fits..." I recited. I struggled to absorb the conflicting information. Carlos, the friendly guy who shared a table with Harvey and me at the art reception, might be both a murderer and a stalker. Or, he could be the victim of an elaborate scheme to frame him for both acts.

The chief and I spent a few minutes brainstorming our strategy until we were satisfied we had a well-defined line of questioning in mind. Then I settled into the testing room and waited for Carlos to arrive.

Detective Val Cooper showed him into the office. Carlos gave me a tentative smile as he took a chair across the desk from me.

I looked up from the paperwork I held in my hand. "I hope you don't mind sharing this office for a few minutes. The chief asked me to review some files here. They are a little short on space."

"No problem." Carlos folded his hands on the table. "Jack and I are here to see if we can fill in some gaps in the investigation. We want to do whatever we can to help."

I raised an eyebrow. "Maybe you could help me figure out a few loose ends?"

"Sure." Carlos squirmed in his seat. "If I can."

"I can't stop thinking about the Crocs shoe prints they found outside my cottage." I stared at him.

"Yeah, I told you before: we all wore them."

"But you didn't mention the customized engraving on the soles." I rested my chin on my fist. "What was that all about?"

Carlos stiffened a little in his seat. "You noticed that?"

"Yes. It's a small detail, but an important one. For example, you always carved an extra 'C' under the Crocs logo."

"Yeah." Carlos cleared his throat. "Several of us wore the same size. I wanted to keep mine separate."

"Did you know the lab has turned in their report on the footprints?" I waved the papers in my hand.

Carlos sat at attention but said nothing.

"The shoe prints found beside the storage shed match the ones outside my home. Every print has an extra 'C' carved into it."

"T-that's impossible," Carlos stammered and wrung his hands. "Look, I was never near the shed. I wouldn't do anything to hurt Ella."

"But you admit to hanging around my home and setting a dead opossum on my steps?"

He groaned and hung his head. His voice was barely above a whisper. "Yeah. I did. Now that we have met, I feel pretty bad about it."

"Why did you harass me?"

Carlos shrugged. "I'm broke. I did it for the money."

"Somebody *paid you* to harass me? Who?"

Carlos raised his palms in the air. "I don't know. Somebody called me before I came to visit Jack. The caller's voice was disguised. They offered me five thousand dollars to pack my Crocs in my suitcase and handle a few errands after I arrived. I thought it was a joke. I packed my Crocs, just in case."

"Then what happened?"

"Jack picked me up at the airport. On our way to the inn, he told me Ella had fallen from a ladder the previous day."

"And?"

"You have to believe me. There was no way I could have caused her death. I wasn't even here."

"Yet your footprints were found by the shed."

"I wasn't there." Carlos looked into my eyes as he repeated the statement.

I set the paperwork aside and closed the folder. "What made you decide to stalk me?"

"The money. The day after Ella died, the same unknown number popped up on my phone. They said you were nosing around and trying to connect Jack to Ella's murder. They told me to scare you off. I checked after the call, and the money was already deposited to my account!"

"Did they tell you to put a dead opossum on my step?" I asked.

"No." Carlos puffed up and pointed both thumbs to his chest. "That was my idea. I figured a dead animal would get your attention better than a note or a phone call."

"You got my attention, Carlos. I nearly had a heart attack."

"Yeah. I figured you would. But it didn't stop you."

I was still puzzled. Carlos admitted to harassing me but denied he tampered with the ladder in the McGregors' shed. If Carlos wasn't in town before Ella's death, how did his shoe prints get into the McGregors' garden?

"Carlos, is there any way someone could have access to your shoes before you arrived? Did you ship your luggage ahead of your trip?"

"No. I didn't bring much. I carried my bag onto the plane."

"If you didn't wear your shoes near the shed, how did your footprint get there?"

I saw the realization dawn on his face before the word came from his mouth.

"Noooooo!" His hands flew to his face.

"What??" I sat on the edge of my seat.

"I can only think of one way that would happen, and it isn't possible. He wouldn't do this to me."

Before he could finish, the chief rapped on the door and leaned his head inside. "Josie, I need to visit with you for a moment."

I excused myself to join Chief Marshall in the hallway.

"There's been a break-in at Ella's apartment. Could you spend a few minutes with Jack in the conference room while I get a report from the officers on the scene?"

"What about Carlos?"

"Val said you made good progress. She will take his official statement while you talk to Jack."

"Anything specific I need to cover?"

"Ask him about his eyesight. Then, see if you can get him to talk about Ella. All he would tell me was he still loved her."

I agreed to keep Jack occupied for a while, but first, I ran to Cozy Cups down the block and returned minutes later with two steaming lattes. Jack smiled when I carried them into the room.

"You are a lifesaver." He reached for one of the cups. "They offered me some burnt brew from the pot in the corner, but I declined."

"The chief said it might be a while, so I thought we could take a coffee break." I set my cup on the table. "What did he ask you?

Jack shrugged. "The usual stuff." He rubbed his eyes.

"I know everybody suspects the 'ex' when a woman dies. I told the chief the truth: I still loved her."

I drank my latte and waited for him to continue.

"The chief said I am the beneficiary on her life insurance policy. It was news to me. Ella never mentioned it."

"Do you think that's why people suspect you killed her?"

"Maybe, but it makes no sense. If I killed her, I wouldn't get the insurance money, right?" His eyes watered again.

"Those eye drops don't seem to be helping," I said. "Would you like some saline solution? I carry it in my purse to help with eye strain – which I've had more of lately, from reading Ella's journal."

Jack laughed. "I'm not surprised. She had the world's smallest handwriting.

"Want some?" I held the saline solution out to him.

"No." He looked down at his hands. "It won't help. Nothing will."

"What is it, Jack?"

He gazed at me for several seconds before he responded. "The doctors say I have something called retinitis pigmentosa. I will be legally blind by my fortieth birthday."

"I've never heard of that," I said.

"It's uncommon and incurable." Jack clasped his hands on the table. "There are clinical trials taking place all around the world. I've applied to participate in one of them."

"But what about your career?" I asked.

"It's time for me to find a new one," Jack smiled ruefully. "It's one of the things Ella and I wanted to talk about. When she mentioned her diagnosis of Essential Tremor, I told her about my own diagnosis. I joked it would take two of us to build a watch in the future—her eyes to see and my hands to set the parts in place."

His calm demeanor surprised me. "Did you believe you and Ella would get back together?"

"No." He spat the word out with bitterness. "I wanted to, but she had moved on."

"Did she tell you her plans?"

Jack's face twisted into an angry grimace. "You're not listening."

He pounded his fist on the table. "She wanted nothing to do with me. I insisted we meet for dinner. She agreed on one condition: it would be our last time. The woman was happy to be rid of me."

After what Maria had told me of Jack's infidelity, I had little sympathy for him. "Do you have any regrets?"

His anger flashed again. "You have no idea what pressure we were under. We worked long hours. Ella had plenty of time for her precious clocks, but none left over for me. She shut me out of her life. Yes, I had an affair. But it was just one time. It was Ella's fault for ignoring me. I found a woman who recognized my talent."

"Didn't Ella forgive you?" I asked.

Jack scoffed. "You've been talking to Maria."

He glared across the table at me. "Ella never quit reminding me of the affair."

He laughed before he commented sarcastically, "It's a good thing she never knew who it was. *She would have died.*"

Chapter Thirty-One

Tuesday Evening

After my conversation with Jack, I left him sitting alone while the chief escorted me down the short hallway where Sam Ternberry had just completed his statement to the detective.

Chief Marshall offered a quick introduction. "Mr. Ternberry, this is Josie Posey, the reporter I mentioned who has a couple of questions about Ella's college days. If you don't mind, I'll excuse myself to return a phone call while the two of you talk."

He started to exit, then glanced back at me. "Meet you back here for a recap before we go to The Curiosity Shop this evening?" I nodded my agreement.

As soon as the chief closed the door, the tall young man extended his hand to grasp mine. "Nice to meet you, Ms. Posey. I'm always happy to reminisce about my college days. What would you like to know?"

"Please call me Josie," I said. "Mostly, I wondered about Ella's relationship with Jack. I understand you knew them when they were dating."

"Sure did. We were all in a science lab together. Jack and I spotted Ella about the same time, but he was quicker than I was. He asked her out before the first bell rang for class. I didn't have a chance."

We talked for a few more minutes, but I didn't learn anything Maria hadn't already told me. I thanked Sam for his time and turned to go. Then I thought of one more question. "You said you ran into Jack at the mall a week before you called Ella."

"That's right."

"Were you in the parking lot? Or somewhere inside?"

Sam grinned. "It was at a shoe store. Jack was buying a pair of Crocs."

I did a double-take and repeated what I'd just heard. "Crocs? You're sure?"

"Yep." Sam bobbed his head. White Crocs. I ribbed him about it because they were identical to the pair he was wearing. He acted a little embarrassed when I pointed it out. Said he was buying them for a friend."

I thanked him again and hurried from the room.

Armed with the news of Jack's extra pair of Crocs, I couldn't wait to get home and dig into the bright yellow folder of data to confirm my suspicions and connect the dots of the investigation. My dining room table looked like a blizzard of note cards had moved through, shoving drifts of white into precipitously high stacks.

Sifting through the piles of notes, I kicked myself for not reviewing the information earlier. When the chief handed me his folder filled with texts and phone records the first day we met in his office, I brought it home. But I only read the easy parts—text messages that led nowhere. I never took the time to look at every phone number to connect the conversations. Now, I took a highlighter from my bucket of pens to begin the tedious process. Two hours later, I felt sure I had the answers we needed.

When the chief called, I was ready to share my theory.

He gave me no opportunity to speak. "Can you still meet at the station before we go to see the professor at The Curiosity Shop?"

"Be there in ten minutes."

The conference room looked as drab as it always did, except the chief had scribbled names and arrows across the surface of the whiteboard. I studied the board, then looked back at the chief's face.

"Are we ready to solve this?" he asked.

"I'm beyond ready."

He filled me in on the afternoon break-in at Ella's apartment. "Professor Davis arrived around noon today. He knew Ella's address and went directly there. He removed a pane of glass from the back door, unlocked the apartment, and entered. Apparently, he wasn't aware of the silent alarm. We caught him searching through her boxes. He made a mess of the place."

"And?"

"He claimed he wanted to find some photographs to share with her family this afternoon."

"What do you think he was looking for?"

The chief tilted his head. "Thought you might know the answer to that one."

"The *32 Complications* painting." I slapped my palm on the table. "He knows Ella's clock sketches are likely to be hidden inside. He wants to own those drawings."

"I agree." The chief poured a cup of the bitter coffee from the glass pot in the corner and took a sip without flinching.

"What did you do with him?"

"We let him go. Devon's on his tail. No doubt, the professor will make another attempt to find the painting. We'll get him."

"Unfortunately, he isn't the only one who wants the drawings. He could claim he wants to protect them from someone else."

Chief Marshall took another gulp of the bitter brew. "That's why we need to figure out who killed her."

I turned to the whiteboard. The original names remained from our previous list, but the chief had erased Alex McGregor's name. "You have updated our suspect list."

"Yes. I talked to him again. Her brother had the opportunity but knew nothing about Ella's valuable clock designs. The other two had the knowledge and a more compelling motive than sibling rivalry."

I studied the two remaining names:

✓ Jack Benjamin (ex-husband)

✓ Carlos Perez (classmate/friend)

"Jack and Carlos were close friends. Maybe they are also partners in crime." I floated the idea to the chief.

He stood and wrote two additional names, big and bold, to the right of the board.

✓ Logan Lavender

✓ Daniel Davis

I smiled when I saw them. "The plot thickens."

He motioned to the bright yellow folder and the stack of note cards positioned on the table. "Tell me what you learned from Jack and Carlos."

"I also learned something interesting from Sam Ternberry," I said.

"Lay it all out," the chief said.

I picked up the note cards and read the top one. "First, Carlos. He admitted he was paid to scare me off the case, but he was genuinely shocked to learn the footprints by the shed matched the ones by my cottage."

The chief waited for me to finish.

"When I told Carlos all the footprints looked the same, he commented there was only one person who could have made that happen."

"His friend, Jack?"

"Without a doubt," I said. "Especially after Sam told me he ran into Jack at a *shoe store* in the mall the week before Ella fell."

"What??" The chief's jaw dropped. "That wasn't in his statement."

"Guess your detective didn't ask," I said. "Sam saw Jack purchasing a pair of white Crocs like the ones he was already wearing."

"So Jack carved Carlos' initial into an extra pair of Crocs to frame him for rigging the ladder."

"Yes. Jack tampered with the ladder. He hoped Ella's fall would look like an accident, but, just in case we looked deeper, he set up his friend to take the blame." I circled Jack's name on the whiteboard and put a question mark beside it.

"Why the question mark?" The chief stared at the board.

"Let me show you something." I walked from the whiteboard to the old metal conference table and spread several sheets of phone records across the surface.

"I finally checked the telephone records you provided. When I compared them to the numbers from Ella's contact list, I made a couple of interesting discoveries."

I pointed to the lists. "The calls highlighted in blue are between Logan Lavender and Jack Benjamin. Dozens over the last two weeks."

"What are the calls highlighted in green?"

"Those are between Logan and Daniel Davis."

Chief Marshall studied the lengthy lists to compare the dates. "Logan was in constant communication with both Jack and Daniel. There were no calls between the two men."

"Now look at the calls highlighted in pink and purple."

The chief noted the single purple highlight. "Jack only spoke to Ella on the phone once in the past two weeks."

I directed his attention to the pink stripes on the pages. "Daniel talked to her daily, with his last call on the morning she died."

The chief scratched his head. "What does all of this tell us?"

"It's odd." I twirled a marker between my fingers. "If the professor was in love with Ella, the frequent calls to her make sense. They planned to announce their engagement to the world."

The chief pointed to the calls between Ella's professor and her mentor. "Why would Daniel be on the phone with Logan as often as he was with Ella?"

"It makes no sense to me," I said.

The chief proposed a theory: "Might have been discussing school business. She was a patron of the program."

"Possibly." I propped my elbow on the table and rested my chin on my fist. "Daniel told me he was disgusted with Logan. He said we shouldn't trust anything she said."

"Anything else?" The chief waited for me to continue.

"Jack called The Curiosity Shop about the same time Ella reported the prank call." I pointed to the entry marked in orange. "There were two calls from Logan's phone to Carlos. "Those correlate to the times Carlos received instructions from an unknown caller."

I noted the yellow highlights. "On the first call, he was offered five thousand dollars to pack his Crocs and travel here. The second call, the day Ella died, the caller instructed him to harass me."

The chief waved his hand toward the pages spread on the table. "I see a lot of communications, but we can't prove any of these precipitated Ella's death."

"We also have my interview with Jack." I held up a second note card from my stack. "He said—and did—several things to make me suspect he killed Ella."

The chief challenged my theory. "People say strange things when they are grieving."

I shook my head. "I've interviewed hundreds of people over the years. Jack behaved like an angry man jealous of his ex-wife's success and happiness. He blamed her for the affair he had during their marriage. He gloated about the name of the 'other woman' involved. He said Ella would have died, had she known. It had to be someone she knew and trusted."

"You have his lover's name?"

I walked to the board and drew a dotted line between Jack and Logan. "Logan was Ella's friend and confidante. Ella would have been crushed to know her sixty-year-old mentor was involved with her husband."

"It's an interesting theory, but the affair took place years ago." The chief shrugged. "Not sure it relates directly to the murder."

"What if they never ended the affair?"

The chief toasted me with his coffee cup. "That would change everything." He walked to the burnt coffee and refilled his cup.

"There was one other thing about Jack that concerned me," I said.

"What was it?"

"The way he drank his coffee."

"What?"

"He held the cup in his left hand."

The big round clock in the conference room ticked toward five. I was pretty sure I'd figured out the scenario of Ella's murder. Jack Benjamin, frustrated that his ex-wife had rejected him just as she was about to unveil a clock design worth millions, killed Ella and framed his friend Carlos by wearing shoes with Carlos' initials at the crime scene. Shoes he purchased at the mall and carved with a 'C' specifically to incriminate Carlos. Jack's lover, Logan Lavender, paid Carlos to scare me away from the case.

"Let's go to The Curiosity Shop." The chief's voice stirred me from my thoughts. "We'll see how Jack interacts with Professor Davis."

We locked our notes and evidence into the chief's office and drove to the McGregors'. I pulled into the parking lot ahead of the chief. When we walked in together, both Thomas and Alex welcomed us.

"Thank you for coming," Ella's father said. "Please join the others on the patio. Sharon and Nellie prepared refreshments, and we've arranged some photos of Ella on the table."

Alex spoke directly to me. "Professor Davis asked about you. You'll find him outside."

I had seen pictures of Daniel Davis, but I was surprised by his height. The man stood at least six foot four and was a commanding presence in the room. At sixty, his hair was still thick and wavy. Chestnut brown, with flecks of silver near his temples. He had aged well. I understood why Ella would be attracted to him, particularly since they were both dedicated to horology.

As I approached, the professor turned toward me and smiled. "You must be Ms. Posey."

I shook his outstretched hand. "Welcome to English Village. What do you think of the town?"

"I'm afraid I've made a bad impression already." He tilted his head and spoke in a confidential tone as though he were sharing a secret. "I stopped by Ella's apartment and set off alarms. I was nearly arrested!"

His charm was undeniable. "Mr. McGregor gave me a key, but it didn't work," he continued. "Someone must have changed the locks."

"So you broke a window?" I was skeptical.

"No. I went to the back door. When I saw the window there was already broken, I reached inside to unlock the door. I didn't think it would be a problem. Obviously, I was wrong."

"The alarm went off."

"Yes. Mr. McGregor neglected to mention an alarm system."

"Did you find what you were searching for?" I watched his eyes to see if

214

he blinked.

His response was unfaltering. "Only a few photographs for the display tonight. I had hoped to bring the painting Maria gave to Ella while they were still in college. Do you happen to know where it is?"

If this guy is a liar, he's a good one, I thought.

"The chief has it," I said.

The professor nodded in acknowledgment. "Good." His eyes flitted to the door where Jack and Carlos stood together. Chief Marshall hovered near them.

"Was there something else?"

The professor lowered his voice to a whisper. "I was afraid Jack had taken it."

"Why would he do that?"

Daniel gave me a piercing look. "I believe Ella hid valuable drawings behind the painting. Jack may have been paid to retrieve it for Logan Lavender."

"We need to talk," I said.

Before he could reply, we heard a commotion inside the shop. A glamorous woman wearing a Lauren Bacall hairstyle and wide-legged Katharine Hepburn pants shoved her way through the door and into the patio, screaming bloody murder. Logan Lavender looked like she'd stepped out of the fashion pages of the forties, but she bolted into the room with a purposeful stride and headed straight for Daniel Davis.

"You!" She pointed at the professor. "You lying, cheating, double-crossing, two-timing weasel. You betrayed me!"

I saw the fire in her eyes and sidestepped just in the nick of time.

She ran toward him and vaulted onto his back. Swung her legs to grasp his waist. Missed me by inches.

I dove for cover.

The professor wrestled to free himself, but the woman held on like a bull rider. She clung to his neck with her left hand and battered his head with a brass spider key clutched in the other.

Daniel Davis spun around. Ducked the blows. Tumbled to the floor and

215

rolled.

"Get off me, Logan!" He roared and bounced to his feet. Gasping for breath, he towered over her as she lay on the floor.

Undeterred, Logan recovered her footing and launched herself into the air, screaming like a rabid raccoon. She rushed at him again, knocked him to the floor, pounced onto his back, and clutched a swath of his hair with both hands, jerking his head backward.

For a big guy, the chief moved fast. In seconds, he pulled his gun and fired a single shot into the air.

"STOP!"

Harvey grabbed the woman at the waist and pulled her away. He held her down while the chief handcuffed her.

Alex McGregor helped the professor to his feet and blocked the exit.

Logan Lavender fought to stand up. She screeched at the top of her lungs. "This is all your fault, Daniel Davis! You knew Ella promised to work with me on her big new project. You dumped me. Wooed her. Gave her a diamond and emerald sundial like the one you'd given me. Then cut me out of the deal."

The professor extended his arm to point at her. "You killed her! I loved her, and you killed her!"

"That's ridiculous. I wasn't even in the country. I wouldn't be here now if your sneaky trick had worked at Heathrow. You slipped a cheap phony prototype into my luggage after we met in London. Then, I told the authorities I was a thief. How *could* you?"

I stood speechless while the two of them attacked each other. Vaguely, I heard Chief Marshall radio for assistance.

Then, another commotion began behind me. Jack Benjamin rushed to Logan Lavender's side.

"Logan, my love." He wrapped his arms around her. "What are you saying?"

"You idiot." The older woman squirmed away from his embrace. "Can't you see I never loved you? All I wanted was Ella's drawings. With that clock of hers, I'd be the talk of the century."

Jack's eyes blazed. "You said we would be together. You said Ella had to go. You said if she fell, she'd quit her job. You said—"

Before he could finish his rant, Carlos plowed into Jack and punched him squarely in the jaw. Jack toppled over a table, smacked his head against the edge of an ornate garden fountain, and collapsed in a heap. Platters of food scattered across the patio bricks. Guests stared dumbfounded at the mess.

Carlos stood a good six feet from where Jack landed. He gasped for breath. "*You* did it, Jack. You killed her and set me up to take the blame."

Jack raised his head and growled back at his friend. "You're crazy. I messed with the ladder, but I didn't kill her." Blood trickled from a cut on his forehead.

Police sirens blared outside. Officers Devon and Walker had arrived.

Chief Marshall shouted instructions like a drill sergeant. "Devon, take Logan Lavender and Daniel Davis into custody. Walker, escort Jack to the hospital in the ambulance. Carlos, sit in that chair. Don't move until I give you permission."

I was already impressed by the chief's quick action, but then he did something that made us all proud. His voice softened as he turned to the rest of us. "Harvey, thank you for your assistance. Thomas, my apologies for allowing a little argument to interrupt this evening."

He tipped his head to me. "Josie, could the mavens sweep up the broken plates and set out new food platters? I'll handle this disruption. The rest of you can continue to remember Ella in a more appropriate way."

Ten minutes later, Jack was on a stretcher in handcuffs, being loaded into an ambulance. The chief excused himself to take Carlos to the police station. There weren't many of us left. Just the mavens, the McGregors, and Harvey.

We refilled our plates. Toasted Ella. And trusted the chief to sort everything out.

I have to admit: I breathed a sigh of relief when I let Moe out for his final patrol of the back yard that night. For the first time since Ella's murder, I felt safe in my cottage.

Chapter Thirty-Two

Wednesday Morning

I slept late Wednesday morning. Even Moe must have known I needed the rest. He dozed at the foot of my bed. The chief's call at nine woke us both.

"Josie, we've done it!" Chief Marshall's voice boomed into my ear.

"That's great news, Chief." My voice cracked as I answered.

"Uh-oh. I woke you again."

"It's okay." I sat up in bed. "I'm ready to get up. Tell me the latest."

Chief Marshall rumbled through a checklist of the loose ends he had tied into neat little knots. "This morning, we took a statement from Logan Lavender. The woman admitted she had a brief affair with Jack Benjamin several years ago. But the love of her life was Daniel Davis."

I wasn't surprised Logan had set her sights on the handsome professor she'd first met when they were both students, especially since they had collaborated to host fundraising events for the Adler Minetti School. "After all those years of working together, she wanted more," I said.

"She believed Daniel loved her," Chief Marshall said. "They saw each other secretly for many years. Then, about six months ago, things began to change."

"That's when Daniel started to date Ella."

The chief revealed another statement Ella's mentor had shared during her interrogation at the police station. "Logan said Daniel claimed he was only after Ella's drawings, not her heart. He promised to share the drawings with Logan."

"Logan would have everything she wanted—her lover and a place in history," I said.

"Unfortunately for Ms. Lavender, the more time the professor spent with Ella, the more he loved her." The chief verified what I had read in Daniel's letters to Ella. "When he finally told Logan the deal was off, she was furious."

"Daniel told me Logan made his life miserable after he broke off their relationship," I said. "Logan refused to believe he chose Ella over her."

"When Logan learned—from Ella no less—that Daniel planned to join her in English Village," Chief Marshall resumed, "Logan could no longer deny the truth. Daniel would never return to her with Ella alive."

"Aha," I said. "That must have been what prompted Logan to contact the one person she knew she could manipulate to take Ella out of the picture. She called Jack and told him Ella planned to marry Daniel and share her clock drawings with him."

"Yes," the chief's gravelly voice took on a somber note. "Logan caught Jack at his most vulnerable state. He was already losing his eyesight and concerned about his future. She convinced him to get rid of Ella and find the clock drawings. Logan would use her contacts to sell the drawings. She promised Jack the two of them could resume their affair and live happily ever after on the money from Ella's clock. Jack believed her."

"Ella's clock design was worth millions," I said. "Logan had no intention of sharing the money with Jack."

"No."

"Hell hath no fury like a woman scorned." I quoted the famous line from *The Mourning Bride* by Congreve.

"That's the truth." Chief Marshall sighed into the phone.

The chief had answered nearly all my questions, but I still wondered who would be held accountable for Ella's death. "Who came up with the idea to tamper with the ladder?"

"The way I see it, Jack and Logan plotted ways to make Ella's death look accidental. When Jack told Logan about Ella's plans to inventory the antique clocks stored on the top shelves of her father's shop, Logan seized the opportunity. She convinced Jack to rig the ladder."

"What if Ella's dad or brother had used the old ladder?

"Jack figured neither of them would climb it. Thomas hadn't been up a ladder in years, and Alex avoided them because of his limp."

I felt a heavy weight in the pit of my stomach. "This murder was well-orchestrated." Somewhere deep inside, I had still hoped the young girl's fall was an accident.

Chief Marshall cleared his throat. "Without a doubt, it was premeditated."

"How did Jack know Ella planned to inventory the clocks?"

"Simple. Ella told him her plans for the day," the chief said. "Jack had hoped to see her, but Ella said she had promised to mind the store that day while her dad and brother were out. He seized the opportunity to take action when he knew she would be alone."

"He did it all?"

The chief nodded. "Jack entered the shed after dark, chipped away parts of the ladder rungs, and exited before dawn. The next day, Jack was ready. He positioned himself in the shadows of an alley across from the shop. He saw you enter to conduct your interview. He watched Ella's dad and brother leave the building. And he observed you drive away. He knew Ella would start her inventory soon afterward."

"And if Ella's fall had only broken her leg?"

"My guess is that Logan ordered Jack to be nearby when Ella fell. If the fall didn't kill her, he was to rush into the shop and strike her head with a common clock tool. They hoped her death would be ruled an accident. As a backup plan, Jack suggested framing Carlos. He had already purchased an extra pair of shoes and carved Carlos' initials in the sole. That's what he was doing when Sam Ternberry spotted him at the mall a week earlier."

"Only a few people would have known about the initials carved in the soles of the Crocs," I said.

"After I finished with Logan last night, I had a few words with Professor Davis. He said Jack and Carlos had been setting up Crocs Capers for years."

"Crocs Capers?" This case was becoming as complicated as one of Ella's watch designs.

"Davis said students often pulled tricks on each other by switching shoes. Carlos once tracked mud into the reception area of the school overnight, wearing Jack's shoes. Jack took the blame for the mess. Later, Jack turned the tables on him. Jack tracked footprints that appeared to enter through a classroom window, circle the workroom, and exit out the same window. Jack used Carlos's Crocs, and his friend was blamed."

"No wonder Jack knew how to frame Carlos. It wasn't the first time he betrayed his best friend to cover his own guilt," I said.

"I imagine Logan told Jack to be resourceful. She probably assured Jack that his friend Carlos would never be blamed for the murder. From what I've seen, Logan was convinced our small-town police department would never suspect murder." The chief allowed himself a chuckle.

"She underestimated you. And she underestimated Ella. Without Ella's deathbed statement to her doctor, we all might have assumed her death was accidental."

"Big mistake," the chief said.

My mind flashed back to the threatening phone calls and the poor dead opossum with the note nailed to his chest. "Did Logan pay Carlos to harass me?"

"She hasn't admitted it yet, but it had to be Logan. She didn't like the questions you asked. She wanted you off the case."

"Logan didn't know it, but those threatening notes only made me more determined to dig into the story."

"Another mistake on her part."

I shook my head to clear the confusion from my brain. "Does this mean Logan and Jack are both guilty?"

"Logan set everything in motion. She fanned the flame of Jack's bitterness and pushed him to action." The chief's voice rang with confidence. "But Jack killed Ella. Logan will be charged as an accomplice."

"What happens now?"

"We finish the paperwork. Right now, Logan and Jack are pointing fingers at each other. He still claims he didn't kill Ella. We will hold them at the jail for the next twenty-four hours while we sort through the charges. I'd vote to convict them both, but we probably can't prove Logan's involvement. Carlos has admitted to stalking and harassment."

"And Ella's clock diagrams?"

"We found them inside the framed painting. Drawn on thin tissue paper. From what I've been told, they are priceless."

"Who owns them now?"

"Ella left instructions along with the drawings. They go to her father," the chief said. "Mr. McGregor said he intends to work with Daniel Davis to make sure someone funds the project. Daniel will select a talented young clockmaker—preferably a woman—to build the clock. When the work is completed, the clock will be sold. Proceeds will compensate the professor and the clockmaker. The remainder will go to Ella's father and brother. It should be enough to support them for the next fifty years. Privately, Thomas told me he plans to fund a scholarship in Ella's name."

At first, I ended our call satisfied with the outcome. I wanted to believe Ella's murder was solved.

But a tiny warning bell rang in my brain, and I had to track it down. The chief had wrapped up the investigation. Except three little mysteries still nagged at me, and I couldn't rest until I had the answers.

I picked up my phone and pressed the speed dial for the chief.

"What is it, Josie?"

"Something doesn't add up."

I heard his huge sigh and imagined him running his fingers through his cropped hair. "Is that so?" His tone was skeptical.

"Yes, sir. I'm sorry, but I don't think Jack killed Ella."

"Want to share with me who did it?"

I explained my concerns, and the chief mostly listened without interruptions. "First of all, there's the jack-in-the-box. I can't picture Carlos coming up with that one. The Toy Shop described a matronly customer who purchased it. Carlos might have delivered it, but I'll bet Logan was in town

222

to buy it."

"That's a long trip simply to buy a toy that would point our investigation toward Jack."

"She didn't fly here to buy the toy," I said. "She came to make sure Jack finished the job. She didn't believe he would kill Ella if the fall didn't work. She was right."

"Is this hunch of yours based on something specific?" Chief Marshall's voice still carried an element of doubt.

"In one of our phone conversations, Logan told me, 'when you want something to be done right, you have to do it yourself.'"

"I wouldn't call that a confession," the chief said. "Anything more?"

"Two things. Last night, when she attacked the professor, Logan wore a necklace identical to the one Ella had on the day she died. The one Moe found buried under the oak tree. She screamed something about how Daniel had betrayed her by giving Ella the same necklace."

"And the second thing?"

"She slammed that spider key against the professor's head like she'd done it before. Only when she hit Ella, the key struck the exact point in her temple where it would do the most damage."

The chief had one more question. "I don't understand how Logan arrived on the scene quickly enough to do all this. What's your theory?"

"That's the easy part. Logan was with Jack when they watched Ella fall from the ladder. He refused to enter The Curiosity Shop to check her pulse, so Logan did it. When she saw Ella lying unconscious on the floor with that lovely sundial dangling from her throat, she exploded with anger. She jerked the necklace from her, picked up the spider key that had fallen from Ella's toolkit, smacked the girl in the temple and left her to die. She took the spider key with her in the hope that Ella's fall would still be viewed as an accident."

"And then?"

"She walked to the park, buried the necklace, and left town. Later, when it became apparent that our small-town police department rejected the 'accidental death' story, Logan instructed Jack to follow through on framing Carlos. Then she paid Carlos to dissuade me from helping with the crime story. Finally, she arranged the jack-in-the-box delivery to point the investigation back toward Jack."

Chief Marshall was on board with the new scenario. "Logan was prepared to frame both Carlos and Jack in order to save herself," he said.

"Hell hath no fury like a woman scorned," I repeated.

A few hours after our conversation, the chief called again. His voice was weary. "You got it right, Josie. Logan Lavender admitted to orchestrating the entire thing. She confessed to killing Ella in a fit of rage. Her attorney will most likely try a 'temporary insanity' defense."

"What about Jack and Carlos?"

"Jack will be charged as an accomplice. Carlos gets off with harassment. He knew nothing of the plans to harm Ella."

"Thanks for letting me know, Chief."

"Couldn't have done it without you...and your mavens, Josie." The chief's gruff voice was music to my ears. The Mahjong Mavens would be pleased.

Satisfied the case was solved, I fastened Moe's leash, and we slipped out the front door. Across the street, Mrs. Abernathy tended her front garden. She sprayed water on a Dwarf Winged Burning bush so full and beautiful it deserved to be on a postcard.

I waved, and she called out to me. "Stop by on your way back. I have treats for Moe."

We headed toward Harvey's blacksmith shop to share the news that Ella's murder case had been solved. It was a beautiful autumn day. The sun was shining. The air was crisp. The sky was October blue.

"This is why we moved to English Village." I reached down to pet Moe's soft coat. "The peaceful, quiet, countrified suburban life suits us."

My fluffy dog tossed his head and pranced along the sidewalk. Clearly, he felt as happy as I did.

Harvey stood in the doorway of his shop, wearing a leather blacksmith apron that hung from a strap around his neck and hugged his narrow hips.

He smiled his lopsided smile, and Moe and I picked up our pace to hurry toward him.

I wondered what could possibly happen next to disrupt our idyllic life.

"Nothing today," I decided aloud. "We play mahjong on Wednesdays."

Acknowledgements

I am forever grateful to the readers who have discovered *Clocked Out*, and completed the book. Your time is a gift. I hope you enjoyed reading this story and solving the mystery alongside Josie and her meddling Mahjong Mavens. I would love to hear from you, so please feel free to reach out through my website or social media.

It is impossible to mention everyone who has supported this book through a multitude of ways, but I would like to try.

First, to the writing community who offered professional guidance, suggestions, editing, and encouragement, I thank you. This includes my wonderful agent, Cindy Bullard, of Birch Literary, and the brilliant editor Patrick Price, at Ask a Book Editor. My talented editor, publisher and friend, Shawn Reilly Simmons, at Level Best Books, deserves a special thank you for her guidance. Thank you, Shawn, for believing in this book, and for improving it with your insightful edits. May you never run out of red ink!

Many thanks, also, to Verena Rose, Deb Well and the rest of the Level Best Books team. And to all the LBB "Besties" and Birch Literary authors who willingly shared their time and their wisdom when asked—particularly Lauren, Heather, Paula, Lynn, Desmond, Ivanka, Gayle, Kama, and Lewis.

I am also indebted to other authors across the country, most of whom I have met through the online resources of Pitch to Published, Pitch Perfect, Sisters in Crime, or Mystery Writers of America: including Jane, Harriett, Amber, Steve, Amanda, and others too numerous to name.

My thanks again to my photographer friend Steve Rasmussen, for the "mysterious author" photo. To artist Lyndsey Mbwauike, for her book cover illustration. And to illustrator Kamilla Sims who created the village map included in this book.

To the real Mahjong Mavens who inspire me every week, and who may see themselves in some of this story: Thank you for believing in me. First, to Diane, who founded our little band of mavens (and whose name was missed in the acknowledgements of book one!), thank you for forgiving the oversight. And, to all the mahjong women who have become good friends through our shared love of the game—Diane, Susan, Karen, June, Carolyn, Jane, and Cheri—I don't know what I would do without you.

I owe my deepest appreciation to early readers who helped proofread for content, consistency, typos and more. My thanks to all of you, particularly those who read the ARC and pointed out errors I might never have seen: Diane Behring, Carolyn Arnold, and Teresa Scantlin.

My gratitude also goes out to all the people who contributed to the content of this story by allowing me to use their name or a family recipe. To the family of Les Anderson, who approved my tribute to his memory through a female character who bears his name. To Karen Townsley for the Dulce de Leche Apple Pie recipe, Susan Neff for the Sante Fe Pie, Mexican Salad, Crispy Polenta Bites, and Bacon and Asiago Cheese Sticks recipes, and my to my sister Teresa Scantlin for our favorite Pecan Tart and Lemon Tart recipes from Mama Dee.

Several close friends have been with me since the beginning of this writing journey. I'm lucky to have them by my side for the adventure. Hugs to Sharon and Larry, Janet and Harry, Jane and Herb, Karen and Bob. I wish Harry and Herb could still be with us to celebrate this book.

Special thanks to my sister Teresa, who always provides encouragement when I need it most. To the rest of the family: sisters Jan and Ann, aunts and cousins, nieces and nephews. Each of you has inspired me in some way. (Yes, this includes you: Martha, Winona and Jeneva, Andi and Abby.)

I can't forget Oliver, our sweet and silly Old English Sheepdog who patrols our property to protect us from birds and squirrels, and who prompts me to head for the gym every morning and the park each afternoon.

Most of all, I want to mention those closest to my heart: our children and grandchildren. Matthew, and daughter-in-law Tatiya, gave us our first granddaughter, Madeline (and have another on the way). Zachary, and daughter-in-law Sarha, presented us with grandson, Zander and, recently, granddaughter Magnolia. We treasure our time with you.

Always, I am thankful to be spending my life with my husband, Bruce, who makes all my dreams possible.

SHARON'S DULCE DE LECHE APPLE PIE

INGREDIENTS

- Double pie crust required
- 1/2 cup brown sugar
- 1/3 cup granulated sugar
- 1/3 cup cornstarch
- pinch of salt
- 8 cups sliced granny smith apples
- 2 tbsp apple cider
- ½ tsp cinnamon
- ¼ tsp fresh ground nutmeg*
- ½ cup Dulce de Leche**
- One egg yolk + 1 Tbs water (for egg wash)

DIRECTIONS

1. Preheat oven to 400 degrees. In small bowl, mix sugars, cornstarch, salt, cinnamon and nutmeg.
2. In large bowl, toss apples, apple cider, vanilla and dulce de leche. Add sugar mixture and toss to combine.
3. Fill pie crust and top with second crust.
4. Combine egg yolk and water and rush top crust.
5. Vent top crust with 4-5 slits.

6. Bake pie 30 minutes at 400 degrees, then lower to 375 degrees and bake
    another 30 minutes. Allow to cool completely.

*Freshly grated nutmeg is a must! Already grounded nutmeg has a different
taste.

**Dulce de Leche is generally located near sweetened condensed milk or in
Hispanic markets.

HARVEY'S COFFEE-RUBBED STEAK

INGREDIENTS

- Beef tenderloin, filet
- 2 $^1/_2$ cups strong espresso or 2 1/2 cups darkest roast non-flavored coffee
- $^1/_4$ cup olive oil
- $^1/_4$ cup molasses (regular strength)
- 1 tbsp brown sugar
- 1 $^1/_2$ tbsp kosher salt (or sea salt)
- 1 tsp cumin
- $^1/_2$ cup ice

DIRECTIONS

1. Place all the liquid and dry ingredients into a large bowl or zip-lock bag and mix until dissolved.
2. Add ice to cool the mixture.
3. Add the filets and marinate for at least 6 hours for best results.
4. Remove steak from the refrigerator thirty minutes prior to preparation.
5. Sear the outside of the steaks for a minute or two until dark and crisp on the outside, then place on the grill to cook.

SANTA FE PIE

INGREDIENTS

- One lb. ground sirloin (can also use shredded chicken)
- 2 tbs olive oil
- 1 cup chopped onion
- One small can of chopped green chilies
- One small jar of mild, chunky Pace Picante (or your favorite picante sauce)
- 3 cups shredded pepper jack cheese
- 1 tbs chili powder
- 1 Jiffy box cornbread

DIRECTIONS

1. Preheat oven to 350 degrees.
2. Sauté onions in the olive oil. When soft, add ground sirloin and brown.
3. Add picante, chili powder, and two cups of pepper jack cheese. Simmer until cheese melts.
4. Mix cornbread according to directions. Add the remaining cup of the pepper jack cheese.
5. Place in the bottom of an 8" X 8" glass baking pan. Pour the meat mixture on top.
6. Bake for 30 minutes. Allow to cool slightly before serving.

MEXICAN SALAD

INGREDIENTS

- 1 bag romaine lettuce
- 12 cherry tomatoes cut in half
- One yellow pepper, sliced into strips
- ½ red onion, sliced thin
- Small can of sliced black olives, drained
- One ripe avocado, skinned, pitted, and sliced (to be placed on top)
- Juice of 1 lemon (drizzle avocado in lemon juice to keep it from turning brown)

DIRECTIONS

1. In a large bowl, combine the above ingredients except for the avacado, tossing to mix.
2. Add the sliced avocado on top and drizzle it with lemon juice.

Avocado Dressing:

INGREDIENTS

- One ripe avocado, mashed
- ½ C sour cream
- 3 T chopped red onion
- 2 T fresh cilantro leaves
- Juice of one lemon

- Dash Tabasco
- ¼ C extra virgin olive oil

DIRECTIONS

1. In a food processor, combine the above ingredients except for the oil.
2. Once the ingredients are pureed, add oil in a steady stream while blending until it becomes a salad dressing consistency.

CRISPY POLENTA BITES

INGREDIENTS

- 1 16 oz. log of prepared polenta, room temperature
- 3 tbs olive oil
- ½ C panko crumbs
- ½ C finely chopped arugula
- One jar of olive tapenade

DIRECTIONS

1. Spread panko onto a plate.
2. Cut polenta log into 16 rounds.
3. Press both sides of the polenta rounds into panko crumbs and cook in olive oil until crispy, about 2-3 minutes.
4. Rest on a paper towel to remove excess oil.
5. Top each with arugula and 1 tsp olive tapenade.

BACON AND ASIAGO CHEESE STRAWS

INGREDIENTS

- 6 slices bacon, cooked and crumbled
- 1 box frozen puff pastry, thawed
- ½ C grated Asiago cheese

DIRECTIONS

1. Preheat oven to 400 degrees.
2. Line a sheet pan with parchment paper.
3. On a lightly floured surface, place a pastry sheet. Sprinkle with bacon and cheese.
4. Place the other sheet on top and press lightly with a rolling pin.
5. Cut into 1-inch strips and twist.
6. Place on the parchment-lined sheet pan and bake for 15 minutes.

MINI PECAN TARTS

(Requires two muffin tin pans. Makes 24 tarts)

INGREDIENTS

Pastry Shells for Pecan Tarts:

- 1 C flour
- Two sticks of oleo (or margarine)
- 2 tbsp sugar
- Dash of salt
- 2 tbsp milk

Pecan Filling:

- Two slightly beaten eggs
- ½ C pecans, roughly chopped
- 1/3 C sugar
- ½ C dark syrup
- 1/8 tsp salt

DIRECTIONS

1. Make pastry dough ahead of time, allow to chill at least two hours before preparation.
2. When ready, divide it into 24 equal parts.
3. Roll into balls and press into pan.

4. Preheat oven to 375 degrees.
5. Mix filling ingredients and spoon into pastry shells.
6. Bake for 18 minutes, then reduce heat to 350 degrees and bake an additional 15 minutes.
7. Allow to cool slightly, then remove from pan.

MINI LEMON TARTS

(Requires muffin tin pans. Makes 24 tarts)

Lemon Tart Pastry Shells

INGREDIENTS

- 1 C flour
- 1/3 oz cream cheese, softened
- One stick of unsalted butter, softened

DIRECTIONS

1. Preheat oven to 350 degrees.
2. Combine ingredients. Divide into 24 equal parts. Roll into balls and press into pan.
3. Bake at 350 degrees for 20 minutes. Remove from oven and allow to cool.

Lemon Curd Filling

INGREDIENTS

- Three eggs
- 1 C sugar
- Two lemons, juice and rind (6 tbsp)
- ½ stick unsalted butter

DIRECTIONS

1. Beat eggs slightly and cook with other ingredients on a double boiler until the mixture thickens.
2. Refrigerate lemon curd until chilled.
3. Spoon into pre-baked pastry shells.
4. Serve.

About the Author

Anna St. John writes cozy mysteries featuring a mature yet feisty former crime reporter, Josie Posey, as the amateur sleuth.

Her debut novel, *Doomed by Blooms*, was released by Level Best Books in February 2023. *Clocked Out* is the second book in her Josie Posey Mystery Series.

Anna is a former journalist, award-winning advertising copywriter, and ad agency owner. She is a member of Mystery Writers of America, Sisters in Crime, and the Kansas Authors Club.

Anna is represented by Cindy Bullard of Birch Literary Agency.

SOCIAL MEDIA HANDLES:
https://www.facebook.com/cozyauthor/
https://twitter.com/AuthorStJohn

AUTHOR WEBSITE:
www.anna-stjohn.com

Also by Anna St. John

Doomed by Blooms, A Josie Posey Mystery

www.ingramcontent.com/pod-product-compliance
Lightning Source LLC
Chambersburg PA
CBHW020133120726
47903CB00007B/2230